DARK DEVICE
OF THE
GREAT CHASM

A Windtracer Tale

by
C. B. Ash

Fabled Horizon Press

Published by Fabled Horizon Press

The *Dark Device of the Great Chasm* is a work of pure, unashamed fiction. In fact, it considers itself rather fancy and quite proud of itself. Names of characters, places, events, organizations and locations are all creations of the author's imagination for this fictitious setting.

Any resemblance to persons living, dead, or reanimated is coincidental. The opinions ex-pressed are those of the characters and should not be confused with the author's, since the characters and the author tend to disagree a lot.

Cover art by Christof Grobelski

Explore more of his fantastic work at: https://christofgrobelski.artstation.com

Map drawn by Karina (@Shepengul)

Explore more of her fantastic work at: https://www.fiverr.com/jlihanks

The world of Awldor created by Starfarer Theta

Explore more of their fantastic work at: https://www.worldanvil.com/w/awldor-starfarert heta

For you.

Yes, you. This is dedicated to you.

The one holding this book right now.

You decided to take a chance and give this a try.

So, this story, and all the adventure, the thrills, the feels is dedicated to you.

Enjoy

Acknowledgements

Stories are not made or told in a vacuum. When they come to life, they need strong arms and shoulders holding them up. At least until they get their legs under them, then wings before they can fly. So, let's break this down, all right?

To start with, this work, or flight of fancy, really wouldn't exist without one Starfarer Theta and the world of Awldor. They invited me into their world and gave me a place in it to play. So, that setting is the source and inspiration for the Windtracer Tales setting, which is just a look at Awldor through the eyes of a different organization, the Windtracer Company.

So to Starfarer Theta, you have my profound thanks now and always.

Onto some acknowledgment!

My heartfelt thanks to Christof Grobelski, the genius who helped me with the cover art. Along with that would be thanks out to Karina (@Shepengul) with her talented work on the map.

Also, deep thanks goes out to the World Anvil platform (www.worldanvil.com) and the World Anvil team! Along with that would be the friends I've made over there, too, that gave me encouragement along the way.

Then would be the folks who followed along with me, chapter by chapter, as I brought this story to life. They were my cheering section, and sometimes an ear to bend. So thanks to: Graylion, Gausscat, Jenks, Tepcat, Chip, Dr. Unity Walker, Jaime Buckley of Wanted Hero, Richard Ritenbaugh of Serial Production, Rob Mortell of Stories Have Power, Ann Kimbrough of Tell Me a Mystery, Leanne Shawler of The Môrdreigiau Chronicles, Shannon W Haynes of Chapter by Chapter, and Alison Bull of Historical Fiction Stack.

Last, there is a special thanks to my mom, dad, Jarissa, Wookiee-gunner. You believed, and therefore so did I.

Now! Grab your hat and coat! Don't forget your journal!

Adventure is waiting on you!

I hope you enjoy the ride, as I know I sure did.

- CB "Kummer Wolfe" Ash

Concerning History

For generations, the Ancient Order unified the world, bringing prosperity like never before seen. Then, it was gone. Swept away by what some call The Great Collapse.

After a thousand years, we still don't know what happened.

But there are clues. Hints. Pieces to the greatest puzzle in history in ruins of the Ancient Order. Remnants of their greatest works.

There are many that debate if the knowledge of the Ancient Order should be rekindled. Its former glory restored to life. Others argue that the Ancient Order's legacy should remain lost. Some even suggest that the Collapse may still be happening now. Certainly, the magic storms and other wild magics that scour the world suggest that something dire lingers from the disaster.

But there are guilds that look to preserve the lost knowledge. The Windtracer Company is one of those organizations that seek to preserve the knowledge of the Ancients. These mercenary-historians scour the forgotten corners of Awldor, into restricted ruins and the dark places. They explore, learn, and share what they find.

They collect this knowledge so that others can learn from the past. Not to rekindle the old Order, but to build something new... while not repeating whatever dire mistake the Ancient Order made.

In the end, the Windtracers hope to decipher why the Great Collapse happened. Through that, perhaps a way to prevent it from happening again.

- Lorekeeper Nicol Oldbuck, 1277 by Windtracer reckoning

1

Summer, 1277, deep in the rain forest of the Chivit Continent

It wasn't my best day.

I tore through the curtain of cobwebs like they weren't even there, then bolted for the doorway. The doors were still open, but the wood I had jammed between them and their doorframe wasn't going to last long. A pathetic groan echoed through the ante-chamber around me, followed by the staccato sound of wood splintering.

Correction, those wooden braces weren't going to last another few seconds. I ran faster.

Stone dust was like a fogbank. My clothes and hair were stiff with it and seeing past it felt like a bad joke. Specifically, on me. Gulping down air, I lengthened my stride, sprinting like a madwoman for the only way I knew out.

Then I was through. Past the stone dust, thick cobwebs, and pale-skinned, giggling, scrambling nightmares with too many arms. Little things that were all too eager for me to sit and stay awhile. I threw myself forward into the wall of heat and humidity that was part and parcel of _Anestri'for_, the 'Great Jungle' on Chivit.

Landing on my hands and knees, I drank in the smell of wet grass and foliage. The feel of damp earth was a delight. Best of all? The sound of the stone doors slamming shut on the writhing mass of bodies with too many arms trying to follow me. They weren't giggling as the doors shut in their face, but snarling.

I hauled my aching body into a sitting position, then placed a dust-covered satchel in front of me. Thunder rolled around in the clouds overhead. I glanced up.

"Hourly thunderstorm. Right on time. At least it's not a magic storm."

"Good job, Tela." I congratulated myself. "Alive, limbs in one piece, and you found it."

Shaking my head, I reached for the flap on the bag to check the condition of my find. The last thing I needed was to get it back to Ishnanor in a thousand pieces. I didn't manage to open the bag. A yell to my right gave me better things to think about.

A man dressed in mercenary leathers, and a belted tunic had shoved his way out of the underbrush. Dirty, mud-stained, he leered at me like a prize or fresh caught prey. I shot daggers back at him with a glare. Sad to say, he didn't seem impressed.

"Here!" he bellowed. "She's here! Tell Vargas! I've found the Wind-tracer! She's got the relic!"

"Hells!"

I was on my feet and past a stand of briza-taeda ferns to my right before the mercenary took another step. Shouts filled the Anestri'for jungle air behind me. I ran faster.

Vargas. It would be him and his hellsdamn Crimson Company out here in the Anestri'for. I vaulted a fallen ruberi rubber tree before darting off along a faint game trail.

The Crimson Company was almost a shadow of the Windtracer Company. A dark, brooding shadow that had a bad habit of stealing relics they didn't poach for themselves. Unlike us Windtracers, they sold anything they stole or poached from a ruin.

By all rights, they ought to be rolling in money. Vargas was to an extent. The Company? Not so much. They had a bad habit of spending too much on wine, weapons, and debauchery. But that didn't take away from their skills. They were deadly fighters and trackers.

I was better.

A throwing ax slammed into a tree, just missing my right hand.

So, I was only a little better. Right then, I needed to be a lot better.

"Idiot! Vargas said 'no killing'. If you kill her, we can't get out of her what she knows about the relic!" growled a voice to my left.

"I was only going to maim her a little!" whined a second.

Sprinting harder, I swallowed the urge to yelp or curse. There wasn't any time. I could hear a group running hard not far behind me.

Beyond the branches, past the caribel trees and long, drooping agenti vines, the jungle thinned out to a sloped clearing. I dimly remembered it when my crew and I surveyed the area three days ago. It was the backside of a hill that sloped down to the riverbank where I had left the others. Perfect.

I ducked past the vines, avoiding the sweet-smelling sticky blossoms, before tearing past the mature caribel. The pendulum-like branches whipped at me as I passed. It stung a bit, but I was all focused on that hill and my crew on the riverbank. Then I broke through. Warm sunlight was a welcome feeling on my skin before I realized one little detail.

This was the wrong hill. It wasn't even a hill.

The hill I remembered was a solid two hundred andels or kilometers away, on the other side of a fast moving watercourse to the north. Its lovely northwest side sloped gently and gracefully toward the shoreline. Here? This was a small cliff that the watercourse spilled over into what looked like, from below, a magnificent waterfall.

It didn't look so magnificent right then.

I stumbled to a stop just short of the cliff's edge and looked over. There was the beach below with the longboat and my crew at camp. The cliff wasn't a straight drop, most weren't. But it was a good two or three hundred nindel or meter descent to the waterfall's plunge pool below.

All I had with me, that I hadn't left behind in the ruin, was a pair of daggers, a whip, compass, and a backpack with the relic. I had even lost my favorite machete dealing with a carnivorous vine bridge back in that place. So, I had literally nothing with me to deal with a waterfall or a long drop.

That time, I did curse under my breath and ran over to the edge of the small river.

It wasn't wide, and there were several rocks that thrust up through the water. I could cross it. The problem was that the water here was moving fast, turning the space between myself and the other side into whitewater rapids. So there was a chance I could get swept into the water.

I sighed. Did I mention I wasn't having a great day?

"Windtracer Tela Kioni..."

The voice from the far side of the clearing behind me drawled out my name with a slow, greasy texture. I closed my eyes for a moment, forcing some of the tension out of my shoulders. Slowly, I turned around, one hand on a dagger to face the speaker, Vincent Takeda Vargas.

"Vargas," I replied, putting some acid under my tone.

He stood at the edge of the tree line, accompanied by a collection of his Crimson Company. Six men and women who looked as dirty and disheveled as anyone would be from running in the muddy, damp heat of the Anestri'for. Basically, the same way I looked.

Vargas? He might be perspiring in that sleeveless long coat and sand-colored 'explorer outfit' he wore. Other than that, he looked as clean as usual. Blond hair was combed neatly back and braided behind his head. There was barely a light tan to his human skin tone. Even the sword and daggers at his belt looked polished.

I still say he keeps scrolls of 'clean me' spells on him hidden somewhere. One day, I'll manage to knock him out and rifle through his pockets to find out.

The greasy braggart strolled out a few steps from under the caribel branches shading him. His mercenaries stood their ground but shot me ugly glares.

"Tela. My dear. We must stop meeting like this."

"Oh, shut it," I snapped. "This wasn't chance. You tracked me and my crew here."

"You didn't make it difficult."

I rolled my eyes. The depths to which I disliked this man didn't have a measurement. Out of instinct, I stepped back until I could tell my boot heels found where the small river kissed the rocky grass. Keeping any kind of distance between myself and Vargas was always a good idea.

"Don't you have an honest living to do somewhere else? Like killing someone or overthrowing a kingdom?"

Vargas made a sour face and waved his right hand in limp, small circles.

"I don't entirely do 'honest', you know that. Work? That I do. Such as taking the delightful relic you've pulled from that wretched death trap back in the jungle. I've at least two buyers, a baron and a guildmaster, that will most likely be at each other's throats to buy it first. I wonder who'll win?"

A fly buzzed at the side of my face. I blew at it irritably and refused to entertain Vargas with a reply. He looked disappointed while he withdrew a kerchief from an inner pocket of his long coat to dab at the sweat on his forehead.

"Set it down, Tela. If you drop it on the ground, I'll let you walk away. No harm done."

The blade scars on my back near my left shoulder itched from the memory of the last time he 'let me walk away'. I halfway turned to my right, holding the backpack over the fast moving water.

"Drop what? This?"

Vargas' usual smug look turned dark and nasty.

"Tela. Don't toy with me, I'm not stupid. A relic with a compass that can detect the direction and strength of magical fields? We both know how valuable that is. The Windtracers have been after it for some time. I'm well aware you won't just throw it away."

I grinned, but there was ice behind my expression.

"To keep it out of your greedy hands? In a heartbeat."

One of his mercenaries, a big orc with a broken tusk wearing dirty red brigandine armor, took a step closer. I shook my head.

"Ah ah, big boy. You're not nearly fast enough to get here before this pitches over the waterfall."

"Tela, be reasonable," Vargas said.

"I am," I snapped, cutting him off. "If you get this," I shook the pack in emphasis, "it'll vanish into some ridiculous private collection and any money you get off it will get burnt on what? A good time in a pub? Well, except for your money, Vargas. You horde it like a dragon."

The blond man sighed as if the weight of Awldor just came to rest on his shoulders.

"Why must you always make this so *difficult?*"

He poured all his emotion and frustration into that last word. So much that I couldn't help but grin wider. Checkmate. I had the upper hand.

Vargas watched me for a moment. I could see in his eyes he was weighing the options. After a few seconds he waved his kerchief at me while he turned away.

"Kill her. The detector will survive the fall."

I *thought* I had the upper hand. Funny how those things change so fast.

The Crimson Company thugs unleashed hell. Three light crossbows sang the same time I heard the others charge toward me. Me? I just dove off the bank into the river.

Water churned around me as the current yanked me toward the falls. It wasn't the best choice I had, but it was better than my alternatives. There was a splash or two behind me. Probably Vargas' mercenaries jumping in to fish me out. I was too busy to notice since I had just reached the overhang of the waterfall.

My feet found the hard rocks at the edge of the waterfall overhang. Planting my boots, I shoved off. There was nowhere to go but down.

2

***Five weeks of sail later. Amates 15, 1277.
Windtracer Company Records Hall, City of
Ishnanor. Planus Continent***

"I can't believe you did it."

I frowned at Lorekeeper Ihodis Jenro and his comment, then set the gray, box-shaped relic on the desk between us. It was no larger than a loaf of bread. The thing was stained, battered, but despite age and travel, none the worse for wear. At least, that is, for a thousand year old relic.

The Lorekeeper's sky-blue eyes lit up at the sight of the relic. A broad smile lit up the centaur's face. He stroked his trim white beard in silence, then nodded. Absently, he tugged at the bottom of his blue vest. It was an old habit from his days as a privateer captain, before the Windtracers. A nervous tick of sorts when he was making a complicated decision.

Ihodis gently scooped up the magic detection device with no small amount of glee. Holding it close, he peered at the inset compass on what I figured was the top of the relic.

"Did what?" I prodded, genuinely curious. "Getting this out of the Obvion Complex in Chivit?"

The older Lorekeeper smirked, eyes twinkling brighter as he peered at me from under those bushy steel gray eyebrows of his.

"Leaping off the waterfall, my dear. Interesting plan."

I snorted a little at that. Words like 'plan' and 'interesting' weren't words I would use to describe cliff diving off a waterfall into the churning water of Kanathi Bay. Especially while being chased by a pack of mercenaries.

"What plan? I was making it up as I went along." I tapped the end of the relic facing me and grinned. "Anyway, we got it. Vargas didn't. Even better? I think it might still work."

"Oh?"

Ihodis turned the device in his hands to scowl at it from all sides. I tapped the small compass embedded in the relic, next to what appeared to be a handle.

"The compass needle moved when I brought it through the Ancient History museum. It turned to point at the Elemental Enchantment Relics."

It could have been Ihodis' lifeday, and I had just handed him his favorite cake, given how fast his grin reappeared. Delighted? That wasn't a strong enough word. The Ancient Order's magic detection relics have always fascinated him. Now he had one that actually might still work.

"Splendid! Just splendid! We finally will get a glimpse into how the Ancients viewed and monitored magics. I can't wait to start trying to decipher how it works. Blessed skies to you, Tela."

Then, the Lorekeeper set the relic back on the desk. He moved it to one side while he scrutinized me for a moment, hands flat against the desktop. Ihodis' expression suddenly shifted from 'delighted' to 'business' in the span of one deep breath.

"But that isn't why I asked you here, Tela. Please, take a chair if you would."

I couldn't help but shoot him a wary, even suspicious look. The old centaur had something in mind. An offer for a new expedition? Maybe. Ihodis was known for his sunny disposition, but right then, his expression had gone chilly. There was something wrong.

It took a moment for me to locate a stray, human-sized chair among the bookshelves and tables. I pulled it over to his desk.

"Ihodis, that look on your face tells me this isn't about that magic detector from Obvion."

"No, not exactly," he said before holding up a hand to forestall the conversation.

His eyes searched the room somewhere behind me. The Lorekeeper pursed his lips a moment, then trotted over toward one of the many bookshelves that lined the room. After browsing one of the higher shelves, Ihodis returned with one of the thicker volumes, bound in green canvas.

"Tell me," he began while he set the book on the desk. "Have you ever heard of the Automatic Crystal of the Eclipse?"

The name didn't ring any bells for me. But hints from discoveries like the Chasm Papers to the Ancient Map of Lluvia had handed over clues about thousands of possible Ancient Order relics. It was impossible to keep track of them all.

I shrugged.

"Never heard of it. Is it something from the Ancient Order? Before the Great Collapse or just after?"

Ihodis set the book on the table, then opened it to one of the bookmarked locations. It was a few pages after that when he tapped an old sketch of a studded dark orb.

"Before." He tapped the drawing once more. "There have been a few obscure references in the collected Lorekeeper records and stories. More if you count references from the Archivists Guild across the sea in Centrum."

"Centrum? That's a good distance across the water. You've been really researching this."

I leaned forward to study the drawing a bit more carefully.

The sketch depicted an orb the size of an Ishnanor melon. Just large enough to hold comfortably with two hands, but not so large that it looked cumbersome to carry. A collection of thumbprint sized studs were scattered evenly across the surface.

Except for what may have been the top, or 'north' on the orb if it was a globe. That section was almost blank, save for a plain circle carved into the surface. There was an odd-looking rune of a rounded square, with a dot in the middle. I frowned at it, then pointed at the symbol.

"That rune. I've studied all sorts of Ancient Order runes from their trade language and other cultures. I don't recognize that one."

Ihodis shook his head.

"I don't either. No one does. What makes this even more interesting is that there are two different accountings of what it possibly does. The first recounts how seers and even wizards of the Ancient Order used these devices for study and at times communication with each other."

"Study?"

The Lorekeeper smiled.

"Yes! Study. Several subjects, I believe. Position of the stars, weather, many other items."

I nodded. Other Lorekeepers had stumbled over references that the Ancient Order used amazing means to communicate over long distances and share what they knew. Why not an orb? It looked simple enough to carry or store.

"You said 'the first'. What else was there?"

"A weapon. Apparently, when used, it could generate devastating magical rays of energy. We have no idea if the Ancient Order devised this to defend themselves from someone or something. But the few partial references we have suggested it was devastating."

I knew where this was going. Ihodis had his moments where he would want to sit and debate various pieces of lore from the Ancient Order. Often he preferred to do that on walks along the lakeshore or in a tea shop in Underside. Here? This didn't seem like that kind of conversation.

"You know where one is, don't you?"

He nodded and closed the book.

"Yes. The *Foxglove* arrived a few days before you returned to Ishnanor. A spice merchant had happened over an old leather satchel with some papers. I happened to be in Underside when he was selling them as 'wrapping paper'."

The Lorekeeper chucked dryly. "The man had no idea what he was selling. But, after a brief haggle, I paid him accordingly and brought the papers back here. They make a reference to one of these orbs and a possible location. One you're a bit familiar with."

I stared. Visions of the Anestri'for and its long list of things that want to eat people leaped to mind.

"Chivit?"

Ihodis raised an eyebrow, then tugged at his vest in a scholarly fashion.

"Why no, my dear. Long Deep."

Just the mention of the place sent a cold chill along my spine. Long Deep. The deepest section of the Great Chasm. The Windtracers had only ever sent one expedition there, and it was mine. I lost almost the whole expedition. It went without saying I didn't have good memories of the place.

"Hells, Ihodis. My last and only expedition to that place was a nightmare! Those I didn't lose came back a little broken. Probably even me."

The Lorekeeper slid the book across the desk toward me.

"Tela. I wouldn't ask if it wasn't important. Also, I've two important reasons to ask you. The first is that you have the best knowledge of the place."

I folded my arms over my chest.

"Which I could recount in absolute horrible detail to any other expedition foolish enough to jump into that death trap. So. What's the second?"

Ihodis let out a long, drawn-out sigh.

"Because this wouldn't be an expedition. It's a *race*. Someone else has learned about the Automatic Crystal and that it could be a weapon. One Baron Marius Apollinare. A cruel, ambitious man. He's hired a mercenary company to get the Crystal for him. The Crimson Company."

I hammered the desk with my fist.

"*Aile Shavat!* Vargas and his band of killers! He *would* be involved in this."

"Yes. And you know Vincent Vargas better than anyone."

I took two breaths to find my composure. A host of memories, most being Vargas trying to murder me in a dozen slow, tortured ways, rushed out from the back of my mind. It took a moment, but I shoved the past aside. At least for now.

"All right. How bad is it Ihodis? If this Lord Marius gets the Crystal, what could happen?"

The old centaur pursed his lips, expression grave.

"Nothing short of conquest. Lord Marius, like some, are keenly interested in the Ancient Order. But he doesn't want to learn about the Ancient Order. He wants to bring back the Ancient Order. Remake it on *his* terms."

Ihodis gestured to the old book on the desk in front of me.

"Like I said, the tatters of records say the Automatic Crystal of the Eclipse can be used to project some sort of magical energy. A Schutz Crystal or a Blackstel Shield might stop it. It might not. The Automatic Crystal might could overpower either defense. We just don't know."

I watched my old mentor for a long, quiet moment.

"You don't think a Schutz Crystal or a Blackstel Shield *can* stop it, do you?"

"No, Tela. No, I don't. What little we know is that the Automatic Crystal of the Eclipse wouldn't have any effect on cities. The walls of, say, Ishnanor, Centrum, Sol, or anywhere wouldn't be harmed. No, the effect of the Automatic Crystal targets people. Only people."

Ihodis tapped the side of his head.

"Their *minds*. The Automatic Crystal of the Eclipse might can summon some special type of magic storm inside a victim's mind, trapping them inside it. A magical storm raging out of control *inside* the victim."

I blinked as nightmares of what a magic storm in a person's mind might be like. It made me shudder.

"Exactly," Ihodis added. "Now, think of doing that to the population of an entire *city*."

3

"So you said 'no'."

I didn't reply. Really, I didn't think I needed to. Instead, I navigated the crowd through Tagrica Silk Square in Underside. The afternoon caravans had come down from the Tugart Marshands with fresh produce and other wares. Some of it was from as far away as the Kingdom of Jata. I figured it was a good time to get supplies and give my friend the news.

"Tela. Really, tell me you said no."

Kiyosi was staring at me in disbelief. I didn't even have to look in his direction to know that. Besides, I could hear that long tail of his swat the air in irritation.

"Kiyosi Valchar. You've known me for *how* long? You know what I told Ihodis about this."

"Oh gods and *ancestors*, woman, you said 'yes'," he moaned. "So you're going to do it. Really. Make another run at Long Deep."

"I am."

My wandering brought us up to a booth that belonged to Nile-vian's Brass Carriage. One of several 'general' storefronts in the Silk Square. I'd shopped there countless times over the years. Especially before heading out on an expedition.

The stand outside the shop was filled with colorful fresh produce just unloaded that day. It was at least some of what I was looking for. Planus is flat, wide open, and a little unforgiving. Fruit can be in short supply out there.

"You do remember that place nearly broke you. It *did* kill a lot of your last Long Deep expedition," Kiyosi snapped.

I scooped up a fresh, purple Immon apple from the stand, then spun around to pin Kiyosi to the spot with a scowl. In his defense, he looked as distraught as he sounded. The worry lines on his forehead under his tiefling horns had worry lines.

"I *do*, Ki. *Vividly*. There probably isn't a day that goes by that I don't remember some little part of what happened."

Tearing my eyes off Kiyosi, I stared at the apple in my hand. A host of bad memories washed over me, triggered by the conversation. My shoulders bunched, tightened as I felt the old, familiar sense of being in danger from all sides. I became all too aware of the crowd. Fortunately, the moment passed quickly this time.

"This is *different*, Ki." I let go of a long sigh. "It isn't just a 'hey, why not go dig up what might have killed off the Ancient Order today' sort of thing. You know just how bad the Crimson Company actually, *really*, are. *Especially* Vargas."

Kiyosi ran a hand over his head, past his horns and through his reddish-brown hair. After a ragged sigh, he tilted his head back to stare at the multi-colored silken shade sails overhead. The large triangles, draped across the rocky cavern roof, fluttered as a short gust of wind raced through the ancient lava tube.

He rubbed the back of his neck while his tail popped the air out of frustration.

"I still wonder if you're obsessed with him," Ki said in a solemn tone. "But I do understand. Vargas is a sadistic man. The idea that he is heading out to find what might be some ancient weapon? That scares me. Mostly because I know he might find it, then use it."

Turning back around, I held out the Immon apple to the young man attending the booth. Only twenty summers if by a day, he sported a dull orange and rust jacket that wrapped across his chest and tied on either side at the waist. It was a merchant journeyman's coat.

His eyes lingered on the enamel pin bearing the crossed key symbol of the Windtracer Company that I wore on my canvas vest. The journeyman grinned, dusted his hands on his trousers, then accepted the apple.

"I'll need a right good twelve tubik of these. Make sure the lot is preserved, dried, or cooked in Travelcake," I said. "Some of the dried beef and Thorn Lemons, too. Have them delivered with the bill to the Windtracer Company, care of Windtracer Tela Kioni."

The young man's eyes lit up at the large amount. Obviously a dyed-in-the-wool merchant, that one.

"Yes, Windtracer. Right away!"

The journeyman ran off to tell the shop owner, Nilevian Annaba, about the order. Nilevian would get it filled pretty quick, like usual. I turned back to Kiyosi and crossed my arms over my chest.

"It would help if that sadistic lunatic would leave me alone and let me, you know, do my work in peace."

Kiyosi didn't reply right away. Instead, my worry-wart of a friend looked slightly more perturbed than usual. I rubbed my hands over my face.

"Look, Ki. You're the best herbalist and physician I know. You're also my oldest friend. If even half of what Ihodis said is true, the Crimson Company does *not* need to find this 'Automatic Crystal of the Eclipse' and hand it over to some baron bent on making his own Ancient Order. For all anyone knows, this crystal may be a part of what brought *down* the Ancient Order."

Kiyosi's expression melted from 'perturbed' into downright 'sour'. So, that was at least progress.

"So, back out there then?" He waved a hand, gesturing in the air at the idea. "Where all sorts of illnesses and diseases could kill us in a slow, ugly death. That's before you get to magical traps, storms, and creatures that could just wink us out of existence." Kiyosi snapped his fingers. "Just like *that*."

I smirked. Some of that expression was bluster and bravado on my part, but not all of it. Going back to Long Deep? It wasn't going to be easy. That place was an old wound for me. But there was more to this than just Long Deep and the Crimson Company.

"If I have the right company with me that I can count on, then it might even be a little fun," I suggested.

Kiyosi let out a low sigh.

"I'd best get packed," he said. "Otherwise, ancestors only know what sort of ancient plague you'll come down with that'll turn you to paste. But," he emphasized this by raising an index finger between us, "we don't go alone. I'll get the crew together. Do you have a route in mind?"

I frowned over that. Planus continent is as flat as a dinner plate. So there were all sorts of ways to 'walk a path across Planus'. Some were just better than others. But, while certain paths were more interesting, that didn't always make them 'better', 'quicker', or 'safer'. The trouble was that Planus was so big, most people didn't have a good idea of what was out there.

"Same route as before, I suppose, using the same means of transport. If he's available, that is." I thought that over for a moment. "I'm pretty sure I heard he's available."

Ki again made with the sour look.

"Tyre? *Tyre Paleros?* He's a cheat and swindler. That old smuggler would sell the chair you're sitting in to make a coin."

I put a hand on Kiyosi's sleeve.

"And he's also a smuggler of the highest caliber with the fastest Windwagon on this side of Planus." I gave Ki a hard look. "You also know Tyre has never steered us wrong. Look. At this time of day, he'll be at the Salty Nightingale." I gave Ki's arm a gentle squeeze. "Come on. We'll go talk to him and make sure he's available for a trip like this."

4

Amates 15, 1277. Salty Nightingale. Underside District on the marsh-side. Where the trouble really began...

It didn't take long to weave through the afternoon crowd of the Silk Square to reach the dark stained oak door of the Salty Nightingale. The pub was set back from the Silk Square down a short close, or alley, from the main market walkways.

Being set back a short distance helped keep the noise from the market down. It also cut down on any snooping eyes and ears. The 'Gale had a very particular clientèle who didn't enjoy eavesdroppers.

I opened the oak door and stepped inside. The lighting was dim, as usual.

Most of the light in the Nightingale came from olive oil hurricane lamps hung on the wooden walls at regular intervals. This made it bright enough to see comfortably, but not glaringly bright. Sometimes the main fireplace was lit, like today, giving the whole place a cozy, welcoming feel.

Inside the doorway, I stopped and just inhaled. The smell of fresh baked cinnamon date bread and slow roasting marsh chicken was like a warm hug. I really loved that bread. Sounds and other sensations caught up to me next, from the mumble of conversations to laughter and the thump of drinking mugs on a tabletop.

By kind tides, there were just so many wonderful memories here for me.

All of that vanished the instant I saw the tree trunk stout figure of Tyre Paleros quietly arguing on the far side of the common room. He was being forced out the back door of the Nightingale by two broad-shouldered men. Naturally, the rest of the patrons kept to themselves, as was the custom.

The smuggler looked more irritated than frightened, but that didn't mean he was in any less danger. Especially since his new 'friends' wore the red trim leather jackets of the Crimson Company. I caught the glint of metal where one of the Crimson Company enforcers kept a dagger-point pressed against Tyre's shirt at his rib cage for motivation.

Fighting wasn't tolerated in the Nightingale. But kidnapping? That was debatable. It also depended if you could keep quiet about the attempt.

"*Ki!* Trouble! Out the back!"

I pointed to Tyre and the two walls of muscle with him. Then I was off like a shot arrow across the room.

Ki said something irate and grumpy in reply, but I missed it. I was sure he'd repeat it later. Out of the corner of my eye, I saw him dart out the front door when I started my run.

This wasn't our first dire merhorse race. If I was running right at the problem, which I often did, I trusted Ki to come at it from the back or side. It was a tried-and-true method to catch a target by surprise. Usually, it worked.

Shouts of surprise, even some cheers, filled the air now that the 'Gale's patrons couldn't politely ignore what was happening. The two

Crimson Company enforcers shot me a look of hot, melted death. This gave Tyre the opportunity to slam a porcelain beer stein against the head of one of his captors. It was a nice try, but it only earned him a swift punch in the mouth that left him dazed.

On my way across the room, I got a better look at Tyre's new 'friends'. They were big. It was as if someone shaved two bugbears clean of their fur, then stuffed their pale naked selves into clothes. But my wiry self is a half a head shorter than the average anybody so 'big' is relative. Still, these two had the look of being a real problem.

All I had on me were two daggers and a whip. Those enforcers were anything but a 'two daggers and a whip' sort of problem. A little extra help was going to be necessary.

I darted around tables and ran past patrons, heading for Tyre and his kidnappers before they could get too far ahead. Along the way, I kept an eye out for anything useful. Anything would do that could give me an edge against those two Crimson Company mercenaries. But this was a pub, not a blacksmith's shop, so I'd have to improvise.

The best I found was a stray wooden plate from a table near the back door and the iron spade from beside the fireplace. It was the best of a poor selection, but it would have to do.

Tyre had already been dragged out into the damp alley behind the pub by the time I had crossed the room. I yanked open the back door and rushed outside.

"Hand over the map, old man!"

Map? That stopped me in my tracks. It was a stupid question. Tyre was the captain of a windwagon. He had dozens of maps.

Tyre was, even for an Ishnanori human, a tall man. He was a good head or taller than me, with broad shoulders from years of hard work. Neither was he out of shape, even if there was plenty of salt to that dark curly hair of his.

But the Crimson Company enforcers were bigger, and there were two of them. One with red hair had Tyre pinned against the far wall of the alley and lifted off the ground enough that Tyre was almost standing on his toes.

"Cough it up or we'll beat it out of you!" Red Hair snapped, spitting in Tyre's face.

A dark grin split Tyre's salt and pepper beard.

"Kiss hell, Chowder-head. My maps are mine and not for the likes of you!"

The enforcer slammed an uppercut into Tyre's stomach, then slammed him back against the wall. It was the best opening I would get in a bad situation, so I dove in.

A fireplace spade isn't the most elegant weapon. It's basically a square, small shovel on a short handle made entirely of iron. But in a back-alley fight, no one cared about elegant.

I aimed low, slapping the flat of the spade against Red Hair's knee. He yowled like a siren, then stumbled back. I kept after him and brought the spade down again. This time, the flat of the iron shovel slapped the knuckles on Red Hair's hand when he grabbed for his knee. That earned me another yowl of pain, and more distance between the enforcer and Tyre.

"Tyre, you all right?"

He coughed then nodded before he forced himself to stand up straight.

"Fine enough. Been hit harder." He suddenly pointed to my left. "*Tela!*"

It was the second enforcer. I hadn't forgotten about him, but he moved a lot faster than I expected. The broad, blond-haired man swung a meaty fist. I tried to block or even duck but missed. The world exploded in stars as I retreated a step and blinked at the sharp pain that flashed from my left eye.

"Should'a stayed inside, little lady. Stick to serving tables."

That comment mixed with Blondy's smug posture made me see red. He swung again, but I was already moving. Sometimes all you need is the right motivation for the job at hand.

I rammed the iron pole of the spade against his forearm while his fist descended. He grunted before I quickly backhanded him across the mouth with the flat of the shovel. A dull metal echo rang in the alley. Blondy stumbled away in a daze, holding his jaw. I glanced over to see if Tyre was holding his own or if Ki had arrived yet.

There wasn't any reason to worry. Tyre had produced a leather blackjack from inside his blue canvas vest and given Red Hair two fresh welts on both cheekbones. It hadn't subdued Red Hair but made him keep his distance. This worked out well since it put the big man in reach of Ki.

Ki had raced into the alley from the far end on light feet. Somehow, from somewhere, Ki had found a short, stout, polished stick. It was probably a walking stick from one of the nearby booths in the Silk Square.

Either way, I wasn't surprised. Ki favored what he called 'natural weapons', like a tiefling tail swipe to just an ordinary thick stick he would pick up from anywhere. Here, he put both to use.

A hard slap with the walking stick to Red Hair's left arm made the man growl in pain. Red Hair sound more surprised than hurt, but the effect was the same. He grabbed the spot where Ki hit him, then tried to step away. But we were in an alley and there weren't many places to go. All that stumbling around must have aggravated the bruise I put on Red Hair's knee because at that moment, the man tumbled to the ground.

Ki didn't hesitate. The physician whipped his tiefling tail across the side of Red Hair's head. The big mad grabbed his face and tried to roll to safety. At least to wherever he thought 'safe' was right then.

Suddenly, I lost my breath when I found myself slammed against the far alley wall. It was Blondy. I was so busy watching Ki and Tyre work that I lost track of my own ugly problem.

I would've cursed, but I didn't have enough air for that. Instead, I gasped and stepped away from the wall, looking for Blondy. He wasn't hard to find since he running right at me.

Blondy lunged with both hands, reaching for my collar or throat. It didn't matter which, since I wasn't there when he tried to lay his hands on me. The moment the man moved toward me, I ran at him, only I ducked under Blondy's arms and stepped to my left. A quick spin, then I slammed the iron shovel against Blondy's right thigh with a hard slap.

My opponent yowled, winced, then stumbled sideways. I backed off to keep some distance between us. Darting around like that took a lot of air and I hadn't quite gotten all of mine back yet. This fight needed to stop soon so I *could* get my breath back. Unfortunately, that's when Blondy charged again.

He ran at me from an angle this time, coming at me from my side, which spoiled the aim with my shovel. Then I remembered the wooden plate in my other hand. Quickly, I hurled the plate like a discus.

My aim was true. The edge of the wooden plate smacked Blondy right between those bugbear-beady eyes then careened off down the alley. Blondy sputtered more than yelped this time, then backed away until he could lean against the stone wall farthest away from me.

No one spoke for the next few seconds. Instead, we all communicated with ugly glares. It spoke hot volumes. I also took the opportunity to gulp down some sweet, sweet air and clear my head. Blondy was the first to break the mood.

He limped carefully over to Red Hair and hauled his partner off the ground. Red Hair still had plenty of fight left in him and so tried to lunge for Ki. Blondy kept a tight hold of his partner's collar.

"Leave it. Not worth it. We'll get the map later."

"The bastard hit me with his tail!" Red Hair sputtered.

"Shut it! Not now!"

With that, the fight was over.

The pair of Crimson Company enforcers half-ran, half-limped down the alley toward the safety of the late afternoon crowds of the Silk Square. I planted my feet, flexed my grip on the iron shovel, and watched them leave. My left eye throbbed in time with my anger. I knew I'll be feeling that in the morning.

Behind me, I heard Ki being his usual physician self, asking Tyre where he was hurt and so on. Tyre replied, but grumbled the entire time about it. The man was forever a bad patient.

My focus, though, remained on the two Crimson Company enforcers until they were out of sight. Once they were truly gone, I turned my attention to Ki and Tyre. Mostly, I was focused on Tyre.

"Tyre. What in the name of the Devlfish's Daughter was that about?"

"They wanted a map," he drawled.

"So I heard," I replied dryly.

"What map?" Ki asked.

Tyre stood up straight and took a couple of deep breaths to get his wind back.

"No idea. They started off asking about my recent trips, trade runs, and the like. Those two never mentioned 'which map'." He tugged and smoothed out the old thick blue-black fearnought coat he always wore. "Really, I'm just disappointed. I remember the day when thugs were properly educated. There was a process to these things. This?" he shook his head. "Just a damn right shame of affairs."

"Oh, the *horror*," Ki said with a sarcastic tone.

Tyre ignored the comment since he was as used to Ki as I was. Ki was simply expressing his usual 'cranky country physician'. Tyre cleared his throat and continued.

"So, I figured they wanted my trade route maps. I get that from time to time." He shook his head. "But those? I won't hand those over to just anyone. Those routes are money for me."

Then the old smuggler grinned.

"But those two are gone for now and my favorite Windtracers are here!"

He clapped his hands together once, then placed his right hand over his heart. After that, he let out a belly laugh that brightened the air.

"What can I do for you two?"

I replied to the Ishnanori greeting in kind with a double clap then a hand over my own heart, and finished with a grin.

"*Yoi T'kalo*."

Tyre had an infectious laugh. Even Ki had started to smile. Unfortunately, my smile was short-lived.

"We're needing something from you, too." I pursed my lips. "Not just your maps though, we need *you*."

The old smuggler's smile widened, colored by humor. He spread his arms wide.

"Well, now it's always nice to be wanted." He waggled a calloused finger at me. "But I'm old enough to know better. So what is it? You two avoiding something? Need passage somewhere?" Tyre wiggled his eyebrows. "I know where we can dump a body or two."

I swapped a look with Ki, who said nothing. Sometimes he was not helpful at all. I sighed at Tyre.

"Passage. We need to get out to the Great Chasm. As close to Long Deep as the Chasm allows."

Tyre's humor melted out and was replaced with a stern, stony look. After a few seconds of staring at me, then Ki, he rubbed the bridge of his nose.

"For someplace like that, you two had best start at the beginning. I'm taking you nowhere until I know exactly what's going on."

5

Tyre stroked his beard, watching me with that measuring look of his while we navigated the late afternoon Silk Square market crowds. It wasn't me he was measuring; it was the whale of an explanation I just gave him.

The colorful shade sail cloth rustled overhead. Light Planus breezes coming through the ancient lava tube were more active than usual today. Market smells from roasted meat, fresh baked cinnamon breads and incense mingled with Underside's ever present musty scent. Silk Square wasn't silent with the chatter of patrons, but Tyre was. He finally spoke up after a minute of walking.

"So, it'll be a race then," he said at last. "Winner takes the prize." Tyre waved a hand, making small circles in the air. "That devil take it all Ancient Order thing."

"Automatic Crystal of the Eclipse," I said.

Tyre nodded a little and pointed at me.

"Yes, *that*," he finished, then paused at a café stall to get his bolat bag filled with fresh tea.

Ki stopped to study the merchant's hand painted wooden sign of available drinks. After a brief glance, he turned away.

"I told her it was dangerous. Double so because it's somewhere down among the plague ridden Long Deep." Ki shot a stern look at me. "Quit poking that bruise around your eye. Physician's orders."

I knew he had a point about the bruise, but I was losing the fight against a bad mood.

"Fine, but it *hurts*," I snapped. "It feels like I got hit with a brick."

Ki snorted.

"You did. A brick with two legs." He folded his arms over his chest as the tip of his tail swatted the air twice. With a nod toward the reddish brown root he had given me, he added, "now, drown it all woman, chew your awari root like I prescribed instead of toying with it. It'll help with the pain and keep that black eye from swelling." Ki sighed. "You're just lucky you've got a hard head."

I replied with a sour grimace, then bit off a chunk of the root in his direction. The chewy honey-pepper flavor of raw awari root was an acquired taste.

At the stall, Tyre smiled, then paid the grizzled tea merchant, who grinned back and gave a slight bow. Tyre raised his bag in a toast to the man, then turned back to our conversation.

"I agree. It's dangerous to head back over to Long Deep."

Kiyosi frowned at me while he gestured with both hands at Tyre.

"See? He agrees!" The realization of that statement sank in. Ki shot a look of astonished horror at the smuggler. "Wait, what? We *agree?*"

Tyre grinned, then took a drink of tea from his bolat bag. After that, he licked his lips.

"I *know!* I'm as surprised as you are, Ki!" The smuggler gently elbowed Ki while we continued on our way. "It was the last thing I ever expected."

One more drink, then Tyre replaced the stopper back in the bag and placed it on his belt. The old smuggler rubbed his hands together. A glint of mischief shone in his eyes.

"So, when do we leave? I can have the *Sheldrake* up and ready within the hour. Certainly, before the evening tide strikes high."

Ki rubbed his eyes.

"Gods of the Cresting Tides, save me from smugglers."

Tyre reached over to plant a meaty, reassuring hand on Kiyosi's shoulder.

"Ah, but they haven't yet, my good physician. So why worry?" His grin widened. "Now, Tela, when do we leave?"

I was laughing too hard to reply, even if it made the bruise around my left eye hurt. This type of conversation went on between the two of them every time before we set out on a trip. By now, it was some sort of strange ritual for them, and really, I didn't see the need to interrupt. Besides, it took my mind off my own private concerns, and nightmares, of the Long Deep.

Once I had the laughing fit under control, I shrugged.

"Soon. Before we go anywhere, we need supplies. I've ordered travelcake but we'll need more than that."

"Oh, I can take care of the rest," Tyre offered. "Other than supplies, what else is left?"

I quirked an eyebrow while I imagined him moving through the Silk Square while he gathered supplies with all the subtly of a Planus buffalo moving through a porcelain shop.

"Ransacking the Windtracer Records Hall for anything I can find on the Automatic Crystal of the Eclipse that Ihodis hasn't mentioned." I sighed. "Mostly because I hate going blind into an expedition."

Tyre gave Ki one last pat on the shoulder, then nodded sagely at me. "Wise as always."

He rubbed his nose, obviously thinking.

"In between stocking up, I'll look over my routes. I've charted two new ones since the last time I've taken you, or anyone, that way. This'll give us three choices to work with if the Planus winds change direction on us."

"Is one faster than the others? What's the difference?" Ki asked, toying with the head of his new walking stick.

Tyre raised his eyebrows at that and pursed his lips while we wandered through Underside toward the Port Side district.

"Faster? No. They're all quick, but take about the same time. Those routes are based on the direction the prairie wind is taking across Planus and what I might be carrying for trade. There's two new farming villages in the deep plains." Tyre winked at us. "So there may be a stop or two along the way, nothing more than that, though."

The smuggler's expression turned serious.

"Also, all of what you've told me explains why the Crimson Company was so eager for my maps. They're looking for a fast route there, too." He stroked his beard again. "That tells a *lot* about what's driving them."

I swapped a look with Ki.

"It does? I assumed it was money. What do you mean?" I asked.

Tyre grabbed the lapels of his long coat before he frowned slightly at my question. It made him look almost scholarly.

"Well, the Crimson Company is mercenary company. A business that peddles a fighting force. If you run that sort of business and rough up merchant captains like myself, you soon run out of people that will carry you and your troops anywhere."

The smuggler smiled grimly.

"So, normally, they would've tried to buy my maps or just hire me to carry them. If either of those offers had failed, *then* I would expect them to try what they did. But no, they started right with the mugging. That's important."

I grunted, then watched the path ahead through the market while we walked. It was clustered with merchants and customers working out late afternoon deals. The steady chatter of people was a humming backdrop that helped me concentrate. Another light breeze drifted through Underside and its underground marketplace.

"I didn't think of that. So you believe they're having to deliver this by a certain day?" I asked.

Ki pursed his lips.

"Or they're under a threat to 'get it done quickly or else' by this Lord Marius that Ihodis mentioned," he added.

That prompted me to give Ki an astonished look.

"What? Vargas and his Crimson Company? Professional ruin poacher *Vincent Vargas]* be afraid of some baron of all things?"

Tyre shook head. "Tela, you've been through far too much to tell me you don't already understand that everyone is afraid of something. Even Vargas."

It was Kiyosi's turn to look thoughtful. The faint hint of a frown that had started a second ago now shadowed his face.

"It must be really something impressive to put a scare into Vargas and his mercenaries."

I didn't reply. Tyre had given me a lot more to think about. We continued down the Silk Square, walking for the Port Side district above Underside. Ki was musing over what medical supplies he would need for the trip in between asking Tyre about the tea he purchased. I kept to my own thoughts.

Vargas, and my dislike for the thieving sadist, had colored my view. I'll be the first to admit it had distracted me. Then there was Long Deep, which loomed large in the back of my mind.

Sure, I played it off with a laugh and a brash comment. But I'd be lying to myself if I said I wasn't concerned. I still carried the scars from that expedition. Scars in my memories and along my left shoulder and ribcage. Those scars were permanent and weren't going away. I even tried paying for a magical cure, which didn't do a thing. I still hear the screams from the people I lost the last time I was at Long Deep.

I shook my head. That caravan of thoughts wasn't getting me anywhere. After a deep breath, I focused on what Tyre had said.

It made sense. Too much sense. But I had no answer for the 'why'. Ihodis mentioned that Baron Marius Apollinare had dreams of a 'New Ancient Order' and that he wanted to remake it on his terms. I didn't think much about it at the time, but 'on his own terms' could mean a lot of things. Some of those things could be very bad.

"We need to set out tomorrow. Soon and fast," I decided.

This broke up the conversation between Ki and Tyre about the subtle variations of tea.

"Good and done," Tyre replied. "The *Sheldrake* will be waiting marsh-side at the camp-ports, ready to move. Should I send my usual fee and contract to the Windtracers?"

I nodded. "Yes. Same as last time."

Ki was squinting and really scrutinizing me now. I never liked it when he did that. It felt like I was being diagnosed.

"What?" I asked after an uncomfortable few seconds.

"Tomorrow doesn't give us much time to research the Automatic Crystal of the Eclipse," he said. "You've thought of something, or just realized something. What is it?"

I pursed my lips, then shook my head.

"What Tyre said makes far too much sense, and I've been too distracted to see it. I'll explain once we've set off."

Ki, who still had that look on his face, nodded.

"All right. So where to from here?"

"While Tyre gets the supplies and what we need, you and I dive into Windtracer records, even any copies sent by the Archivists Guild from over in Centrum, for anything that even mentions the Automatic Crystal of the Eclipse or this Baron Marius Apollinare."

Tension flared in the back of my shoulders. A premonition? It might be, but I ignored it.

"Because what we don't know might kill us."

6

Amates 19, 1277. Somewhere on the Planus continent, aboard the Sheldrake, moving northeast of Ishnanor.

There had been a lot to think about in the four days since we left Ishnanor.

I untied the canvas shade, then rolled the cloth up to the top of the window frame to let in some air and clear my head. There were too many thoughts fighting for my attention. I needed them all to be quiet for a while. The soft prairie wind rushed through the window, so I pulled the tie from my hair to let my dark braids fall loose in the breeze. It felt good.

Outside, the wagon's sailwings fluttered and creaked. Rigging between the wagon and its pontoons softly complained, while Tyre's Planus buffalo team towed the floating wagon along over the tall prairie grass.

I took in a long breath. The wind, which almost never stopped blowing across the Planus prairie, was filled with comfortable, earthy scents. The smell of sweet flowers mixed with faintly bitter dry dust and prairie sage moved in the surrounding air. The tension behind my eyes melted, then slid off of me.

Another few seconds wandered by while I watched the flat landscape. I sighed, then opened my worn leather journal to leaf through the hastily scribbled notes I took down in the Windtracer Records Hall.

Ihodis had left out a few details, but not many. The book he had shown me and the papers he bought off the spice merchant had cleared up a few questions. Neither one was a complete study, but they held some interesting details.

The book was a copy of a cartographer's journal who had explored the ruined city of Elka in 977 AGC. This cartographer, one Foldor Gilstock, had found what he thought was an alchemist's workshop. Among old reagents that nearly blew his head off was a diagram of an 'Automatic Crystal', thumb-sized studs and all. Foldor wasn't sure about the drawing, just that he felt it was important.

Then there were the papers. These were written by a woman named Nilna Sestoros about a century ago. She was an herbalist who had been roped into more dungeon delving that she wanted to by her brother.

On one of their trips, they explored the tombs around the Samat Pyramid in the Oniruuru Desert. There, much like old Foldor, she found an alchemist's workshop with diagrams as well. But as a bonus, with these diagrams was a crude explanation of how the Automatic Crystal did, or might have, worked.

This last was how Ihodis had learned how the crystal might be for communication or be some device that generated lethal rays of magic. But thanks to both accounts, I now had a better portrait in my head about the Automatic Crystal of the Eclipse.

I used both Foldor and Nilna's accounts to fashion my own sketches of an Automatic Crystal for reference. This inspired my own conclusions, or really theories, about the relic. I didn't think this was a weapon at all, but something else.

A device that could be used for communication but also be a weapon with 'deadly magic rays' just didn't work for me. Foldor and Nilna's accounts made the 'for communication' part pretty clear. My own theory was that the things were for academic study.

As for those 'lethal rays', it could be the Crystal was missing a component to make it work? Now that made more sense to me. After all, not everything dug out of a ruin was a dangerous weapon. In fact, most things weren't.

After four days, I still had questions with no answers and not enough information to fill in the gaps. But puzzling over all of this had kept my mind busy while we traveled. I really needed the distraction.

I was so buried in my own thoughts I didn't hear Ki walk up behind me. That was a bad habit I really needed to fix.

"Reading your notes again?" he asked.

I jumped, or really twitched, in surprised before I turned around. Ki was freshly scrubbed and dressed in his usual traveling attire, complete with a denim blue shirt that offset his tiefling sea-blue coloration.

"Can't help it," I replied. "Ihodis is really onto something here. This could be a major find if it still exists."

Ki folded his arms over his chest and nodded.

"It could. Especially if you're right about your idea that the crystal is really some sort of academic teaching tool." He pursed his lips. "How are you doing?"

I gave my left eye an experimental blink, then opened it wide. That last made me wince.

"Better. Still sore, but better. The awari root helped. Thank you, Ki."

A faint smile, almost sad, crossed his lips.

"I didn't mean the eye, not entirely. What I meant was you." Ki tilted his head to the side just a hair. "I saw that shaking fit you had in the Records Hall when you thought no one was looking. It had me worried."

I looked away to stare at the window frame, then the grassland rolling by outside.

"It's nothing. I just needed to get my head together after the fight."

Ki was quiet for a time, then sighed.

"All right. Just remember, when and if you want to talk, I'll listen. Either as a physician or your friend."

That made me smile, if even just a little.

"Deal."

Ki joined me at the windwagon's window. I propped myself against the side of the window frame while he leaned against the windowsill. The view of Planus trailed by at a steady pace while we floated several hands high over the wheat-tall prairie grass. The tug of Tyre's buffalo team on the wagon kept a methodical rhythm.

I ran a hand over my journal, then opened it to where the drawing of the Crystal filled an entire page. To be honest, my thoughts weren't on theories about the relic and why the Ancient Order made the thing. When I looked up from the page, I saw Ki watching me.

"So, which is it? Your theories on the Crystal? The Crimson Company?"

"What? I'm *that* transparent?" I asked with a faint smirk.

Ki shook his head with a wry smile, then looked back out the window.

"Transparent? No."

He took a deep breath.

"We've been friends a long time, Tela. As your physician, I've patched you up more times than I care to remember. Something about your notes is chewing at you as if you had a Gelpa ichorworm on your back."

I raised by eyebrows and glanced down at my journal.

"No, not a Gelpa ichorworm. Not again."

Running my hands over the leather binding of my journal, I rattled my brain for the right words. A long moment later, I used the best ones I could string together.

"It isn't about the relic." I pursed my lips, then continued. "Sure, I'm thinking over my theories. I can't help that. What little we found mentioned more about the Ancient Order using Automatic Crystals for teaching and to talk to each other than hurting people." I shook my head. "But no, not that. Not even the Crimson Company. They're a big problem, but we've dealt with that barrel of rotten spike-fish before."

"So, it's the baron, then?" Ki asked in a soft, concerned tone.

"Yes. The baron." I sighed. "There were only three references to him and one of those we had to pry out of a thieves' guild. The other two just didn't make any sense."

Ki shrugged.

"Some people *do* live to be three hundred years old or so. People with an elven bloodline for one."

I lightly slapped the journal against my hand.

"But he's *not* an elf. He's human, or supposed to be human." I paused, as my thoughts lost the tug of war against my frustration. "*Just* a normal human."

Ki pursed his lips, then squinted at the prairie outside.

"A three hundred-year-old human," Ki said. "With possibly two birthdays on record, if that thieves' guild was being honest about it. I mean, they also kept calling him everything from a vampire, to a lich, to a dragon."

"I just wish we could have learned more about him." I sighed. "Just to know who we're up against. He gives me a bad feeling I can't put my fingers on."

"But we've already learned a lot," Ki replied. "We found there is nothing about his lineage, who he owes his allegiance to, or any of the details that the nobility wear openly like jewelry. That says volumes, Tela. All we have is that he's a three hundred-year-old human who lives in the city of Sol. That means he's spared no pain to keep a low profile."

He glanced at me with a concerned look.

"In Sol, of all places."

I nodded slightly, even though I didn't feel any better about the entire situation.

"Then it's good then we didn't collect an entire crew for this expedition. Just you, me, Tyre, and his first mate, Eviera."

Ki chuckled.

"Four in a race against the Crimson Company and their odd backer." He stood upright, then rapped his knuckles on the windowsill with a faint grin. "With four, we should be nimble and draw almost no attention."

"That's the idea," I replied in a tight, low voice.

"Town ahead," Tyre shouted from the front of the windwagon. "Place called Banye. We'll be stopping to rest the buffalo, trade, get some rest for ourselves and supplies."

Eviera trotted past us from the front of the windwagon. The centaur was pulling back her copper-gold hair in a tight braid. I've known the lady for about as long as I've known Tyre. Her eyes were hard and shoulders tense, like she was back in her pit-dueling days.

"Evi, what's wrong?"

The lady centaur paused at my question and finished her tight braid.

"There's a lot of smoke rising from Banye," she replied.

Her tone has always been deep, with a matter-of-fact edge to the words. The edge was sharper this time. "Far too much to be chimney smoke. Something's wrong ahead."

7

I was covered in soot. Wood smoke, which stung my eyes, was everywhere.

Where there weren't spots of soot on me, there was grime. I smelled burnt hair, which I think was mine, but I hadn't had time to check. Overall, I felt like a dusky-skinned Chivit smudge leopard in a bad need of a nap.

The fire, bad as it was, hadn't spread very far by the time Tyre pulled the *Sheldrake* into Banye at a hard gallop. One building at the edge of town was already a bonfire, and the one closest to it was smoldering. Kiyosi and I were out of the *Sheldrake* before Tyre had his buffalo team pulled to a full stop.

It took a solid half-hour of hard work to get the fire under control. Banye, like any town, used a fire brigade to haul water by bucket from the ancient fountain in the town square. To my surprise, they also had a small hydraulis pump on a wagon. I had only ever seen those pumps on a ship, and the ones used aboard ship would never work on a wagon.

Tyre and I took turns hauling buckets with the fire brigade, or helping people escape the smoldering building before the flames next door grabbed it. Ki and Evi took turns on the hydraulis pump lever with the Banye locals.

But now it was over.

I leaned against the side of the hydraulis pump wagon and stared at the charred skeleton of the sole building that hadn't survived. Orange motes rose from the ruin like scattered rain falling up to the sky. Nearby, at a hastily erected tent, Ki was treating locals for everything from burns to smoke poisoning. Evi stopped next to me while I was getting my breath back.

"This is one way to get welcomed into town," I joked dryly as I glanced over at her.

Evi let out an amused snort. The lady centaur was as grimy as I was and looked no less tired.

"I'd prefer a quiet drink at a warm tavern myself," she said, folding her arms over her chest. "Anyone say what caused it?"

I shook my head.

"No. I haven't heard a thing." I sighed, then pointed at the makeshift physician's tent nearby. "Ki might've though. He's been seeing to the locals long enough. Someone might have said something by now."

Evi stared at the charred remains while she let out a long breath. I followed her gaze. Orange embers winked from the broken timbers while flecks of black, bitter wood dust few off in the light breeze. The building next to it was intact, but the wall that faced the burnt ruin had warped slightly from the fire's heat. That alone would take some repair.

Towns out here are built using adobe mud but relied on wooden timber frames and sometimes even wooden walls. That Wafer Willow wood was *always* dry. Fires on Planus are often lethal because of the winds and dry air pushing the fire across buildings. More than one town had been destroyed in minutes that way.

I sighed.

"Thank the Goddess of the High tides that fire never left the first building. I just hope no one was hurt."

"Not a bit! The only thing hurt was my pride, and that'll recover."

Evi and I turned around toward the cheerful, scratchy voice behind us. It was a balding, older halfling man, slightly short and stocky, who was walking our way. Most Banyians I had seen so far wore a simple linen shirt, trousers, and a short sleeve knee-length outer tunic. It was typical Planus clothing style, as best I knew of it. But not with this man.

In place of the outer tunic, he wore something like a wool and leather surcoat. It was covered with a collection of pockets and tool loops. I had never seen a thing like that in my life. But, given the well-cared for tools, writing stylus, and a journal peaking out of a book pouch at his belt, I guessed he was an inventor of sorts. Maybe even the local tinker or blacksmith.

His grin was as bright as noonday. A large, white spotted charcoal cat as tall as my knees wandered next to him. A Planus smoke cheetah if I remembered the breed right. The man stopped short of us, looked over at the ruined building, and sighed.

"It was just my workshop. The older one." He sniffed and tried to pat the soot from his own clothes with little success. "I'd be tearing it down and rebuilding it soon, anyway. I shouldn't have put it off so long."

I swapped a quick, suspicious look with Evi. She folded her arms over her chest again, then pawed a little at the ground with a front hoof.

"Sorry about the workshop...?" She let the obvious invitation for introductions hang in the air.

He looked back at us, eyebrows raised. "Hm? Oh! Just caught up in my own thoughts there." The man placed a hand over his chest and smiled. "Good winds. I'm Mikasi Zenia and this over-sized ball of fur at my feet is Nicodemus. He's a lump, don't mind him."

I placed my hand over my own chest.

"*Yoi T'kalo*. I'm Tela Kioni, this is Eviera Zerveli. We just arrived on the *Sheldrake*."

Evi nodded.

"Kind tides."

"Tyre's windwagon! So I saw." Mikasi squinted at me. "You're a Windtracer from the Windtracer Company, aren't you?"

I blinked in surprise, then realized I was wearing my old locket with the Windtracer Company heraldry on it. It had fallen outside my shirt during all the fire-fighting. Ki always did tell me that I was as subtle as a hammer when it came to keeping a low profile. I tucked the locket back under my shirt in a fit of self-consciousness.

"Ah, yes. Yes, I am."

Mikasi rubbed his hands together.

"Wonderful! I have some ideas and notes on a few devices I'd like to share with you. Water pumps, a device that uses lights for sending messages, that sort of thing. I would love to get your thoughts on them."

The little man waved a hand at the rest of Banye and its tiny sprawl of buildings.

"Once you've cleaned up, I'll be at the Buckhorn down the road."

I blinked and looked over at Evi. She glanced in the direction Mikasi had waved.

"An inn?"

Mikasi nodded once.

"Exactly! Though around here, we call it a boardinghouse. Buck-horn Boardinghouse. It's a fine place. We'll talk and get something to eat if you're hungry. I'll bring my journal!"

With that, he was off down the road with his smoke cheetah trotting happily along beside him, tail raised. I rubbed the sides of my head.

"Wait! What about your," my mind stumbled over itself for the right words. I blinked and pointed at the ruin. "Workshop?"

Mikasi didn't even pause. He simply raised a hand and waved.

"I'll rebuild later! That old place needed a good cleaning, anyway!"

A headache was trying to worm into the back of my skull. I rubbed the sides of my head again.

"What just happened here?"

Evi raised her eyebrows at me and smirked.

"We got invited to a mid-day meal. I wonder if it's formal?"

I shot her a pained grimace. Evi just laughed.

Two young men wandered by, thanked us for the help, then left with the wagon and its small hydraulis pump. Tyre, sooty as the rest of us, walked over right after that while five or so Banyians finished tossing sand on the last of the burning rubble. He gave us a bright grin, then hooked his thumbs in his broad leather belt.

"So. I saw you met Mikasi."

I shifted my look from Evi to Tyre.

"Yes," I replied slowly. "He's... a lot."

Tyre's deep chuckle rumbled in his broad chest.

"He is, but that's just his way. Can't be still that one. He's always inventing one thing or another." He waved a hand at the burned ruins. "That was probably the result of some new device he dreamed up. Cresting Tides knows what it was, as I'm sure the fire claimed it."

"He invited us to a meal and some conversation." Evi explained. She nodded slightly toward me. "I think mostly because he noticed she's a Windtracer."

Tyre added a chuckle to his grin.

"Oh, count on it. Probably means he's got some idea he wants a second opinion on." He jerked a thumb at the retreating wagon with its hydraulis pump. "Could be an improvement to his hydraulis pump there, or some device to let a person fly. Who knows?"

I pursed my lips and resisted the urge to fidget. The race to the relic was on my mind. There was no way to know if the Crimson Company had found transportation and where they were right now. Were they behind us? Or *ahead*?

That last thought made me grimace.

Tyre spread his arms wide.

"Oh, come now. We won't be in Banye long and Mikasi is only dangerous to mostly himself. You, my lady, need to relax while you can. Besides, we'll be with you."

He gestured at the physician's tent.

"I'll even go harass Ki into coming along. He's so uptight, he's ten years overdue for a truly relaxing meal."

That last comment made me grin despite my list of worries. Tyre had a point. What could it hurt? It might even help.

"Hells, Tyre," I said with a dry laugh. "All right. I don't know about anyone else, but I want to be clean first and not feel like an over sized soot-stain. Besides, you're right. If your Mikasi friend invented a small version of a hydraulis pump that fits on a *wagon* instead of only a *ship*, maybe I can learn a thing or two. I might even relax."

8

Amates 19, 1277. Town of Banye, in the Buckhorn Boardinghouse. The only inn in town.

Scrubbing off the soot was far easier than hearing what Mikasi had to say. I nearly dropped my mug. Fortunately for my food, I didn't.

"Wait. What did you just say?"

Mikasi, his own mug partway to his mouth, looked around the table at us wide-eyed.

"Say what?" He asked slowly. "All I said was that I realized what I had overlooked when I read the Cesibus' notes again. He used a counterweight in his design that I hadn't accounted for. I was tired and missed that."

I shook my head.

"No, not that. The part about Cesibus himself."

"He was a blacksmith, really an inventor, during the time of the Ancient Order." Mikasi looked even more confused than before.

I set my mug on the dark, rosewood wooden table and stared at Mikasi. This news, really a revelation, was amazing. The clank of plates, hum of chatter in other parts of the boardinghouse and other sounds floated through the surrounding air. In that moment, I had even forgotten about the heavenly spiced barley beef stew in front of me, despite how hungry I was.

The name of Cesibus meant absolutely nothing to me. I hadn't heard or read even a hint about him before. That wasn't unusual. The Ancient Order lasted a long time before it fell. They had a lot of inventors during those years and only and only a small cupful had been rediscovered.

Learning that Cesibus even existed *was* important. But what this overly energetic halfling inventor just causally suggested? That was something else entirely.

"You can *translate* Ancient Order manuscripts that easily? You can *read* their language?"

Mikasi sat very still and cradled his mug close to his chest. His eyes darted around the table while he pursed his lips.

"Well... I..." The inventor took a quick drink of whatever that dark, bitter looking liquid was in his mug. "No. Yes?" His eyes wandered over his tin plate of food in front and the long boardinghouse table. "Maybe?"

He squinted at us.

"Mostly?"

I blinked before I sat back in my chair and ran a hand over my dark braids. Words? I lost those. What could I say? Windtracer Company, the Archivists Guild, and so many more were still struggling to translate what the Ancient Order left behind.

Yet here, in a dusty little town in Planus, was a halfling inventor who had done just that.

While I might have lost my words, Ki was right there to help. He sat forward, pinning Mikasi to his seat with one of those narrow squint-eyed expressions that Ki used so well.

"Mostly? What is 'mostly'?"

Mikasi drew his mouth into a tight line while he fingered the rim of his elm wood mug. After a second, he shrugged.

"Mostly is mostly." The inventor frowned with the expression of someone who had misplaced a thought. He even patted the breast pockets of his surcoat as if he had left it there. "Just mostly," Mikasi concluded after a moment's consideration.

That worm of an ache had found my head again. I rubbed my eyes. "*Aile Shavat!*" I swore in a soft voice.

I took a quiet few seconds to collect my patience before I placed both hands flat on the table in front of me.

"All right," I sighed. "I do want to hear more about this Ancient Order blacksmith, Cesibus, and I'm going to want to take notes. But. You said Cesibus wrote something down you overlooked. So, was that from a document *written* by Cesibus, or was it from a collection of works someone *translated* from Cesibus?"

Mikasi emphatically shook his head.

"Oh, Cesibus wrote it. I translated it myself."

I slapped the table lightly out of mild frustration. The halfling inventor jumped in his chair, startled.

"I'm sorry. Sorry." I raised my hands to try to make some sort of peacemaking gesture. "It's just, this is important... I didn't mean to startle you."

Tyre took a long drink from his own mug. He lightly tapped the table with a finger.

"Mika. Take a deep breath, old friend, and let's start back a bit. When did you learn to read anything written during the Ancient Order's time? The language is dead."

A glimmer of light dawned in the inventor's eyes.

"Oh. Oh!" He shook his head again. "No, I can't read just *anything* written by *anyone* from the Ancient Order. I can read Ancient Order papers and scrolls if they're written by Cesibus. Anything else?" Mikasi shrugged. "I might could read a little of it, but I'm not sure."

"Progress," Evi rumbled, then devoted her attention to the bread, meat, and slaw on the plate in front of her.

I gave her a sour glance, after which I frowned slightly at Mikasi.

"So, Cesibus wrote in some sort of dialect?"

Mikasi pursed his lips again and took a quick drink from his mug before he answered.

"No. Not a 'dialect' really." He gave me a bright grin. "Though I understand why you'd think that! But no. As I understand it, Cesibus was worried about other people stealing his work. So he wrote in a sort of 'code'."

"Code?" Ki asked. "What kind of code?"

Mikasi set his mug down before he fished the journal out of his belt pouch. Almost exploding with excitement, he pushed the half-empty place aside, then spread open his journal in front of us.

The pages were weathered and filled with notes, diagrams of pumps, and other devices. A half dozen cloth bookmarks divided the journal. Where there weren't bookmarks, there were loose, small, hand-drawn maps or pieces of scrolls.

I can't say I'm an expert at the Ancient Order written language, but I can manage a rough translation of key phrases here and there. What I saw on those pages made no sense to me. It was nothing I had ever seen before. I squinted at the scrawl of letters, which didn't help one bit.

Mikasi tapped the pages.

"See? It's brilliant. Cesibus normally wrote his notes in a mathematical shorthand. On this page, I was just copying what he wrote." He fished a loose piece of paper from the depths of the journal. "Here is one of Cesibus' original papers."

The paper was obviously old, and a bit fragile, given how much care Mikasi took with it. Instead of Mikasi's narrow scrawl, this paper was covered in notes written in a slanted, fluid handwriting. Mikasi touched a finger to certain spots on the relic.

"He used symbols and icons that normally are only used in device designs. Here, he uses them to represent similar words. But that wasn't enough!"

The inventor rummaged around in a pocket of his surcoat, and produced a small, palm-sized rectangular mirror. He placed that up against the edge of the ancient paper.

"He wrote all his letters, notes, everything backwards, so you had to use a mirror to read them!" Mikasi giggled a bit. "I mean, you'd need a mirror unless you learned to read it backwards like he wrote it."

"Which, you have?" Ki suggested.

"I had to when I lost my first pocket mirror."

I leaned forward to stare at the reflection in the mirror while they talked. True to his word, the writing on the yellowed paper now made more sense. Briefly I read the notes, taking time to work out the abbreviations and mathematical 'symbol shorthand'.

The paper, this one anyway, was notes and ideas on controlling the flow of liquids to produce certain results. There was a drawing of a device similar to a hydraulis pump as well. I suspected this had been a part of a journal the blacksmith used some centuries ago. At the bottom, Cesibus remarked on the nature of light and magic. How, based on his own measurements, he knew that light 'flowed' in 'waves', which he wrote was crucial in using it to convey messages. Cesibus wondered if magic behaved the same way.

I sat back in my chair, stunned. The implications left me speechless. It took me a second to catch up with the conversation going on around me.

"Gods of the Cresting Tides," Kiyosi said softly. "And you said you learned to read this... 'mirror language' on your own?"

Mikasi smiled again.

"I did. It took me some time to puzzle it out, though. But because Cesibus used so many mathematical symbols, it helped me decipher the rest of what he wrote."

Ki shook his head slowly.

"Astounding. Really damn astounding."

I grabbed Ki's arm to get his attention before I tapped the last lines of Cesibus' notes in Mikasi's journal.

"Ki, look here. This part where Cesibus wrote about 'flowing light'." I gave him a stern, meaningful look. "If he's read about Cesibus' studies involving light..."

Ki was better with translations than I was. It took him only a few seconds to read the reflected notes. I could see it in his eyes that he finished my thought and came to the same conclusion.

He took a deep breath as he leaned forward on his elbows. I could hear his tail gently swat the chair leg.

"Mikasi, I know you might be busy, what with your workshop having burnt down and all..."

The older man chuckled. He waved a hand in the vague direction of the burnt building.

"It's like I said before. That old place needed a good cleaning. I'll get to rebuilding it soon. After all, it's not where I do most of my work, anyway."

Tyre chuckled.

"You got your wish on getting to 'clean' there, Mika."

Ki shook his head at that, so I jumped in.

"Well, if you're not busy right now, would you be interested in looking over some drawings of an Ancient Order relic? We would love to know what you think. They possibly used the device for... several things, but we're not exactly sure what. We've a lot of wild guesses, but nothing really seems to fit."

The inventor's eyes lit up.

"I would be *delighted!*" he said with enough enthusiasm for two people. "Is this part of a Windtracer expedition?"

Now it was my turn to fidget. Mikasi was just so *excited* about anything with the Windtracers that it made me a bit uncomfortable. I managed a weak laugh.

"Ah, yes," I replied slowly. "It's an expedition and we really don't have a lot of time to spare."

Mikasi abruptly pushed back from the table, then stood up. He tossed two coins on the table by his plate. At his feet, I heard Nicodemus yawn before cheetah claws tapped the wooden floor. The unmistakable sound of a cat stretching after a nap.

"Let's get started! Where are your designs?"

I blinked, desperately trying to keep up.

"Aboard the *Sheldrake*. I'll need to go get them."

Tyre cleared his throat.

"Mika, where's your *actual* workshop? The one you *don't* usually burn down?" he asked with a grin.

The inventor pointed to the south end of Banye.

"Other side of town. Two story, mud-brick building. It has a blacksmith's forge in the back with a custom hydraulis pump next to it. It's one of my more recent designs to help cool down forged materials and reuse the water."

With that, Mikasi was off again, like he was hurled out of a slingshot. Nicodemus trotted along happily beside him. I glanced over at Tyre and Evi.

"He really doesn't do 'slow', does he?"

Tyre laughed, one of those belly laughs that could shake the heavens. Evi was also chuckling while she finished her meal.

"No, he doesn't," she said.

Tyre drained the last of his drink, then set the mug down on the table.

"Mika's been that way for all the years I've known him. Sharp as a well-honed knife, and gets very focused when he's got a goal in mind."

"Sounds like someone else I know," Ki said dryly, with a sideways glance at me.

I gave him mildly sour look.

"I don't own a Planus cheetah," I replied in flat tone.

Ki lifted his mug for a final drink.

"If it keeps you out of near-death experiences, I'd be in favor."

I rolled my eyes at him.

We quickly finished our meals. I needed to run down to the *Sheldrake*, gather up my satchel with my journal and other notes. After that, I would head for Mikasi's workshop. Ki elected to go right to the workshop with Evi.

It was obvious, at least to me, that Ki was eager to see the inventor's workshop and notes. Especially any more journal entries by Cesibus. Ki was as bad as I was about such things, even if he didn't like to admit it.

Tyre joined me on the trip back to the *Sheldrake*. He wanted to check on his buffalo team and going with me made a good excuse to do just that.

On the way out of the Buckhorn, a ghost of motion by a small side window of the boardinghouse caught my eye. It seemed like just someone passing by the window getting on with their day. But it wasn't what they did that made me hesitate. It was how he looked.

It was a big man, human, broad-shouldered with red hair, wearing what I thought was a red-trimmed leather jacket. The same sort of jacket the Crimson Company preferred to use.

He also had a black eye that looked only a few days old.

I stopped in my tracks and stared at that window. Without a word, I raced out and around to that side of the building. The man was already gone.

Tyre trotted up after me a second later.

"Tela, is everything all right?" he asked, concerned.

I lightly rubbed the side of my head near my black eye and frowned.

"It's fine. Just... distracted." I smiled at Tyre. "Let's get my satchel, then catch up to the others."

9

***Amates 19, 1277. Mid-afternoon. Town of Banye.
Walking down the south side of town.***

The trip from the *Sheldrake* to Mikasi's workshop didn't take that long.

As farming and ranching towns on the prairie went, Banye wasn't that large. Only one hard-packed dirt street meant it was easy to navigate. This quick trip also wasn't very exciting, other than the conversation.

"So," I said slowly to Tyre as we walked. "When were you going to tell me that you set me up?"

That earned me a look of feigned shock. It didn't last long. Another one of Tyre's 'amused with the world' chuckles rumbled in his chest.

"About now, most likely. I didn't figure it would take long before you realized I brought us to Banye on purpose." He shrugged. "Tela, you've been stewing over those notes about that Autowinder What-sit..."

"Automatic Crystal," I corrected him.

Tyre nodded.

"Right, that. The Automatic Crystal. You've been stewing over your journal ever since we left Ishnanor."

I started to reply, but he held up a hand to stall me. The wind kicked up around us, stirring a faint trail of dust with the smell of prairie grass and wildflowers.

"Hold the plum line and let me get this out," Tyre said. "You've been chewing over this so much that you've skipped at least a meal or two." He gave me a sideways glance. "Don't think I haven't noticed."

There wasn't a good reply to that. Tyre was right. I *had* skipped a meal or two in favor of redrawing some part of the relic. If I wasn't sketching, I was reading copies of Foldor Gilstock or Nilna Sestoros' journal entries. Maybe I had been a bit focused. It wasn't like I was starving myself.

Tyre waved a hand at Mikasi's adobe brick workshop ahead of us at the edge of town.

"So, I used the route that would bring us through Banye. Mika's erratic, but I've known him a bit longer than I've known you. The two of us did some ruin poaching back in the day and he's one of the sharpest minds I know." Tyre shrugged at me again. "This way, you have someone about as smart as you to toss ideas around with."

He let out a slow sigh, then focused on the walk ahead of us.

"I meant well, Tela. This," he waved a hand in a slow circle, "expedition? Race? It's important. I understand that. But you're important, too. There's a good chance Mika can give us a fresh look at what seems to be an old problem. Which means we'll have a leg up on the Crimson Company with knowing what's ahead."

I *really* wanted to be irate with him, but I couldn't. Tyre was a good friend. In many ways, he was more like a favorite uncle. When I was a little girl, he had always been there for me. Especially every time I tried to stow away aboard the *Sheldrake*. I rubbed my eyes with one hand while I squeezed the leather strap of the satchel slung across my chest with the other.

"All right. Yes, I've been a bit... focused? Focused." I held up my hands for emphasis. "I'll give you that. Also, maybe I have needed to consult with someone to get some fresh ideas. Ki can listen to me babble about the same thing only so much. Besides, Ki's studies lean toward medicine, medicinal magics, herbs, languages, and the like. The Automatic Crystal is a little outside of what he knows."

I pursed my lips before I smiled at Tyre.

"So, all right. Mikasi is odd. *Really* odd. But if he has some new idea or better way to look at this thing we're chasing? I might hug him until he turns blue."

Tyre barked out a short laugh.

"Bargained fair and true," he replied while he gestured to the front door of Mikasi's workshop.

The outside of the workshop was just as Mikasi described. It was a plain, dark tan adobe brick, two story building, similar to a handful of other adobe brick buildings in Banye. A blacksmith's shop, which was little more than a tacked-on room with one wall removed, extended from the back.

Inside, Mikasi's place was *far* more interesting.

The entry way was just that. A table, chair and not much else. Past the entryway was a room lined with stained bookshelves made from an orange-gold cedar. They were slightly warped from age and the weight of haphazardly stacked books with the occasional specimen jar.

I didn't recognize the specimens, and I wasn't sure I wanted to. All I knew was that the jars contained either an unusual plant, or some small dead creature, floating in a blue-green fluid. So, I kept my distance from those. The books were more interesting, anyway.

They were leather bound journals like the one Mikasi carried. Only these were thick with bookmarks and odd scraps of yellowed paper sticking out of them at odd angles. What little handwriting I saw on the outside matched Mikasi's own scrawl. I couldn't help but wonder, what other Ancient Order papers did the little inventor have tucked away in there?

I didn't have much time to think that through, since the next room was Mikasi's actual workshop. It smelled of glue, boiled dye, tannin, and a bucket of other odors I couldn't begin to identify. That last sentiment almost held true for the collection of inventions scattered around the room or hung from the ceiling.

A flock of small, hand-held hydraulis pumps sat gathered on one table. Nearby, a halfling-sized backpack frame with a pair of long wooden cylinders in place of the pack itself leaned against one wall. I had some guesses as to what it was for, but I wasn't entirely sure.

To my left, on a long cedar table, was a modest-sized telescope and a miniature spyglass. Both were bolted into their own stands. The telescope was pointed out through the window at the sky. But the spyglass? It was pointed at a flat plate of glass on the table. Then there was the one thing that really caught my attention.

Attached to the ceiling was a harness sporting a pair of wings. The hinged wings were bat-like with what might be an oilcloth stretched between the wooden wing 'bones'. It looked like the whole thing was designed to collapse into the harness and pack. I stared at it, fascinated.

"I designed it as a means to let someone fly. Like a bird or a dragon!"

I fought down a real urge to jump or yelp. Mikasi had wandered up next to me while I was lost in my sightseeing. That was a bad mistake on my part. I really needed to be more mindful of what was around me.

"Does it work?" I asked while I caught my breath.

He shrugged.

"In principle. But I've only ever tried it with smaller ones carrying a bundle of carrots, or a straw doll." Mikasi clapped his hands, then rubbed them together. "So, you had something you wanted me to look at?"

I raised my eyebrows at that before I opened my satchel to pull out my journal, then flipped it open to my notes.

"Yes, this. The Ancient Order called it an Automatic Crystal of the Eclipse."

Mikasi frowned over the notes and sketches. Occasionally, he would nod or tap a part of a drawing with a finger when some small part caught his attention.

"This is *very* interesting. An 'Automatic Crystal' you say?" He scratched his chin. "It reminds me of something."

"Well, there's a lot of guesswork over what the thing actually did." I pointed at a set of my notes on a page. "Here's what *I* think it was for..."

It turned out Tyre had a good idea. I needed someone to have an old-fashioned debate with me over the Automatic Crystal. Mikasi was just what the physician ordered.

We talked for at least an hour, maybe more. I lost track of time. Mikasi had cleared off his workbench for us, mostly with a sweep of his arm. Scattered bits of string, coils, toothed wheels, and things I couldn't identify either found the floor or wound up piled at the far end of the table.

The conversation started with what I learned from Ihodis in Ishnanor and the journals from Foldor Gilstock and Nilna Sestoros. Then I tossed out my own theory that the relic was actually used for study and learning.

Mikasi replied in kind with new ideas. It wasn't long before something took shape. Something completely unexpected.

I rubbed the sides of my head as Ki set a cup of coffee on the table next to me. Where he found the coffee, I had no idea. I barely paid it any mind.

"Wait. You mean this could be something that 'pumps light'? How does that even work?"

Mikasi shrugged. "Light *does* flow. I've been over everything Cesibus wrote, and his mathematics make so much *sense*." He waved his hands like he was fanning flies. "But no, I don't mean literally 'pump' light. Think, like a spyglass with a candle on one side!"

"The light is focused," I said with some thoughtful hesitation. "Channeled like... water moving through a hydraulis pump."

"Like water," Mikasi repeated with a bright grin.

Kiyosi placed another cup that matched mine next to Mikasi. The dark rich smell of roasted coffee teased my nose.

"Both of you. Drink," he ordered. "It's been hours. At least most of a day."

I did a double take at both the cup and Ki as my mind soaked in the idea about what he just said. Through the window, the last of the afternoon sun was sitting low over the plains, turning prairie grasses and rocks an amber gold. The day was almost done. Ki smirked at me.

"Right. Drink," I replied and grabbed the cup. Mikasi did likewise.

Ki wasn't wrong. It did help. The tension around my eyes relented while the deep roasted flavor of the drink spread a gentle warmth through me. I took another sip, then set the cup down.

"So it *could* be used for study or teaching. If your notes here, and your equations there, are even close, then those knobs on the Crystal's surface allow a person to adjust the crystal's actual facets on the inside."

Mikasi nodded vigorously.

"Indeed, yes! Which changes how the light passes through," he said. "A person could use a strong light, then point it at say, cloth, and let you see the finest detail of the weave. Like you suspected, a teaching or study tool."

I drank more of my coffee.

"That would explain why references to Automatic Crystals have been found in old alchemist workshops."

Mikasi pointed at a simple drawing of two spheres with lines running between them.

"Yes! Also, here it seems reasonable that focused, flickering light could travel between two Automatic Crystals. It could easily be a way to send messages."

"Like using mirrors to reflect sunlight to send ship to ship messages. Only," I hesitated at the implications. "This wouldn't be just simple words. The ball shape with all those facets would be like dozens of mirrors working together. This might have been able to send complicated messages. Maybe complete sentences?"

Mikasi raised his hands over his head as if cheering.

"Like an entire *language! A written language of light!*"

I just stared at the drawings and equations in astonishment. Then my thoughts wandered down a dark alley, as they often did.

"It sounds almost magical. If this focused light, and someone sent a magical light through the Crystal while adjusting the facets..." I let the words hang in the air.

"The spell would be altered, focused. Most likely enhanced while it passed through," Ki added from the other side of the worktable. "Granted, the magic I've studied is healing magic, but still... certain healing magics do involve light. Magical light that can affect the body or mind. Also, healing magic can cause harm instead of mend harm."

A dead silence hung in the room. The implication was ugly, but there it was.

"It *could* be used as a weapon," I said softly. "All those facets might let someone 'tune' a spell passing through it. I'm not sure if a city's Schutz Field could effectively stop magic like that if it was a focused, altered spell designed to affect minds... or steal a person's health."

"Gods of the Cresting Tides," Ki whispered.

Tyre frowned, darker than I had ever seen before.

"And that... that right there... is why we need to make sure the Crimson Company doesn't lay a grubby finger on the thing," he growled.

"Maybe no one else," I whispered.

10

**Amates 20, 1277. Just past midnight. Town of
Banye, aboard the Sheldrake, trying not to wake
anyone up.**

Sleep was a lost cause. I tossed and turned until I finally gave up
and slipped out of the bunk. My mind just would not let go of the
yesterday's conversation.

I knew I shouldn't worry. Everything we talked about, every idea,
was just a guess. A 'maybe' of how we thought the Automatic Crystal
could work, not how it *did* work. All the talk of it being used as some
sort of weapon could be wrong. That could just be a product of the
twisted little part of my mind that kept me from sleep.

So, if that was the way of it, why didn't I feel any better?

I slipped on some clothes and stepped out of my bunk room.
Worry drove me to pacing, and the tiny sleeping quarters aboard the
Sheldrake weren't big enough for that. They were the right size to hold
a single, roll-up futon mattress, a small wooden footlocker for your
gear, and not much else.

The windwagon was quiet while I walked silently across the dark
common room to the gangplank to let myself outside. It was better

to pace out there. If I had tried it in the *Sheldrake's* common space, I might step on one of the windwagon's Nightingale boards it used for security. Those would wake anyone up.

I grabbed my maecri along the way and was glad I did when I stepped off the gangplank onto the grass. The nights on Planus are always cold, no matter what time of the year. Fortunately, the tailor who made my maecri made sure they sewed my long coat from a sturdy cotton weave. That extra layer chased off the chill.

"Can't sleep?"

I turned to see Evi walking around the *Sheldrake* in my direction.

"No," I said with a faint smile as I stuffed my hands into the maecri's pockets. "Wish I could. Too many thoughts rolling around in my head."

Evi put her hands in the pockets of her own centaur-sized maecri. After stamping a hoof against the ground in thought, she sighed.

"Makes sense. Lots to think about." She replied wistfully. "Mikasi made some good points, but you have to know he was guessing like anyone else."

I glanced at her, then looked down the main street of Banye. It was quiet. There was plenty of moonlight out, casting a healthy pale twilight over the town. It gave everything a peaceful look. Almost like a painting from one of those street artists in Ishnanor.

"I know." The words hung in the air while I let out a slow sigh. "All that talk of a 'weapon' could just me overreacting."

Evi snorted.

"You? Oh, no. I can't see that. You're so *calm* and even-keeled."

That made me laugh, which got Evi started.

"Thanks, Evi. I needed that."

"Don't mention it. Anyone can get lost in their own head." The centaur shrugged, then swatted the air with her tail. "Anyway, we now

know a sight more about the Automatic Crystal than we did before
we got here. Probably the best we're going to know. Now? Well, now
we go get the hells-damned thing."

"Just like that?"

Evi grinned.

"Just like that."

A shriek broke the night. It was a familiar, high-pitched voice coming from down the street. This was accompanied a moment later when
a certain halfling we knew burst out from between two buildings. He
raced in our direction, tool-encrusted surcoat flapping along behind
him.

"Help! They're gonna take me!"

Four more figures, men cast in shadow, raced out after him. They
may have been stalking him, but now it was more like a wolf pack
running down its prey. One of the hunters stood out, despite being
smeared in lampblack and dark clothes. He was a large human man,
thick at the shoulder, with an unruly crop of red hair.

It was Red. The brute from the Crimson Company we fought
behind the Salty Nightingale in Ishnanor. This time, it looked like he
brought more friends.

"Mikasi!" I ran toward him.

"Tela! Hop on!" Evi called to me before she called out over her
shoulder. "Tyre! Ki! Trouble!"

I didn't waste a second. Once I was on her back, Evi galloped toward
the halfling inventor. Red and his pack of thugs picked up the pace.

The silvery-gray moonlight gave me a pretty good view of the four
Crimson Company mercenaries. They were all armed with at least a
dagger, but two brandished wooden batons.

Me? All I had was a lot of anger. My weapons were back aboard the
Sheldrake. Evi, from what I could see, only had a pair of daggers on

her belt. But the centaur also had hooves and a long history as a street fighter.

I started to miss that fireplace shovel and wooden plate from the Salty Nightingale at that moment.

"Down the middle!" I said, and pointed at the mercenaries.

"Gladly," Evi replied. With a feral grin, she galloped around Mikasi and right at the Crimson mercenaries.

They were determined, though. The mercenaries held their course and tried to dodge around Evi to get at Mikasi. But a centaur galloping right at you? That isn't something to take lightly. At the last moment, the lot of them lost their nerve and dove to either side, cursing and yelling. Evi barked out a deep laugh.

We circled to a stop a few paces away from the bunch. I slid off Evi's back and hit the ground, running toward the nearest would-be kidnapper. He was a thin, wiry man about my build with dusky skin like mine and no hair. Like the others, he was scrambling to his feet. Sad for him, he only made it partway.

I planted a sharp kick in the man's midsection that robbed him of his air. He collapsed to the ground, gasping, curled into a ball. There wasn't time for anything else, and I'm not one to kick anyone while their down, so I moved on to the next brute.

It was Red.

"Hells and High Water," I swore.

"I remember you," he snarled and flexed his fists. "I owe you a beating."

In a fight, I'm not much of a talker. This wasn't any exception. I raced in low as Red charged at me like a mad buffalo. He swung one of those massive fists at my head, but I ducked under it and sidestepped to his right. On the way past, I slapped his elbow hard for good measure.

Red hissed when he felt the sudden, sharp strain of his elbow bent the wrong way for a second. But he recovered quick. He shook his hand once, then sliced that same fist down to backhand me. I danced away before I replied with a sharp kick against his right leg. It was the same leg I slapped a few days ago with the iron fireplace shovel.

I'm not sure how much of that really hurt, but he reacted. That kick pulled a yell and two curses out of Red while he stumbled back. There was pure murder in his eyes. I glared daggers back.

Red was taller than me, square build, with a better reach, and a good bit stronger. Me? I had no weapons, was quicker, wasn't as out of breath, and had a belly full of hot anger. It might have been the anger, but the way I saw it, I liked my odds.

Behind Red, I saw Tyre and Ki sprinting in our direction. Ki raced toward Evi, holding out a short staff. Meanwhile, Tyre collected Mikasi to get him out of the street. That took a lot of worry off my mind.

I didn't know, and hadn't ever asked, if Banye had a justicar or anyone that kept the peace. But by now, what with the all the shouting, one ought to be running our way soon. At least, I *hoped* they would come running soon.

Just then, Red moved in at me faster than I thought he could. I sidestepped, batted one fist away, then another, but missed the third. I should have kept moving. That was a costly mistake.

His uppercut knocked the wind out of me. I doubled over and hit the ground hard. Red lunged for me with both hands, but I rolled away, gulping in air.

I didn't have any time to recover, as Red immediately lunged at me again. With a hoarse wheeze, I rolled aside once more but hammered the heel of one boot against that same spot on Red's right leg. This time, I knew he felt that.

Red howled like a prairie banshee. But I was too close, so he managed to backhand me for my trouble when I got partway to my feet. That tossed me aside into the dirt. My cheekbone stung. I grimaced and shook my head before I hauled myself up to one knee.

Then a miracle called Ki appeared as my whip landed on the ground between myself and Red.

"Happy Lifeday!" he quipped, before he charged another of the Crimson Company with that new walking stick of his.

Red and I glanced at the whip, then at each other. For a second we froze, gasping in air. We dove for it. Red was a second too slow.

I grabbed the whip, and sidestepped to my right. Red landed hard where the whip had been and got a face full of dirt. Quick as a blink, I lashed out and cracked the whip over the big man's head. Red flinched, swearing a string of curses I didn't quite catch, then crab-crawled backwards.

He climbed to his feet in time to face a drawn crossbow aimed at his nose.

I didn't know the person on the other side of that crossbow. He was a thin, older human man, dressed in the Banye clothing style. Neatly trimmed, steel-gray hair, stern look, and ice-blue eyes that glittered in the evening light screamed he didn't tolerate foolishness.

The most important part? The man was wearing a round Justicar's Amulet with its typical image of a griffin holding a hammer.

"I think you're done with the fighting for tonight," the justicar said to Red in a drawn out, gravelly, low voice. "People *were* trying to sleep and I normally like it *real* quiet around here."

Red froze, eyes on the crossbow. Slowly, he put up his hands in a sign of surrender.

"*Mikasi!*"

The shout was from Tyre, and it wasn't happy.

I bolted away from the justicar and Red, looking for Tyre. He was over near the Buckhorn Boardinghouse, running around the side of the building. Behind me, I heard the justicar shout something that sounded like 'miss' or 'wait'. There wasn't time for pleasantries, so I would have to apologize later.

Tyre and I reached the back of the Buckhorn about the same time, and I saw what had him so upset. Another quartet of men, Crimson Company mercenaries, by the cut and style of their jerkins, were riding off at full gallop into the night. One had Mikasi, the halfling hastily bound and gagged, thrown over the saddle of his horse.

"Evi! Ki! They got Mikasi!" I shouted and raced for the nearest horse or buffalo, or anything I could ride to give chase.

They had a head start. I just hoped I could catch them before the night swallowed them whole.

11

I bit off another piece of Awari root and grimaced. The taste of Awari didn't improve the more I chewed on it. That spicy, fibrous texture also didn't go well with coffee. It may help with the new bruises, but it didn't take the knots out of my frustration.

The night wound up swallowing Mikasi and his kidnappers whole before I took out after them on a horse. Not that I didn't try to find them. I set out on horseback along the last route I saw the kidnappers. Evi, the Justicar, and others from Banye joined me on the search.

Justicar Landry Copeland wasn't irate with me for any part of this mess. There was enough sign at Mikasi's workshop that gave a clear portrait of what happened. Mikasi was well-liked by the locals, especially Justicar Copeland, who considered the inventor a good friend. I could feel the frustration, and the anger, in the air while we looked for tracks.

We didn't find any; it was too dark and the ground too dry.

It was still night when we returned to Banye, exhausted and in a dark mood. I slept for several hours after that, harassed by nightmares fueled by what happened. Angry tears, exercise, and a brief yell at the morning sunrise later, I mostly had my head together.

So there I sat in the *Sheldrake* on a bench by my favorite window, chewing Awari root. The others had gone back out to beat the bushes for any idea of where the kidnappers took Mikasi. I couldn't go. Kiyosi said I needed to get some sort of rest after sleeping too little and fighting too hard.

I rolled my eyes at that, then bit into the bitter-spicy Awari. One day I would remember to beg or bribe Ki to fix the flavor of these things. Maybe dip them in chocolate or something. But since he liked them bitter and spicy, he probably wouldn't. After a sip of coffee, I sighed and looked out the window.

Planus prairie wind drifted in with its scent of dirt, wildflowers, and grass while warm sunlight drove a few aches away. Behind me, the methodical churn of the *Sheldrake's* rotating boiler provided a low rumble in the air. Together, they did more than the Awari root to soothe my mind and frustrations. It helped me think about the Crystal, Mikasi, and this whole situation.

The creak of the gangplank rattled my thoughts. I saw Ki come aboard, covered in a fine cloud of Planus prairie dust.

"Anything new?" I asked.

Ki raised his eyebrows, before he shrugged out of his maecri to knock some of the prairie off of him.

"Yes, some."

He slapped the coat twice, then waved the dust away from his face. The musky smell drifted through the common room.

"We started at the back of the boardinghouse, then followed the first set of hoof prints leading out of Banye. We lost them about where you did at the first rocky hills to the East. But Justicar Copeland picked up where the Crimson Company turned down a shallow stream bed to hide their tracks."

I scowled at my coffee.

"Hells and dark water! I *knew* I should have checked that stream," I groused.

"Don't start," Ki chided me. "The only reason Copeland saw *anything* was because it was daylight. None of us would've seen the tracks in the dark, even with the moonlight."

He sighed and hung his maecri on a nearby wall peg. After that, he joined me at the window.

"That trip the kidnappers took along the stream made them move south for maybe half an hour before they moved east again. Copeland lost the tracks when the kidnappers crossed a wide stretch of broken rock. We came back to get some food and water before heading out again. So, I came to check on my favorite irritable patient."

I shot a sideways glance at him and saw his all too cheery grin. It's really hard to be mad at him when he's like that. I pursed my lips and ignored the twinge from my bruise on my cheek.

"I'm mostly fine," I said with a sigh. "Just an ache here and there."

Ki studied the fading black eye and the fresh bruise on my cheekbone.

"I know that saying 'stay out of fights' is useless, but you could duck better next time?"

I considered pouring my coffee on him, but that would be a waste of good coffee. Instead, I settled for a deadpan glare.

"So funny," I replied in a sour tone. "Anyway, what you're saying is that the kidnappers have a huge head start on us and they're somewhere east of Banye? That's all we know?"

"For now," Ki said while he gently touched around the recent bruise on my cheekbone. Fortunately, the Awari root had stolen away the sensitivity there, so I didn't wince.

I shot a dark glare at Ki that made him jerk back.

"We need to get him back," I growled.

He held up his hands in defense.

"Of course we do." Ki arched an eyebrow at me. "Once there's been a quick meal and more Awari in you for your bruises, then we work on getting him back."

I blinked, then sighed again. Shaking my head, I looked back out the window.

"I'm sorry, Ki. You didn't deserve that. I'm just," I let the words hang in the air a moment, "frustrated."

He gave my shoulder a reassuring squeeze.

"I know, Tela. So am I. We all are."

Ki squinted at me like he struggled with a thought.

"How in the High Tides did they *get* here? The Crimson Company I mean. I thought we left them behind in Ishnanor?"

"I can answer that one," Tyre replied somberly from behind us. "A few other things, too."

The big man walked off the gangplank then across the *Sheldrake's* common room, hands buried in his fearnought long coat. I glanced over while he approached as I leaned a shoulder against the window ledge. Tyre didn't look as confident as I was used to. Right now, he looked both embarrassed and more than a little angry.

The wind stirred through the window again. Tyre took a deep breath before he continued.

"While everyone's been out beating the bushes into salad, I've been having a chat with our new 'friends' the Justicar locked up for 'disturbing the peace', as he called it."

I felt a bit useless and out of touch. That was a terrible feeling. Everyone was busy doing *something* while I was 'resting'. I savagely bit off another piece of Awari root in frustration.

"That bunch of Crimson Company we fought last night? They say anything?" I asked.

Tyre's expression turned pensive.

"Not to me, not directly. Most of they said to me was insults when I had them all together."

Then Tyre smiled with a slight twinkle in his eye while he hooked his thumbs in his wide leather belt.

"But then I learned they talked to each other some, and one has a habit of talking when he's nervous."

I swapped a puzzled look with Ki.

"You did something," Ki said to Tyre. "You're being all 'you' again, which means you did something."

"Ki, stop," I said while I waved a hand at him. "Tyre, what *did* you find out?"

"Well, I figured out the skinny one, the one you kicked in the gut at the start of the fight, is a nervous talker. So I took turns talking to each one of them alone. The skinny one? I rattled his nerves enough that he told me a little more about what was happening here. Turns out, he's not comfortable kidnapping people."

Tyre gestured out the window.

"We were all wrong about the fight behind the Salty Nightingale. They weren't trying to get my maps. They wanted to slow down any Windtracer expedition from leaving Ishnanor. Vincent Vargas knew all too well you'd ask me to take you out to the Great Chasm, Tela. So he sent muscle to steal my maps, break one of my legs, something."

Ki crossed his arms over his chest.

"Well, that obviously didn't work."

Tyre chuckled.

"No, it didn't. But it also means they set out from Ishnanor about when we did, if not a few hours before. Probably a few hours before."

I rubbed my eyes.

"*Aile Shavat!*" I took a deep breath. "What about Mikasi?"

Tyre nodded and raised a finger.

"About that. You two will like this part. Vargas has information about the Crystal, too. Our talkative little friend mentioned seeing copies of two journals that Vargas is keeping in a strongbox with something else. He doesn't know what, just that the strongbox is stuffed full of papers and straw."

"That Baron. Marius Apollinare." Ki frowned and lightly scratched his chin while his tail swayed in thought. "Notes and research from the Baron?"

"Copies of those journals by Foldor Gilstock and Nilna Sestoros, too, probably," I added. "Anyone can get those from the Windtracer Record's Hall. They're on public display."

Tyre nodded again.

"True. But in any case, Vargas can't make sense out of it. Not *any* of it. He's been raging about it for days. *That's* why he went after Mikasi. He needs a translator."

I set my cup down.

"Did you get him to say *where* the Crimson Company is now?"

Tyre's bright, mischievous grin lit up his beaded face while he spread his arms wide.

"Now Tela, of course I did! They're a few hours east of here, past a snake-like dry riverbed. He wasn't much for description, but he mentioned an odd rock pile with white and tan striped rocks stuck up sideways and looked like a tree trunk." His grin got wider. "I'm pretty sure I recognized that rock pile he talked about from a couple of trips I've taken out that way before."

I immediately stood, then raced for my maecri hung on a nearby peg in the wall.

"What are we waiting for?"

"Food. Water. More Awari root in you." Ki answered dryly. "Maybe a plan?"

I shot a scowl at him.

Tyre held up his hands to slow me down from running out of the *Sheldrake*.

"Ki's right on that last one, Tela. Planus is flat out there, you know that. Sound carries on that prairie wind. Vargas isn't stupid. He'll have guards out around the Crimson Company campsite. If we're not careful, they'll hear us coming long before we get there."

He jerked a thumb back toward the gangplank.

"We need to talk with Copeland and figure out a way to slip over there without being heard. Scout it out quietly and lay an ambush? I prefer to do those at night. Ambushes go off better that way."

"Vargas will have moved his group by nightfall," Ki suggested.

Tyre shrugged.

"That can't be helped. Besides, Mikasi won't be eager to help Vargas, and Vargas won't risk killing Mikasi. Vargas needs Mikasi's mind too badly. That'll slow them down." He took a deep breath, then let it out slowly. "I'm just not sure how to get in close to where their camp is."

"We need to *see* their camp first," Ki replied. "There might be dry riverbeds, gullies, or all sorts of landscape we could use. Surely there has to be something that will let us get close enough to see that."

An idea sprang to life, fully formed in my head. It was risky, and probably even stupid. But it if worked, we could get a good look at where the Crimson Company was camped. It could even give us a way inside to get Mikasi back.

"I have an idea," I suggested with a smirk, then looked at Ki. "You're going to *really* hate this one."

12

Amates 20, 1277. Town of Banye, early evening. Working just inside Mikasi's half-open forge in the back of his workshop. The best time for a stupid idea.

Ki stood outside Mikasi's forge, hands folded over his chest, his expression a thundercloud.

"You call this a *plan?*" he grumbled while he watched me adjust the buckles for the tenth time.

"No," I told him. "I call this 'making it up as I go along'. Besides, this is only *part* of the plan. You're in the other part, remember?"

I didn't blame him for being a worrywart about this. It really was a stupid idea. But given the situation, none of the *good* plans were going to work. So, all we had *were* the bad ones. But even Ki had agreed that my calculations made sense after hours of debate.

My idea? To borrow Mikasi's 'wing pack' to give me a little silent boost over any Crimson Company sentries at their camp. I thought of the wings and cloth backpack as a 'wing pack' since I wasn't sure what Mikasi called it.

The weight of Mikasi's invention felt off balance across my shoulders. It had to be modified from 'halfling sized' to 'human sized' so I would fit into the thing. The 'getting it to fit' was a work in progress.

I slipped off the wing pack, then punched another set of holes into the right strap to adjust the buckle. After that, I put it back on. It felt better with the pack not tilted to the left.

The device wasn't heavy at all, even though it contained a large set of folded bat shaped wings with thin wooden wing 'bones'. It was a little bulky though, but nothing uncomfortable.

Mikasi had done good work. The oiled cloth was thin, almost silk-like, and the 'bones' were hollow wooden tubes. The weak point was the joints. I made a few adjustments there to shore up their strength. Hopefully, they would hold.

I twisted side to side to test the balance. After that, I tugged on a pair of rope and leather pull handles to extend and retract the wings. Everything seemed to work as expected. That was a good sign. I noticed Ki's expression was getting more concerned by the moment while I checked the device.

He shook his head, then massaged the base of his horns. The dry evening Planus winds had picked up in volume like always and stirred the grass outside the covered forge.

"I can't believe I'm helping you do this," he groused. "You could literally fall to your death. I don't see why we can't just sneak out there in the dark."

"You are," I replied. "Along with Justicar Copeland, Tyre, and a couple of others, so I have a way to get Mikasi out of there in a hurry."

Ki rubbed his face before he blew out a long sigh.

"Right. True."

He reached over to a bag on a nearby chair and produced a small buckled leather pouch that he handed to me. It was one of his alchemy field bags. Inside were four vials. Two held a bright red liquid and the other two a thick, brownish-red oil.

"Medicine and elixirs?"

"Just in case," Ki replied with a shrug. "You know, to make sure everyone comes back with all their correct parts. I brewed and enchanted those up while you were sleeping. The liquids are for drinking and the oils are for burns, cuts, and so on. The usual arrangement."

I closed the alchemy field bag, then slipped my belt through the loops on the back. It rested snug against my hip. In the meantime, Ki walked outside a few steps away from Mikasi's half-open blacksmith shop.

The moon was bright again that night, and already high in the evening sky. Ki produced a spyglass from a pouch at his belt and searched the eastern horizon with it. I watched him lower the spyglass after a moment to scowl at the view.

"What is it?"

Ki glanced at me, then back to whatever had his attention. Pale, ghostly clouds dotted the sky, and one sparked with distant lightning. Grass and shrubs waved in the evening breeze. He shook his head.

"I've been thinking about this ever since Tyre told us what he learned from that mercenary." He gestured to the dark skyline. "There's nothing, and that's wrong."

I stepped partway out of the blacksmith forge to join Ki. The midlands of Planus were mostly a flat prairie, interrupted by the occasional rocky badlands or banded mounds of stone made from ancient lava flows. The eastern side of Banye was just typical prairie, or an 'ocean of grass'. I squinted at Ki.

"What?"

He shook his head.

"If the Crimson Company set out of Ishnanor about when we did, they would have been moving in our same direction. Especially since they came here for Mikasi."

His frown deepened as he waved a hand at the skyline.

"Where is the *dust?* We should have seen dust from buffalo, horses, or whatever they are using to move across the prairie. At night, like now, where's the campfire? There should be at least a dot of light. The night's clear enough we can see for miles."

I blinked, then looked out again. He was right, there was nothing.

There had been other windwagons that left Ishnanor when we did. Those were either headed north to the kingdom of Jata, or south to the Belari water-towns after a day traveling alongside us. We were alone after that. At least, it *looked* like we were alone.

"No campfire might just mean they've set up a cold camp with no fire. You know, so they can keep out of sight," I suggested.

"Maybe," Ki said before he pursed his lips. "But that doesn't explain the lack of dust. Planus is dry this time of year. Herds of buffalo, teams pulling windwagons, most anything kicks up some dust. Sure, the wind carries it away pretty quick, but it's been days. We should have seen a hint of *something* moving in our direction by now."

"Magic, then," I countered slowly.

The words tasted bad in my mouth. Magic to hide a group moving over the prairie for several days didn't come cheap, and it wasn't common. It was also sometimes unpredictable.

"Again, maybe... even probably." Ki sighed. Worry lines creased his forehead under his horns. "I worry a lot, probably too much, but that's me being a physician. Now? It's me being a friend. Be careful, Tela. You're my oldest friend. Something about this just sits all wrong."

I smiled a little and glanced down at the wing pack's straps across my shoulders.

"I will, even though it doesn't look like it."

Ki returned my smile.

"Fair enough."

I adjusted, or really fiddled, with the buckles on the wing pack again. This time, I made sure the waist belt was attached.

"Now, if I'm right, I'll get there pretty quick," I said while I buckled the waist belt around me. "They probably have most of their guards along the west side of their camp to watch for anyone coming from Banye. So, I'll try to reach land along the southeastern side."

Ki nodded while he put away his spyglass.

"We'll have horses, or whatever we can find, in that south running stream bed waiting for you once you get Mikasi out of there. The rise of the land on either side of the stream should mute the sound of the horses." He folded his arms over his chest, then gave me a half-shrug. "I hope, anyway."

My smile bloomed into a grin.

"It'll be fine, Ki, and I'll meet you there with Mikasi. We won't have any new bruises, cuts, or anything that needs tending."

Ki arched an eyebrow at me with a deadpan expression.

"You say this now."

"Ready?" Evi asked from the street in front of Mikasi's workshop. She held up a long coil of rope. "I've got the rope."

I took a deep breath, then straightened my back. The wing pack creaked in response.

"I'm ready. Let's get Mikasi back."

13

Amates 20, 1277, later that same evening. Middle of nowhere in the prairie.

I wasn't ready.

We rode east out of Banye, following Justicar Copeland to the shallow stream bed. The stream was barely there. It was just enough water to keep the plants fed and possibly give the local wildlife something to drink. During the rainy seasons, it was probably impressive.

The others continued on south while Evi stayed with me. Once they were out of sight, we put my idea in motion.

Evi held onto one end of the rope while she took off at a gallop. I held the other end while riding on her back. The centaur raced across the prairie into the evening wind. After a few seconds, I let out the wings.

It took me a few tries and false starts. Once, I nearly fell face first into the dirt, but it worked.

I flew.

Also, I nearly screamed. But I kept that to myself.

Sheer terror gripped me like a vice when the wind yanked me into the air, but only at first. Then came the wonder.

The night sky was clear, rich with stars and moonlight. Cold Planus winds carried me along faster than I imagined. I shivered. My clothing was all linen and cotton. That was almost, but not quite enough, protection against the chill.

I decided if I *ever* had to do this again, I'd wear something a bit warmer than a maecri long coat. The coat seemed to slow me down a bit and wasn't quite warm enough. But I had to work with what I brought with me.

In the distance, I saw a gray haze settled over the ground. A cloud, or light fog, was all piled up near what almost looked like a large vernal pool. It was one of many that are scattered across the Planus prairie landscape. I was a good three stores in the air. From that height, I could almost make out the glow of a campfire and a few tents along the shore.

Ki had been right. The Crimson Company was using magic to hide themselves. Either it wasn't very strong at night, or it worked better against anyone on the ground. I sighted a wonderful piece of flat dirt to the southeast of the camp to make landfall.

When I was a little girl, I liked to watch the flying marsh squirrels and fisher bats that lived in and around Ishnanor. I remembered how they glided through the air or landed on a perch. It gave me a vague idea of how to come down safely without breaking my fool neck, or anything else.

I glided through the prairie night like the world's most demented looking bat-squirrel-woman that ever lived, complete with a feral grin. After a brief struggle with the wing pack, I figured out how to tilt and turn myself toward the ground. It wasn't a sharp fall, but more like a slow descent. In the meantime, I took a long look at the Crimson Company's camp through the magical fog.

It wasn't a large camp, so Vargas hadn't brought the entire company, thank the Tides. A cooking fire dominated the center of the camp, with tents arrayed around it in a rough circle. They had pitched four large tan canvas tents near the pool. Several smaller, ashen-colored ones sat scattered out in a semi-circle to the west. A rough ring of poles surrounded the camp. Each supported small oil lanterns that glowed a sickly yellow.

This looked like a small fighting force of ten or even twenty strong, which wasn't good news. Either way, that was a lot of people more interested in bloodshed than history to dig up an Ancient Order relic. But that was something to think about later. I needed to focus on avoiding guards and not getting any broken bones.

I sailed silently over two, maybe three sentries with no one the wiser. The fickle Planus wind was dying off, so the ground was rushing up at me fast. I arched my back like a marsh squirrel and used the wing pack handles to tilt the wings, slowing my fall.

Even without a marsh squirrel's bushy tail, my gamble paid off. I hit the ground at a fast run and only tripped twice when the wind grabbed at me. The second trip dropped me sideways into the dirt in a small cloud of dust. There was an ugly crunch as the wing pack took the brunt of the fall. The right wing was a mess of shattered wood and torn cloth.

I wiped dirt from my face before I pulled myself out of the battered wing pack. Mikasi's wonderful invention had done what it needed to do. Even if it wasn't broken, it would slow me down. I took a last look at the fantastic device.

"Mikasi, you're a *genius*," I whispered.

After a glance up at the night sky, then ahead to the fog-shrouded mercenary camp, I added, "I owe you a wing pack."

I raced for the camp. Tall clumps of prairie grass and the occasional rock pile gave me a little cover along the way. The Crimson Company had posted most of the guards to the west of camp. Only a handful were on duty elsewhere.

They weren't hard to avoid. The sickly yellow light thrown out from the lanterns was a different story.

A light breeze toyed with the lanterns, which made them sway. This caused the light and shadows around them to shift and move. That was rougher to avoid, but I managed. I lost myself in the tallest Redbrush reeds along the water's edge, before I eased past the line of lanterns without drawing any attention. Once inside camp, I started my hunt.

I found where they had stashed Mikasi five minutes later.

He was inside one of the four larger tents. I could hear him inside muttering to himself. It sounded like he was chewing over some idea or design. He also wasn't alone.

One of the Crimson Company stood guard outside the main entrance of the tent. He was a broad-shouldered, hawk-nosed man with cold eyes and an old knife scar that decorated his right cheek. A well-cared for short sword and pair of daggers suggested he was long accustomed to fighting. This was someone I wanted to avoid.

Another mercenary strolled around the tent itself. He was thinner than his companion, but no less armed. The man was dressed in the same leather-trimmed, brick-red armored coat typical to the Crimson Company.

I kept still, crouched in a patch of tall reeds in the tent's shadow. The guard walked his rounds, eyes darting toward any little movement. Thankfully, he didn't notice me. It gave me the feeling that these two weren't trying to keep people out, but Mikasi in. Once the guard went on his way, I hurried over to the tent wall. I took a quick glance around, then scurried inside under the tan canvas.

Mikasi was sitting at a chestnut wooden camp desk in the middle of the tent. The desk was his size and just large enough for him to work.

Papers filled with half-finished equations and drawings were piled around him. He jumped up when he saw me, scattering the desk's contents everywhere. The surrounding tent housed haphazard stacks of backpacks and other bags. It appeared to be a storage tent put to use as a cell for the inventor.

That was when I saw they had him hobbled with rope strapped to his ankles. I sighed.

Shock and excitement flooded Mikasi's face. He glanced between me and the front of the tent.

"Windtracer!" he said in a sharp whisper. Terror replaced excitement. He turned pale, then quickly stared at the tent entrance.

I ran over to him before he got any louder. The straps on his ankles were leather, with locked buckles. That was a problem for later. The rope connecting them? That I could deal with. I started work on the knots.

"How did you find me?" he asked in a low voice.

I shook my head. The knots refused to budge. Fortunately, I came armed. The rope was tough, but wasn't a match for my dagger.

Mikasi glanced back at the tent entrance, then ran a hand through his unkempt, thinning hair. From what I could tell, Vargas and company hadn't mistreated him aside from hobbling him. Mikasi looked haggard and disheveled in his rumpled clothes stained with prairie dust. He tried to say something else, but I interrupted him.

"*Quiet*," I replied in a hushed tone while I sawed at the rope. My dagger sliced through the last of it. "Now. Time to go. Grab *anything* you've written. The others are waiting for us outside camp to help get us back to Banye."

Mikasi shook his head emphatically.

"No. We can't!"

I cut a sharp glance at the tent entrance. The shadow of the guard outside hadn't moved. I pinned Mikasi to the spot with a frown.

"What do you mean, 'no'? You want to *stay?*"

His eyes went wide.

"*No!*" he hissed through clenched teeth. "No, I don't. But you don't understand. That man, their leader..."

"Vargas?"

"Yes! Him," he replied. Mikasi gestured at the chaotic mass of papers. "This is only part of what I've written. That Vargas fellow has more complete notes I've already finished with his own documents and relics."

I rubbed my eyes. For some reason, I thought rescuing Mikasi might be easy. Then I realized what he had just said. I grabbed the inventor by his shoulders and almost shook him.

"Wait. *Relics?* What do you mean by 'relics'?"

Mikasi managed a half-shrug despite my grip.

"I mean relics. He's got journals like you do, some of the same ones, but he has more than that. Vargas has *part of an Automatic Crystal!*" Mikasi held up a fist. "A chunk about that large. I want to say it had broken off some time ago, but I don't think that's true."

My frown tightened into a scowl.

"What do you mean?"

"It's more like a 'puzzle' piece than a 'broken' piece. I think all those seams in the old drawings are edges of pieces. That would mean the crystal could be assembled in different ways for different uses, not just 'adjusted'."

I sat back on my heels and blinked. The implications of what he said swam through my mind, making it difficult to concentrate. I let go of him to sheathe my dagger, then rub my face. This wasn't even the last thing I expected.

"Here? That is *here?*"

Mikasi nodded with his typical manic excitement.

"Yes, here!" He grabbed a bundle of papers he had been writing on a few seconds ago, then waved them at me. "The calculations were right if that lone piece is anything to go by. Movable facets? All we considered? I think it's *all* true!"

I pursed my lips in thought. Should I even dare? The answer was painfully obvious.

"All right. He doesn't need to keep that. Where's Vargas' tent?"

Mikasi stabbed a finger to his left.

"That way. The large one with the fancy banner embroidered on the tent flap."

I rolled my eyes.

"Of course it is." I glanced at the front of the tent with its looming shadow of the guard outside. He still hadn't moved or noticed us. "Listen. We can slip out the way I got in and go over there to grab it. Then we head out of camp."

Mikasi was already shaking his head before I finished.

"No, we can't."

"What?"

"Vargas comes to see how I'm doing every about every hour." Mikasi waved an arm at the tent entrance. "He'll be by any time now. I'll keep him occupied while you get the relic and as many of the notes as you can. You'll have to come back for me."

I squinted at him.

"You sure?" My frown returned with a vengeance. "Are you sure you can convince Vargas that nothing else is happening? Vargas isn't stupid."

Mikasi nodded once with the most determination I'd ever seen since I had met him.

"I can. Please, get those notes and that relic. Then we can run out of here!"

I gently squeezed his arm and tried to give him a reassuring smile. Mikasi didn't look any more reassured than I felt, but it was worth a try. Without another word, I slipped back to the tent wall where first entered.

Grass crunched and the shadow of the guard on patrol loomed large against the cloth. Then, he moved on his way. I took two breaths to steady my nerves, then scurried back outside to my previous hiding place.

At the tall reeds, I squatted down to collect my thoughts.

All I had to do was slip inside Vargas' tent. Once inside, I had to find Mikasi's notes and this piece of an Automatic Crystal then get out. After that, I needed to collect Mikasi, then run like all hells for the others outside of camp.

It was a straightforward plan, and with Vargas distracted, it seemed reasonable. I couldn't think of anything that could go wrong, other than, well, everything.

I raced off through shadows and water reeds toward Vargas' tent.

14

Amates 20, 1277. Still evening. Still swimming nose-deep in trouble. Inside an overly fancy tent in the middle of nowhere.

Vargas kept his tent guarded about as well as the other one. Like before, timing and a bit of luck helped me get inside. Once the guard on patrol vanished out of sight, I slipped under the waxed tent cloth.

The interior was dark, with the only light being a dim glow that seeped in past the front flap. Scents of old hay and musty, weathered canvas hung in the air. They didn't blend well with the lingering fragrance of Vargas' cheap cologne. I stood still and winced in the half-light while I let my nose get used to the clash of odors.

This was the largest tent used by the Crimson Company, but 'large' didn't mean 'spacious'. Military field commanders often use tents like this. Those tents are just large enough for a sleeping bag or cot, a folding field desk with a chair, and a backpack or two. This particular tent was a shade larger, but not by much.

Here, Vargas had added his own touch. The folding desk supported a nest of papers, a quill pen, and inkwell. The edge of a journal peeked out from underneath the stack. On the main tent pole, a brass-gilded mirror, only about two hands wide, hung from a small peg. A folding coat rack with the Vargas family crest burned into it completed the decor.

In comparison, the lurid, blood-red embroidered emblem of the Crimson Company draped on the outside of the tent looked almost tasteful.

I shook my head. Even in the middle of nowhere, Vargas tried to be 'fashionable' about his military campaigns and expeditions. In my opinion, Vargas and 'fashionable' parted ways a long time ago.

But what did I know? I was the child of two ship captains. Fashion wasn't a useful tool for me.

It took a second, but my nose finally surrendered to the sting of odors. Carefully, I slipped over to the front of the tent, and 'closed' it with one of the frog-knot buttons. It wouldn't stop anyone determined to get in, but it would give me a few seconds' warning if they tried. After that I got to work.

The papers on the small desk turned out to be a set of maps that covered what anyone knew about the Planus continent. Large parts of Planus were still unexplored, especially the east coast that is dominated by the Great Chasm. These particular maps focused on the middle region of the Chasm.

I knew that area all too well. It's the deepest, and worst, part of the Chasm that holds a lot of unpleasant things, like Long Deep. The spot is due east of Osidore, the largest of the water-towns in the Belari river region. Based on the route drawn on the map, Vargas considered taking the Company that way after Banye.

It was a good route, but not the only one. I kept that in mind before I set the map aside. Quickly, I sifted through the other maps for any sign of Mikasi's work. There was nothing.

Frustrated, and a little frantic, I turned to the rest of the tent. Tyre had mentioned learning that Vargas had papers stuffed in a strongbox with straw. That had to be where the crystal piece was kept. Unless Vargas had it with him.

I finally found what I was looking for stashed underneath the tent's folding cot. The modest-sized strongbox was no longer than a person's forearm. I put it at about nine sizu long. It was crafted out of a stout, dark wood that had the light fragrance of juniper and linseed oil. A metal hasp and lock kept the box closed.

It was tempting to grab it and go. But what if, after all this, it was empty? Or just held socks or something? I winced. It would be better to check it now.

Breaking open the box was out of the question. That would be too noisy. I spared a nervous glance at the front of the tent. The guards were still there. I even heard one yawn. Feeling time trickling away, I shoved my nerves aside, then pulled my small pouch of skeleton keys from an inside coat pocket.

It took half of a long, nerve-rattling minute and four skeleton keys later to get it open. Inside were the straw and papers as described. The top document was one of Mikasi's diagrams. It was another of his 'light pump' ideas. Below that was select pages, copies of course, from the same journals I had. The ones written by Foldor Gilstock and Nilna Sestoros.

The real prize? It was in the straw at the very bottom.

A fist-sized piece of the Automatic Crystal lay cradled in a straw nest. It was quartz-clear, except for one side, which was slightly curved and had a dark charcoal tint. I wasn't sure, but that dark outer part looked like a separate piece of crystal. The deep smoky charcoal on the outside reminded me of obsidian.

Raised knobs and long, smooth grooves had been carved into the clear portions of the crystal. I agreed with Mikasi that this wasn't broken. This looked like it should fit together with something else, like a puzzle piece or a key.

I turned it over. The dim light of the tent played off and through the facets. Reflected light shimmered with a ghostly aura, which eclipsed my hand for a moment.

There was more there that nagged at my attention. But this *wasn't* the time for any sort of intense study. That would have to wait. I stuffed the papers back into the box and closed the lid. The crystal was going into my long coat, just in case. The lock clicked shut when I heard the tent flap move behind me.

I was on my feet in a second, then raced for the back of the tent. A shadow loomed large from guard strolling by, taking his own sweet, agonizing time. I bit down on a hard curse.

"Find anything interesting?"

Tension shot up my spine like a cold spike. I took a deep breath and forced myself to relax. After that, I turned around to face the speaker.

I frowned.

It wasn't Vargas.

I had no idea who this man was.

He wasn't a guard or dressed like any member of the Crimson Company. From shirt to boots, his clothes were far too tailored, trimmed, and polished for that.

This man was tall, lean, with a strong air of 'dignified' mixed with a generous helping of 'above all this and you'. A human, whose straight, dark hair was pulled back and kept contained neatly behind his head with a burgundy cloth tie. It was embroidered with saffron-colored thread in some frilly design.

He was the very picture of a low to middle aristocrat from Sol or any of the other major cities. One that got outside just enough to chase away that pasty-pale look of pampered nobility.

Except for his amber-green eyes.

Those eyes were bright. Hungry. They belonged to a wild animal on the hunt, not to a person.

I gripped the crystal chunk in my hand until my knuckles turned white. His eyes flicked down to that, then to the strongbox in my other hand. A slow smile wormed up at the corners of his mouth.

"You *must* be the Windtracer that Vargas rants on about. If you're here, and no one spotted you, then I see Vargas has *every* right to be worried."

The man slowly inclined his head.

"Baron Marius Apollinare, at your service, m'lady. I think we have something to discuss."

15

Amates 20, 1277. Evening. In the middle of way too much trouble.

It was getting to be a very long night.

The baron gestured to the white canvas cot behind me before he reached for the sole chair in the tent.

"Please, have a seat."

I scowled and stayed right where I was.

Lord Marius hesitated, then shrugged.

"Or we can stand, if you prefer." He clasped his hands behind his back while he considered me for a moment. "Well, now you have a piece of the Automatic Crystal, *and* most of the notes. If reputation is anything, being a Windtracer, you've done your own studies. So, I doubt you need anything we have other than that portion of the device."

My eyes flicked to the front of the tent, then back to the baron. The guard outside hadn't moved, but I also wasn't sure I still saw any shadows. Despite me trying to be subtle, Lord Marius caught the shift in my glance. He arched an eyebrow.

"Don't worry. No one will interrupt us. Master Vargas is busy. He's getting his hourly dose of frustration from trying to talk to our mutual inventor friend, Master Mikasi. The guards are also busy. They're elsewhere looking for your allies because I doubt very much that you're alone."

I kept still when he said that, but inside I felt a stab of white-hot panic run through me. Have I led everyone right into a trap? Was I *that* predictable? Maybe I was. I shoved the thoughts aside. There would be time to worry about that later. I needed to get away and warn the others as fast as I could.

"What do you want?" I asked, my voice low and tight.

Lord Marius chuckled. It wasn't a pleasant sound.

"Nothing complicated. Unlike Vincent, I prefer diplomacy over brute force."

"So, you hired Vargas and his mercenaries," I scoffed. "Nice diplomacy, m'lord."

"Fair," he replied with a slight nod.

Lord Marius glanced down at the ground, then at the stained canvas tent walls. I got the idea that he wanted to pace. Ki looked that way when he wanted to do just that while talking about something that was on his mind.

"Hiring Vincent Vargas and his Crimson Company was an unpleasant necessity. *Useful,* mind you, but despite that, they're still a blunt object. No, the diplomacy I'm referring to is an arrangement." He gestured toward me. "An understanding between scholars."

I didn't fall off the turnip barge yesterday. This was a stall if I ever heard one. But Lord Marius was only a few feet away from me. If I tried to duck under the wall of the tent, he'd be able to grab me in a second.

Out the front? That was no good. The baron stood right in the way. Even if I made it past him, I wasn't sure that I believed his story that the entire Crimson Company was out beating the bushes for Ki and the others.

I was caught, or at least I was for right now. My mind raced, trying to pin down some reasonable escape route. There wasn't a way around it. I had to play along with whatever this was.

"What sort of 'understanding'?"

Lord Marius shrugged.

"We combine our efforts. A contest for something as rare and ground-breaking as the Automatic Crystal?" He grimaced. "Absurd. Almost offensive. We should work *together*, m'lady."

I stared at him, a little dumbfounded, while his words sank in. My thoughts had just become a shattered piece of glass and I couldn't find all the pieces. After a slow breath, I found my words.

"Join you?" I nodded to the front of the tent. "I doubt your pet mercenaries would like that. We've got some bad blood between us."

The baron raised his eyebrows. A smile wormed up along the edges of his mouth.

"Oh, I'm aware." His eyes lit with a burning intensity that made me want to fidget ever so slightly. "But isn't tolerating those brutes a small price to pay for this particular discovery?"

The baron held his hands out in front of him. It was like he was reaching for something in the air or giving a speech.

"This relic is a *significant* discovery. It would be the greatest turning point in history since the Great Collapse! Together, we could unlock its secrets! I'm sure you're aware the Automatic Crystal is said to alter light or magic, and possibly even affect thoughts, yes?"

An uneasy feeling was bubbling up in the back of my mind. Lord Marius was going somewhere with this. I just wasn't sure where. It was a slithering, cold idea of a thing that danced in the shadows of my mind, just out of my sight.

"Yes. There's some theory about that," I replied cautiously.

"Pardon my manners and familiarity, but Tela, think of it! It would open the door to creating a new, fully working Automatic Crystal of the Eclipse! A device giving us firm and direct control over the elements, over magic itself."

Lord Marius clenched his fists.

"With it, we could usher in a new Order! Wars, conflict between cities would end. Magic storms? Soothed and conquered. Even *controlled* for more productive purposes! Awldor would know *peace*."

There it was. That dark, slimy thing had just crawled into the light. I forced down another silent wave of panic with a deep breath while I tried to stay focused.

"You said 'we'," I replied.

The baron's eyes grew a bit brighter.

"I did. Who else could do this, *should* do this, but us?"

Lord Marius spread his arms wide, his uncomfortable smile in full force. I had seen that look before. It was the smile of someone drunk on dreams of power.

"Tela, I've studied your expeditions. Read about them in depth. *Memorized* them. You are *brilliant*. Don't you see that? You're far beyond the other Windtracers. Together, we would build this New Age! Mold it to our vision!"

I could actually hear the capital letters in most of those words. It had finally happened. After all these years, I found something far more dangerous than Vargas or more terrifying than the worst magic storm. A fanatical baron who had dreams of a 'new world order' and the means to make it happen. I needed to find a way out of this mess, and fast.

A heavy silence filled the tent.

"What if they don't agree with you?" I asked in a soft voice. "Some of the cities and its people?"

"They will," he replied quickly. "If they don't, we will bury them in dust and history."

Lord Marius held out his right hand.

"So? What is your answer? You can't tell me you're not tempted."

I didn't need a single second to think it over.

"No."

The baron's posture didn't shift, but his expression turned wooden.

"No? Don't be hasty, Tela. We could remake the world."

I took a slow, deep breath to steady my frayed nerves. Unfortunately, it didn't work out all that well. I still had this tremendous urge to run for the hills, or grab a repeating bow, or both.

"That's what scares me," I said. "You've talked a lot about bringing 'peace' to Awldor. It sounds like along the way, you'll be leaving it in pieces. So, what? You'll throw away what won't fit in your vision? Those are people with lives, m'lord. Not a broken chair."

The baron let his hand fall to his side. He shook his head slowly.

"I thought that you, out of anyone, would understand my vision. What the Automatic Crystal means if it's in the right hands."

I've been in all sorts of ruins with any manner of twisted, murderous traps, undead, or nameless horrors. They never made me as uncomfortable, or angry, as I was right at that moment. I flexed my grip on the piece of crystal in my hand. The solid mineral felt comforting. It kept me grounded.

"Oh, I understand. That's the problem," I replied. A hard tone slipped into my words. "When anyone says 'in the right hands' they mean 'their hands'. All so they can be in control, or at least think they are."

I shook my head.

"No, Lord Marius. Your hands aren't 'right'. Mine aren't either. That relic," I stopped myself when I remembered I held a part of that relic in my left hand. "These *relics*," I corrected myself, "should be studied by scholars, then placed on display so anyone could learn about them. Yes, these relics might be the path to a better world."

I fixed a hard, angry gaze on the baron.

"Or they might have caused the Great Collapse. If they did, then it'll be a cold day in the Last Watery Hell before I let you or *anyone* else use a fully assembled Automatic Crystal of the Eclipse."

Lord Marius pursed his lips. The wooden expression melted into something sad, bitter, and harsh. He must have thought this conversation through a dozen times. I suspected, in his mind, it never ended this way.

"I'm disappointed, Tela. Somehow, I thought you had more foresight than this. A shame, really. It would have been easier with you by my side."

The baron sighed.

"But you've made your choice, and choices always have consequences."

His hand darted to a pouch at his belt. Panic screamed in my mind and I hurled the strongbox at him. The baron ducked to his left, allowing the box to fly past his head to slap the front of the tent.

In one motion, I drew my dagger, then thrust at the man's chest. It was the fastest I had ever drawn a blade in my life. My aim was accurate. Timing? Perfect. My dagger slammed into the left side of his chest, cutting through cloth and spearing his heart. He grunted from the impact.

Instinctively, I yanked the dagger free while I sidestepped away as far as the tent allowed.

But the baron didn't move.

He wasn't surprised, or even in shock. All he did was stand there. Lord Marius just stared at the jagged hole in his chest. I suddenly realized why.

There was no blood.

The baron wasn't bleeding. I had *stabbed* him and he wasn't *bleeding*.

In place of any blood, there was a faint trickle of what looked like charred dust or gray sand. A wisp of black smoke oozed out from the edges. Lord Marius didn't seem upset, only frustrated. He glanced at me from under his eyebrows with a look that made my soul shiver.

"Like I said, Tela, choices *always* have consequences," he whispered.

I didn't see him raise his own piece of an Automatic Crystal until it was too late.

There was a flash of light that robbed me of the tent, Lord Marius, and everything in front of me. It felt like a storm howled in my mind while it tried to claw its way out of my skull.

I screamed.

Then, I didn't remember anything else.

16

Amates 21, 1277. Early morning on the prairie after having been tossed out like a sack of potatoes with no coffee in sight.

The mercenary tossed me into the dirt, which caused nearby insects and a prairie ferret to run for safety. The fall knocked some of the wind out of me and I gasped in the dusty, dry air. I glared up at my captor through the first rays of the morning sun.

She wasn't impressed.

The woman smirked back with a toothy grin, complete with orcish fangs. Lean and hard muscled in a sleeveless jerkin, she planted her hands on her hips. She was built like some used to heavy labor, like a miller.

"Tied up and left out on the prairie," she said with a small shake of her head. "Bad way to go. Glad it's you and not me."

I scowled but didn't give her the satisfaction of an answer. Instead, I fought off a sneeze brought on by the stench of prairie dust, dead grass and bitter dirt that hovered in the air.

It went without saying; I wasn't in the best mood. The morning sun and lack of coffee didn't mingle well with what Lord Marius had done to me with that piece of the Automatic Crystal.

My head throbbed. It wasn't the worst headache I'd ever had, but it was close. The nosebleeds that came with it were an unpleasant bonus.

What with all the theories, fighting, traveling, and running around, I had completely forgotten what Ihodis had warned me about back in Ishnanor. But the rumor of the Automatic Crystal's mind magic storm effect was nothing compared to reality.

The Automatic Crystal *could* unleash a magic storm inside a person's mind. I'm pretty sure that is exactly what Lord Marius hit me with. Like any magic storm, it's a nightmare come to life. But this type of magic storm does more than just try to batter your mind to mush. It takes a toll on your body, too.

I squinted down at the spot just above where they had tied my wrists together. There on my forearms, between the ropes and my sleeves, was a healthy patch of small bony scales. They were a lot like the raised bone scales on an alligator's back.

These were a dusky color that matched the rest of my skin, but looked like they belonged on a reptile instead of me. A stab of panic shot through me anytime I glanced at them.

The rest of me felt cracked. Exhausted. Maybe even a little stretched out of shape. Along with that came a strong feeling of being thirsty or hungry, but I couldn't tell which. It was like that gnawing, almost lightheaded, sensation that comes after a long climb or run through the swamps.

When I didn't reply to my captor's comment, the woman shot a sour look at me, then walked away. Vincent Vargas appeared in her place. I shifted my glare to him, but he wasn't any more impressed.

"Where's Lord Marius?" I asked in a dry, hoarse voice. "Too busy burning other people's minds with the relic to see me off?"

Vargas was fashionably dressed as usual, from his tailored tan shirt and 'explorer' outfit to his brown waistcoat. Blond hair was combed, pulled back, and braided down his back in one of the current Ishnanori styles. It clashed with the customary sneer on his face. He looked down his thin nose at me, then waved that stupid silk handkerchief he always carried in my direction.

"Dealing with your mess, I expect," he remarked. The reply sounded casual enough, but I could hear the irritation laced through the reply. "Clever plan really, I'll give you that. Distract Lord Marius and the rest of us to buy time for Master Mikasi to make good his escape? Typical, irritating, 'you'."

I did a double take at Vargas. Mikasi had *escaped?* Also, Vargas hadn't gloated over catching Tyre, Evi, or any of the others. I hoped that meant they also avoided the Crimson Company.

Of course, Vargas could be lying, and it wouldn't be the first time. But that seething anger over losing Mikasi seemed genuine enough.

I shook my head a little, then tried to focus on what Vargas was saying. Fortunately, he had been too busy talking to notice I had gotten distracted. He let out a long, frustrated sigh.

"So, while the little inventor isn't the fastest runner, he apparently can hide rather well." Vargas waved his handkerchief at the prairie. "Even in this desolate place, he vanished."

It took a second before his usual sneer returned in full force.

"At least I'll have the joy of leaving you behind. Not quite how you left me behind, but good enough! What do you think, Tela? Which will get you first? The heat? The sand jackals?" His sneer bloomed into a full, malicious smile. "Or the crab ants?"

"You arrogant *ass!* I didn't leave you behind!" I snapped. "You knew we had to leave. The traps were going off everywhere. But no, you had to run back into Long Deep! For what? A silver amulet?"

"It was *my find!*" he raged back, fists clenched.

"You were treasure hunting! We were there for records and you were there to line your pockets!"

I watched him reach for the spider pendant he had under his shirt out of reflex. Anyone acquainted with Vargas knew he wore that thing all the time. He never let it out of his sight. Not that he has any choice about it. I struggled to sit up but wound up leaning on one elbow.

My temper was at full sail. If I could have slapped him down with a glare, Vargas would be on the ground by now.

"We went back in looking for you," I replied with a growl. "Ten people *died* because you got greedy! *Ten!* Almost every last one of us! I hope *that,* and living with the curse on that pendant, was worth it."

I looked away, which meant staring an angry hole in the dirt where I lay. It was that or glare at the horizon.

Neither of us spoke for a few seconds, and even his two Crimson Company bodyguards kept quiet. The sound of the wind running through the prairie grass shook the accusing silence.

"No. It isn't," he said in a quiet tone. "All those voices whispering to me, especially at night? No. It isn't worth it at all."

I glanced back over at him as he turned to walk away. There was a curve to the man's shoulders I missed before. It was the appearance of someone who carried a heavy burden they couldn't, or didn't know how to, put down.

"Hey. Vargas?"

I kept my voice low, in an even tone.

Vargas stopped, but didn't turn around. I watched him take a deep breath, then sigh.

"What?"

I bit my lower lip while I scrounged words together. It was a lot simpler just to hate the man. He was still responsible for those people that died in Long Deep, and the bloody path he's followed since then.

But all of this was bigger than the bad blood between Vargas and myself. What Lord Marius did with the Automatic Crystal made that all too clear. Then there was the matter of the baron himself.

"Be careful," I replied. "There's something wrong with all of this and Lord Marius. I don't mean his grand plans or whatever he's told you. Not that. I mean the man... or *whatever* he is."

Vargas glanced at me over his shoulder with a curious expression.

"How do you mean?"

I locked eyes with him.

"I stabbed him and he didn't bleed."

Vargas frowned.

"You did what?"

The morning sun had climbed partway into the near-cloudless sky. I could feel the heat starting to beat down on me. It can get hot quickly out on the wide, flat lands of Planus. Sweat trickled down my cheeks while I blew out a heavy breath.

"I stabbed Lord Marius, and he didn't bleed," I repeated, forcing myself to stay calm. The memory was fresh in my mind, along with the shock. "At least, it didn't look like blood. It was more like dust."

There was another long silence while we stared at each other. I could see it in his eyes that this was new information. His expression was as dark as a thundercloud.

"A contract is contract." His voice was low, almost gravelly in its intensity. "Even if the arrangement is getting worse all the time."

At that, he walked away, flanked by his two Crimson Company mercenaries. I could've yelled at him to break the contract. To not be an idiot and die for a business arrangement. But I knew better.

A part of Vargas was still the man I remembered from his days as a Windtracer. Contracts were sacrosanct to him. They were tied up with his personal honor, even if it landed him in trouble. What happened with him and his silver pendant was a shining example of that. So, instead, I waited impatiently for the three of them to ride away.

The prairie heat continued to bake me while I struggled with my bonds. The rope was secure, but I was still able to move my hands a little. I curled up and fumbled near the top of my right boot.

They had taken my whip and daggers from me, and any other obvious personal items. I hoped they hadn't had the time, or the inclination, to search for my not so obvious tools.

It took a few minutes, but I opened the flap on the inside of my right boot. My fingers touched the blunt end of the thin, palm-length knife I kept hidden there. I grinned.

My grin faded when I heard howls echo on the light wind.

I froze, then slowly looked to the horizon. In the distance, thought the tall prairie grass, I saw a pack of tan-furred jackals rise into view. There were five of them. It was mid-morning, which was late for Planus sand jackals to be out for a morning meal. But it happened sometimes.

Slowly, I drew the palm-knife out of my boot, then sawed at the rope.

Then the wind shifted direction, and I saw the lead jackal look right at me.

17

Amates 21, 1277. Mid-morning. Alone with my thoughts, and a little more. The latter wasn't the best company.

I knew exactly where I was. Out in the middle of nowhere.

It had been about an hour since I had cut myself loose from the ropes. After that, I picked a direction and started walking through the dry prairie heat. I could tell where 'east' and 'west' were just by the position of the sun. North and south were a bit harder.

For those, I pointed my left arm toward the rising sun and my right to where it ought to set. That had me facing south. I double checked this when I found a crab ant tower. Crab ants build these tall tower mounds out on the Planus prairies, taller than most people. Along the base, about halfway up, the mound stretches out in a wedge-shape. That part always runs north to south.

So, I had my directions. Did I know where Banye was? I had no idea. But I wouldn't find it by standing still.

The jackals had been my constant companions since I got free. I figured they had to be shadowing me out of either curiosity, or were just waiting for me to collapse from the rising heat. Which, if I did collapse, they would probably attack me in a second. I just needed to hold out a little longer. Sand jackals don't like heat, which is why they hunt at early morning or evening. So I expected they would leave sooner than later.

They also weren't much for conversation and kept about a stone's throw away from me. But the jackals were someone to talk to, even if they didn't reply much past the occasional yip.

"I *know* that I should have remembered what Ihodis told me about the Crystal." I wiped the sweat from my face. "But I've been busy with the Crimson Company getting in the way, and talking out ideas with Mikasi…"

My words trailed away when a gust of wind blew past that cooled me down a bit. I closed my eyes to enjoy the sensation. The sweet wildflower scent stole a little of the tension out of back. But I could feel the tingle of a faint sunburn on my skin.

I glanced over my shoulder at the jackals. It could have been the heat, but I thought I saw the lead jackal nod at me. I sighed, then looked back at the all too flat horizon. It was an ocean of wild grass. The bright sunlight over all of it made me squint. I kept walking.

"You're right, I should have paid more attention." I shook my head. "Been more careful."

A series of sharp yips from the jackals made me turn around. They had kept about 10 nindel away from me for most of the morning, or roughly 13 paces. Like I said, close enough to hit with a rock if I wanted to throw one. Now? They were three times farther away.

Most stood and looked around in different directions, tense and alert. The big one that I considered their leader sat down and stared at me. I almost thought they were looking for a nearby threat, but the leader didn't seem alarmed like the rest.

"What?" I asked with a shrug.

Then the ground dropped out from underneath me.

I shrieked and fell into pitch darkness for a few seconds before I careened off a gentle slope of gravel with an unpleasant crunch. Two bounces and a tumble later, I found a nice, flat, smooth piece of black volcanic rock to cushion my fall. Immediately, I rolled to my right until I was outside the circle of sunlight cast from above.

Broken chunks of the prairie rained down from the hole. They shattered against the dark rock where I had first landed. Over by the cavern wall, I curled up to make myself as small a target as possible while the debris cascaded down.

Eventually I uncurled, then looked up, once the avalanche of dirt and rocks stopped falling. I slowly stood, ignoring the chorus of aches along my sides and left leg.

The hole, now roughly large enough for a buffalo to fit through, was a good two stories overhead. A pile of gravel and rock reached most of the way back up, but stopped short of the ceiling. I scowled and studied the distance from the top of the pile to the opening. I wasn't sure if I would be able to reach the hole, or if the edge of the opening would support my weight.

There was only one way to find out.

It took me three attempts to scramble to the top of the gravel pile. The edge of the hole was rough and thicker than I was tall, so it should more than handle me climbing on it. My problem was I couldn't reach it. When I tried, the gravel would crunch and shift, nearly throwing me downhill.

I was trapped.

That dark and ugly thought ran around in my head for a moment, looking for a place to take root. I mentally shoved it aside with a shaky breath. Thinking like that wouldn't do me *any* good. This wasn't the time to panic. I took slow deep breath of stale, dry air, then carefully scrambled to the bottom of the pile.

"All right, *think*. This makes no sense. How is there a cave out here under the prairie? And how in the Cresting Tides did its ceiling cave in under *my* weight?"

I paced, but stayed on the illuminated part of the ground. There was more space to this cave I was in, several paces to either side, but I wasn't ready to explore it. Not yet. I needed to think this through.

There was a familiar yip from above. I glanced up.

Five sand jackals stared down at me, ears raised, curious. I grimaced at them.

"You could have warned me sooner, you know. Also, how about a little help here?"

They didn't bother to reply. Instead, they raced off in a cloud of dry grass and dust. Their leader was the last to leave after he twitched his ears at me twice. I shook my head.

"Right. I get it. Pay attention," I muttered. "Like they understood anything I said, anyway." After a long sigh, I resumed pacing.

On each pass, I eyed the gravel. That it was even there just bothered me. Gravel, best as I understood, was usually in rivers or lakes. I had never heard of gravel, especially this much, building up on its own underground. I stopped pacing.

"Unless it had help," I said slowly.

Wide-eyed, I raced over to kneel at the pile and study the stones. Bank gravel, like from a river, was smooth and a variety of colors and sizes. Those colors stood for various kinds of rock carried down from different locations along the river's path.

These stones didn't look a thing like that.

The gravel here was roughly all the same size. They were a collection of small, light-tan stones that looked like they came from the same source. Not limestone but sandstone or granite? They also hadn't been worn smooth. I had seen gravel like this only once before.

"A *mine!*" My voice echoed in the half-lit expanse. "This isn't a cave! It's a tunnel, or a mine." That thought sank in. "A ruin? Out here?"

My excitement shoved away any sense of caution. I hurried over to the nearest wall outside the well-lit spot in the middle of the chamber. Rock dust swirled around me when I skid to stop. If this was a mine, or even a tunnel that once belonged to a building, there should be marks on the walls where miners smoothed out the natural rock. I slowly ran my hands over the wall.

There was worked stone all right. The dry, chilly walls hadn't been smoothed out by miners, they had been built.

These were marble, perhaps even granite, brick walls. There was no mortar. These immense bricks, as best as I could feel, had been cut and laid so precisely, they didn't need it. I squinted in the dim light for a better look.

Each mottled blue-gray stone was as tall as my head and easily twice as long. It gave me a better sense of where I was.

This place was *old*. Ancient Order old? Maybe, but I didn't know enough to tell. There were a lot of ruins across Awldor, like the Temple of Draosis in the Anestri'for jungle, that were built after the Great Collapse. Sometimes well after the Collapse.

Still, this changed everything.

Tunnel or mine, that meant the pile of gravel had to be waste rock. Stone that would have been tossed away from where the main dig happened. I wasn't that far underground. There had to be stairs or some other way back up to the prairie, I was sure of it. All I had to do was find that way up and not get killed.

My only light was from the hole in the ceiling, so I wouldn't be able to explore very far. But it was worth a try. I placed one hand against the wall and walked into the darkness.

Then the ground shuddered from an earthquake.

18

Amates 21, 1277. Probably still mid-morning. Definitely still no coffee. At least the ground had stopped shaking.

Nothing says 'hurry' like a cave in.

The earthquake rattled the hallway and split open the bricks. Chunks of stone rained from the ceiling, then shattered close to my feet. I hugged the wall while I ran. Jagged cracks in the floor chased me until it was too dark to see them.

After a few seconds, the earthquake stopped. Darkness buried the hallway and everything near me in an inky blackness.

Panic flared and that ugly thought of being trapped returned. It battered at me and tried to take root in my head, this time with more enthusiasm. My heart hammered in my chest. Every breath was an effort. I clenched my jaw, kept one hand on the chilly wall, and tried to search for any hint of light.

A faint crack of light peeked through the darkness behind me. It was enough to show me that the ceiling had collapsed. Somewhere, past all that, lay the hole where I first fell in.

Bitter, sour dust hung in the air and clung to my skin. That light fog of powder filled the hallway. I sneezed, followed by a cough. The dry dust, with the intense darkness and stale air, made the hallway feel tight. I had no choice but to keep moving.

My hopes for escape rested on experience with other ruins; mostly Ancient Order ruins.

Ruins are nothing more than old buildings that people used for some practical purpose at one time. It's true that some contain 'secret doors' for many reasons. But the 'long, twisty, maze of passages' you read about? That's a myth. Ancient cultures made buildings with a purpose. All hallways lead to somewhere.

The problem was, I couldn't see. Not really.

After a few minutes, or even an hour, I had my first break of luck. My left hand found a door.

I ran my hands along the rough surface to search for a handle. The wood was dry, like everything else down here. It wasn't easy to determine the door's age; lack of light made it even harder. But, if old enough, I might could break through.

It felt old. But Ancient Order old? I wasn't sure. Wood can rot in a place like this. It just takes a lot longer.

The door felt intact but brittle when I lightly tapped on it. Four centuries? Five? That was my best guess based on the stonework I saw before the ceiling collapsed. So not Ancient Order, but still old. If this *was* part of a mine, it could be a storeroom. A storeroom meant a chance to find something for light, like a candle, a lantern, or something to tie together for a torch.

I found the lock and handle after a second.

"High Cresting Tides, you'd better *not* be locked," I snarled.

It wasn't.

I hauled the door open with a little effort. It was a little swollen, which I thought was odd, but this wasn't the time to figure out why. After a deep breath, I kept to my 'left hand on the wall' rule and stepped past the doorway.

The room lit up. A sharp sizzle echoed with the sudden light. I bit back a sharp yell and covered my eyes, though I cried just a little from relief.

This wasn't a storeroom.

It was a workshop. At least, it looked like a workshop to me.

Old, dry crates were stacked against one wall with faded letters scrawled on their sides. I couldn't read the language, and it didn't look like an Ancient Order dialect. It looked closer to one of the miner's cants of ancient Dwarven clans. It surprised me to see it here.

Bags and forgotten debris were scattered across three short wooden tables against the wall to my left. Metal scraps, cut lengths of rope, and broken wood lay on the floor. A wide, cold forge dominated the far wall. Faded papers with barely legible sketches hung from a wooden board to the left of that forge.

But it was the lights that really got my attention.

Fist-sized orbs hung in each corner of the room. They hummed while giving off a dim light, no brighter than a fading sunset. For a room ten or fifteen paces wide, it was enough.

The room's only door turned out to be as old as I thought, but lacked any of the Ancient Order's typical style. It was plain, almost utilitarian. Even though the door may not have been Ancient Order make, the room was with its smooth walls and impossibly graceful overhead ceiling arches.

I slowly stepped further inside, a wide grin on my face. A faint, pungent smell of brewed tinctures and other herbal ingredients hung in the air.

"An alchemist's workshop," I said excitedly. "Maybe an herbalist's? No. An alchemist or artificer. An herbalist wouldn't have a bucket of parts lying around."

The smells were sharp, and I stifled a sneeze. After I rubbed my nose, I hurried over to the closest orb. I needed light, and I recognized those from other Windtracer reports.

Sun Orbs, like the ones on the wall, were a common sight in many Ancient Order ruins. They varied in size, and often no longer worked. Ancient Order records suggested a special type of enchanted stones fueled the Orbs. Those stones could absorb and hold sunlight or lightning for decades, sometimes longer.

No one knew how to make those enchanted stones anymore, not even the Helians who had a habit of re-purposing Ancient Order designs. Finding one Sun Orb, much less four, that still worked? That was rare.

A chain suspended each orb from a hook attached to the wall. They were pretty high up, but I could still reach them. I removed one from its hook with extreme care.

"You are the prettiest thing I've seen all day."

I think if I grinned any harder, I would have sprained my jaw.

The orb was smooth with a clouded, glassy surface. It felt cold but wasn't heavy. In fact, it barely had any weight at all. Most of the weight was the chain used to dangle it from the wall hook.

It hummed cheerfully in my hands while it gave off its sunset glow. The sound was like a dozen distant bees working away at a clump of yellow Honey Hynoxi flower-vines. It was a little mesmerizing.

I shook my head, then forced myself to concentrate on the surrounding room. Now that I had light, I could rummage around for anything to help me escape.

The best I had after a quick search was a pile of almost nothing. I had found old broken brass gears and cracked wooden rope spools piled in open wooden crates. Dusty lengths of chain, brittle rope, and small bags of ore topped my list of supplies. The only thing that had any potential was old, torn sections of a parchment map that I found tacked to one wall.

I cleared a space on one worktable, then laid out the map pieces in a row. They had obviously been part of some larger map. Age, and more than likely prairie weasels, had done most of the map in. What was left depicted chambers and tunnels of what I thought was this complex. Only, what I saw there made little sense.

The tunnels on the map crossed over each other like a spider's web. I was close to the surface, so either there were a lot more tunnels below me or there was something on that map I just wasn't seeing. Frustrated, I held the map piece against my Sun Orb to get a better look at the details.

Numbers and faint lines appeared like ghosts on the parchment. A few notes, written in what I think were more miner's cant dialect, lined the margins.

"*That's* why you don't make any sense," I said with a heavy sigh. "Those aren't all tunnels. Most of those are guidelines."

A wild idea sprang to mind, and I quickly held the other pieces against the orb. Each drawing had similar lines and numbers. I re-arranged the torn pieces on the table. This time, I matched them as close as I could, using those guidelines I found.

They weren't a perfect match; I needed the rest of the map for that, but it was enough. I suddenly understood what I missed before.

"This room is *movable*," I said, amazed. "Like at the Natoce Ruins with that lever and pulley system to move entire rooms around inside that giant underground shaft."

I turned my back on the map pieces to take a good, long look at the workshop. This time I saw the little details I overlooked before in my rush to find some light.

A thin layer of dust covered everything. Large cobwebs lined two corners and decorated one side of a workbench table. Half-broken gears, empty stoneglass vials, and a few ruined books lay strewn across the floor among bits of gravel. Not even the forge was spared.

Thin, ugly cracks ran along its length, even into the pair of narrow chimneys that vanished into the ceiling. That forge would never work again in that condition.

Light gouges or scratch marks marred both forge and walls. They looked like claw marks. Large claw marks. There weren't any blood-stains, so whatever happened took place a long time ago.

"There was a 'last stand' here," I whispered. "Whoever it was, they didn't go quietly." I shuddered, then frowned. "Just like at Natoce."

The Windtracer expedition to Natoce wasn't a disaster, but it was a lesson to take older ruins seriously. What they found there, those things from the deep pit, were lethal. That expedition had a full group. Here? I was alone. If this place was anything like that, I was in more trouble than I thought.

Just then, the room quaked. It hurled cracked pottery, loose gears, and more to the floor. I grabbed the table to stay on my feet. The shaking stopped after a moment. I scowled at the room while my eyes wandered over the debris.

"If this place uses movable platforms with buildings on them, how is it having a normal earthquake?"

I held my light higher, then glanced at the open door with the thought of leaving.

"This place shouldn't 'shake'. It should sway like crates held up in a cargo net."

That's when the floor dropped out from under me.

I didn't fall far. The entire room had dropped a hand-breadth or so. It was just enough to pitch me to the floor along with anything else left on the nearby tables. I caught my Sun Orb before it met an ugly demise against the unforgiving stone tiles.

The motion of the room, and my fall, was all too familiar. It reminded me of the last time I was aboard a ship during high winds at sea. I ignored the fresh bruises along my legs while I stumbled to my feet.

I shook my head and scooped up the scattered map pieces. After that, I headed for the door.

"Those aren't earthquakes," I said to myself. "That's the platform ropes giving way."

A chorus of faint giggles stopped me at the doorway. There was the unmistakable skitter of claws on stone nearby. The workshop lurched again, this time sideways to the right.

That's when I heard the distant, faint, ragged sound of a saw tearing through rope.

19

Amates 21, 1277. Underground, unarmed, in the middle of nowhere, with only one light. Things have been worse...

I wanted to run out the door, but that would have been a mistake. Instead, I eased through the doorway and looked around.

The light from my Sun Orb gave me a better look at my situation. The direction I came from was a jumble of broken rust-tan brick, earth, and stones. I already knew that, but it felt good to check in case I missed something in the dark before.

What I didn't know about was the other side of the hallway.

Instead of an ancient, perfectly set, brick wall was empty air. The wall I remembered on the other side of the hallway ended ten paces to my right, toward the collapsed section. Had I used my 'hand on the wall' trick on that side, I would have run out of wall. Worse, I would have fallen off the platform.

I shuddered.

The sound of a saw chewing on rope echoed in the air. There was also a giggle and the light skitter of claws on stone. A lot of claws. I had no good way to conceal the light from my Sun Orb, so instead I kept still. The faint noise wasn't from down the hallway, it was from *above* me. I frowned. That didn't make any sense.

This entire complex was right up against the surface. At least, that's what I thought. Was the first hallway I ran through sloped down? I couldn't remember. It was a little hard to think. I was starting to get tired, hungry, and thirsty.

"Just keep moving," I whispered to myself. "Keep. Moving."

I crept farther down the hallway, or platform balcony, as fast as I dared. The balcony eventually spilled out into an open courtyard made of multi-colored stone tiles spread out in a mosaic pattern at my feet. They glinted through the dust under the light of my orb.

The small tiles were a sea of color, from light blue to green, and more. They had been set into a careful design, like a painting. The tiny, colorful tiles were set together into flowing circles and curves. It made me think of a river running through a meadow.

Other than behind me, there weren't any walls around the courtyard; just blackness. Empty air. This was a platform suspended over a pit.

It was an exciting, but uncomfortable thought. I eased forward and inspected the rest of the courtyard.

A set of stone stairs led from the tiled courtyard to the top of a building. The building looked too wide to be the workshop I ransacked earlier. That suggested this platform had more than one building. That felt important, but I was too focused on escaping to think it through.

Opposite the stairs at the far end of the courtyard was a small, waist-high column no thicker than my arm. There were six levers at the base and something round at the top. It looked no larger than my fist in the gloom.

The urge to go study those levers, and that small pillar, yanked at me. But so did the stairs; they could be a way out.

I chose the stairs.

There would be time to study this place later with a full crew at my back, provided the ruin hadn't collapsed by then. Not to mention that sawing sound on the rope? The claws and those giggles? My nerves were done with that.

Near the top of the staircase, I heard the sawing and other sounds again; this time much more clearly. I crouched down before I eased my way onto the last step. Careful to keep my Sun Orb low so the light wouldn't give me away, I peered onto the roof. I couldn't see much, but what I could see was plenty.

The roof was large enough for four buildings the size of the workshop I found. It was more long than square, and holes dotted the surface where parts had fallen in from age. Above me was the actual cavern 'ceiling'. That confirmed my suspicions. The hallway I took after I fell into this place had to have sloped down. I just didn't notice it at the time.

All of that was interesting, but two things in particular caught my attention. First was the impressive rigging that held the platform up, and second? The small mob of miniature dragon-like figures busy to cut it all down.

Kobolds.

My best guess? They wanted to take the ruin apart to use the pieces for something else. Kobolds did that with anything they got their paws on. They had done a good bit of damage, but there was a lot of rope left to cut before they sent this platform crashing into the pit.

Destructive kobolds were the last thing I needed, but I could cope with that. A clutch-clan of kobolds would have some path back to the surface. Kobolds built their warrens in tunnels or caves, but lived a lot of their life above ground. They would also have something to eat and drink if I managed to negotiate with them.

I had dealt with kobolds before. It was back in Ishnanor when the trade ships came up from the Belari river region. Belari has dozens of kobold clans in their water-towns. Each extended family, or clutch-clan, has their own unique markings. I memorized a few of them.

This lot didn't have any of those tattoos, but it didn't mean they might not be reasonable. I stood up and cleared my dry throat. After I stepped onto the roof, I lifted a hand at them.

"*Buzet'el*".

I wasn't that fluent in Belari-scal, but at least I knew how to say 'hello'. For kobolds, it translated more to 'you eaten yet?', since they always seemed to be hungry. At least, it was a friendly greeting.

Kobolds at the rigging stopped sawing at the tarred ropes. The ones on the roof dropped their conversation and spun around to face me. For three uncomfortable seconds, no one moved.

Then, the kobolds on the roof drew knives before they ran right for me.

"*Aile Shavat!* I was just saying 'hello'!"

I turned on my heel and bolted down the stairs, heart pounding. A pack of six kobolds raced after me. Once I reached the courtyard, I looked around for some place to hide. There wasn't anything. I could have run for the workshop, but I didn't want to get trapped inside. Also, I didn't know if that door would hold up against being attacked.

Claws skittered on the stairs behind me. I clenched my jaw and spun around.

They had claws and knives. Me? I had a Sun Orb and my little boot knife. Those weren't great odds, but I refuse to lie down and die. I drew my boot knife before I swung the Sun Orb around by its chain in a circle at my side. It may not last long, but it would work as a temporary flail before the glass shattered.

The kobold pack scrambled down into the courtyard and spread out around me in a semi-circle. One of them let out a small, manic giggle.

Frustration, fear, and a lot of pent-up anger from the past day boiled over.

"You want a fight?" I yelled. "Come on, then!"

The mob hissed or shrieked before they ran at me all at once, knives at the ready.

"*Ah'sa'kee!*"

That yell stopped all six in their tracks. It caught me off guard, too. I may not speak much Belari-scal, but that was one phrase I knew from a half-dozen dock and bar brawls. It was as close to a 'kobold battle cry' as any of the Belari clans got. Loose translation? It meant 'go to it'.

It also didn't come from any kobolds around me.

The yell came from the buildings. Another pack of kobolds, three times larger than the bunch surrounding me, swarmed into the courtyard. They raced out of the hallway-balcony opposite the one I first came from. This new group brandished everything from knives and bows to pots and pans.

They were a different clutch-clan just going by their tattoos. My six would-be attackers turned their back to me, shrieked a reply I didn't understand, then charged the newcomers with murder in their little reptilian eyes.

I glanced between the two groups as I realized what was going on here. This wasn't a bunch of kobolds ripping apart a ruin for raw materials. It was one clutch-clan trying to kill off another one.

This was a clan war, and I was right in the middle. I shook my head and sighed. There was only one thing I could think to do.

"*Ah'sa'kee!*" I screamed, then charged the nearest kobold that wanted to kill me a second ago.

The fight was on.

20

Amates 21, 1277. On a platform, in an unknown ruin, under the middle of nowhere in the plains. This was getting to be a really long day.

I've been in fights before, but this was different. From the outside, it looked like a rolling mess of kobolds clawing at each other. It wasn't. This was every bit a skirmish between two small armies.

Each side had their own leader, who directed the overall battle strategy. There was also the kobold who controlled the tactics for their part of the mob. Most had daggers, long knives, or hammers. Some even brandished improvised weapons like pots, pans, or whatever they could find.

It may sound haphazard, but in the hands of someone with a bit of fighting skill, even an iron skillet can hurt as bad as any war hammer.

Despite all of that, and having no armor, I waded into the middle of that battlefield anyway. It turned out that my Sun Orb was tougher than I thought.

My first swing caught the nearest kobold by surprise. The orb slammed under his jaw with a solid whack. He stood up straight on his toes before tipping over backwards onto the courtyard tiles.

The newcomer kobolds, which I dubbed 'Bluescales' for their blue tattoos, must have decided right at that moment I was on their side. So their 'Master-at-arms' running orders from their leader shouted a few of those my way. My Belari-scal is pretty weak, so I missed most of what he said, but I understood the intent.

I was suddenly adopted as their new 'basher'.

They directed me to come in from the left. Their only other basher came around on the enemy's right with a pair of iron skillets. The rest of the Bluescales would harass the enemy in the courtyard, or the few running down the stairs from the roof.

It was a pincher tactic that put the enemy's back to the stairs with no cover.

The whole thing lasted a fierce, bloody twenty minutes, if I had to guess. In the end, the enemy kobolds were killed, caught, or chased away. I was cut and bruised within an inch of my life, but I still met up with my fellow basher on the battlefield.

We grinned like lunatics at each other, hugged, and cheered our victory with the rest of the Bluescales.

After that? I passed out.

I had a lot of strange dreams that involved caverns, chanting, and twisted memories of the previous battle. Several involved fighting Baron Marius over a dark pit.

Eventually, I jerked awake. I was lying on a grass bed in a room I didn't recognize. More working Sun Orbs hung from the walls and cast the room in a bright late afternoon glow. My wounds had been bandaged and treated, but I had a thin headache. There was also a dry, cotton sensation in my mouth. A kobold wearing a blue and yellow trimmed tabard, belted at the waist, sat beside me.

He was chanting something under his breath while he lit a thin, brown-black stick. Once it smoldered, he stuck it in a ceramic holder near my head. It smelled sharp, like burnt cinnamon or scalded mint.

I slowly sat up. The surrounding room was more of the same ancient brick walls, only cleaner and less cracked. This place contained woven grass mattresses, short tables, and even a workbench. I saw jars, mortar, pestle, and other herbalist tools there.

The room was half the size of the workshop I had visited before. Even though it was small, the kobolds had put this place to good use.

"Healer?" I asked and winced. My voice sounded hoarse and felt a little raw.

The kobold nodded slowly.

"Magic?"

That time he, at least I thought it was a 'he', shook his head.

"No," he replied in a soft tone. "I've already done that." He gestured to the smoldering incense stick. "This is for soothing the nerves. You were yelling in your dreams."

I dredged up the scattered nightmares, then shuddered.

"I've had a rough time of it."

The kobold grinned.

"I could tell. You needed healing, so I have cast a few spells. Mostly, you needed water and ointment." He touched a hand to his chest and nodded. "I am Odro, the Healer for the Tirak."

"Tela. Tela Kioni," I replied, then reached up to rub the side of my head when my headache threatened to get worse.

The bandages on my hand made me hesitate. I sighed, then rubbed my temples.

Odro chuckled, which for a kobold sounded like a cross between a snicker and a hiss.

"Thank you for helping my people, Tela."

I nodded.

"Honestly? It seemed like a good idea at the time."

"We do appreciate it." Odro tilted his head a little to the right and frowned. "But, and I am just curious, why are you here?"

I glanced at him but didn't reply right away. What do I dare tell him? Anything? Then again, what would it hurt? I was in a kobold warren out in the prairie and didn't know where Ki, Evi, Tyre, or anyone was.

That feeling of being lost and alone pressed down on me. It was like being wrapped in a wet blanket of wool that pinned me to the ground.

When I didn't reply, Odro pursed his lips while his frown deepened. Despite his reptilian features, down to those yellow eyes, it was the same 'physician frown' that Ki always gave me.

"You had a small fever after the fight," Odro explained. "You had been poisoned. The fever made you rant on about many things. People. Places. Mostly people. You sounded very worried about them. Oh, and always there was a crystal. You mentioned that more than once."

I took a deep breath, then sighed.

"Good to know I can't keep my mouth shut."

Odro chuckled again.

"You had a *fever*," he stressed. "You were badly cut and were exhausted. On top of that, the magic-sickness was quickly breaking you apart."

It was my turn to frown. I looked at my arms, then what I could see of my legs through cuts in my trousers. In between the occasional bandage, pale white scars from healed cuts crisscrossed parts of my skin. Some looked like they may have been pretty deep. Scars from magic healing weren't new to me. I took it as proof of Odro's claim about having cast a few healing spells.

But healing magic and ointments only cure the physical wound. It doesn't take care of the 'phantom pain'. The mind wants what it wants, and right now, mine wanted to remind me in no uncertain terms that I put myself through some serious danger. So every move I made came with a mild ache.

"All right," I relented. "My crew and I, my friends, we're looking for a crystal. Something from the Ancient Order called the Automatic Crystal of the Eclipse." Odro's comment on my condition sank into my head. "Wait. What do you mean 'magic-sick'?"

He shrugged, then gestured to the scale ridges along my forearms, then to my surprise, my *face*. I felt icy needles of panic race along my spine and I sat very still.

"Magic-sick," he repeated.

"What's wrong with my face?"

I almost couldn't get the words out. Deep down, I knew what he meant about 'magic-sick'. There was only one thing it could be: the magic storm that Baron Marius hit me with while using that piece of the Automatic Crystal.

The healer didn't reply right away. Instead, he studied me in silence for a moment.

"It's what can happen when anyone is magic-sick, like from too much altering magic, or being caught in a magic storm." He tapped his own cheekbone. "Kobold eyes. You had human eyes before? Now you have kobold eyes. It's something that can happen."

I clasped my hands together to keep them from shuddering.

"So the 'magic-sickness' is turning me into a kobold?"

Odro shook his head.

"No. It's trying to kill you by transforming you into," he paused, thinking, "... something else."

Words like 'magic-sick', 'poison', and the rest shattered my thoughts into tiny pieces. Before I could ask anything else, Odro turned around to pick up a small box just big enough to hold a pair of shoes. He fished around inside, then withdrew an all too familiar piece of a clear crystal with one smooth, charcoal-black side.

A piece of an Automatic Crystal of the Eclipse.

Odro chanted a short phrase, and the thing glowed sharp yellow.

I nearly shrieked.

21

Amates 21, 1277. Coming face to face with what I believe is true.

I took one look at that chunk of crystal in Odro's claws and wanted to crawl up the side of a wall.

Instead, I stumbled to my feet, then staggered back a step. It was all pure instinct. A reaction to just seeing the thing. The fact it was lit up with magic didn't help one bit.

It took a few breaths before I collected myself. My heart was hammering in my ears. The memories of what Baron Marius did were still raw. I focused on what was real, what was around me. The smells of hay, herbs, and what I swore were peppers roasting on a fire nearby.

Odro, at first, had flinched at my panic attack, but now he studied me with that physician's expression on his face again. I watched his eyes flick between me and the glowing crystal in his hand. A brief frown crossed his face. Odro whispered a short phrase while he passed his free hand in the air above the crystal. Magic evaporated in a tiny shower of faint, glowing bits of light.

Stress bled out of my shoulders while I watched the magic fade out.

Without another word, Odro put the crystal in his lap. He held up his hands in a show of peace.

"The stone is just a tool. I don't mean you any harm. In fact, I've been using it to heal the worst of your ailments. I can tell you were caught out in a strong magic storm. A bad one." He lowered his hands. "I don't know what happened before, but now? You're a *guest* here. You helped my people. Let me help you before the magic-sickness kills you."

A silence settled in the room between us, then dragged on for another few seconds. Two Tirak kobolds appeared at the doorway; Odro waved them away.

It took me another ten seconds before I found my words again.

Even then, I needed another slow breath to get my nerves to calm down. What happened in the tent between Baron Marius and myself was only what? Yesterday? Last night?

I nodded sharply.

"All right," I said solemnly. "I've had a bad experience with an Automatic Crystal piece like that one." After a second I added, "it's where the magic storm came from."

Odro looked puzzled at that. I settled back onto the thin, woven mattress while he picked up his crystal.

"This?" he asked. "One of these?"

I caught the faint note of concern in his voice.

"Yes. One of those," I replied uneasily.

Odro looked thoughtful for a moment before he whispered an incantation in Belari-scal and waved his left hand over the crystal. A soft glow radiated around his scaled fingers before it descended on the stone. The crystal picked up light and amplified it, like a palm-sized lantern. Odro aimed the yellow-white glow at the scaled sections along my forearms.

It took every ounce of willpower I had to ignore the spike of fear that shot through me. Odro cleared his throat.

"I don't mean to poke my snout in where it doesn't belong, but... what happened?"

I fidgeted slightly and stayed quiet.

Odro glanced up at me from his work, and nodded.

"I shouldn't have asked," he blurted. "I'm very sorry."

Odro had an easy manner of asking questions, much like Ki did. That didn't help me put into words what happened. I wasn't comfortable talking about that nightmare; wouldn't be for some time. Instead of an answer, I tried to dodge the question.

"You hardly have any accent. Where did you learn to speak Planari?"

He chuckled. "Ishnanor. I worked as a Shield's Mate aboard the *Wavecrest* for the Eastledge Merchant Company. We sailed along the Ishnanor-Belari trade route."

My curiosity perked up. I squinted at him. "But you wound up here?"

Odro shrugged.

"After a few years, yes." He glanced at me sympathetic expression. "I really am very sorry for prying."

That made me fidget again. This time I didn't try to change the subject, instead I kept quiet. But the silence turned painful. I found what I wanted to say after that.

"There's a man named Baron Marius who has one of those crystals. He wants enough of them to build a complete Automatic Crystal, I think. He's hired the Crimson Company to help him. After he gets it built? I think he plans to use it like some sort of weapon."

The memories of what Baron Marius put me through rushed at me. I winced.

"A very horrible weapon."

Odro hesitated at the word 'weapon'. The yellow-white magic running through the crystal sputtered as he lost concentration on the healing spell. He raised his brow ridge, which passed for 'eyebrows' on a kobold.

"A weapon?" he closed his left hand into a fist, which ended the failing healing magic. Odro leaned forward slightly while he examined my forearms. "I see. Is that why your people are looking for it?"

I didn't fall off the cargo wagon yesterday. That hesitation in Odro's reply? I almost missed it. He was testing me. Would he attack me if I gave him the wrong answer? I glanced at the chunk of crystal in his hand. A thousand different ideas about what Odro, a spell caster, could do with it came to mind. I didn't like any of them.

But I never saw anyone use this crystal during the fight against the invading kobolds. There was something going on here I didn't understand.

"No."

I realized how sharp I said that the instant the word left my mouth. A deep breath later, I tried again, but in a softer tone.

"No," I said. "I'm a Windtracer. We don't do that. Learn about it? Study it? Yes. If we're lucky, it'll have some clue why the Great Collapse happened to the Ancient Order. Maybe it'll just open up new ways for life to get better. But a weapon? No."

Odro's posture relaxed slightly. It was subtle, but I saw it.

"I've heard that about the Windtracers."

He looked lost in thought.

"Yes, good." Odro lifted the crystal over my arms before he resumed the healing spell. "I was worried that I made a bad choice in welcoming you to our clutch-clan."

Odro directed another few seconds of healing light through the crystal and onto my forearms.

"But this means there's a lot for you to learn before the runners return with your people."

Shock replaced the warm comfort I felt from Odro's healing spell.

"What?" I tried not to shout, but did it anyway. I blurted out, "you know where my crew is at?"

He nodded.

"For about a day. We understood you weren't working with the mercenaries. Nothing good comes from dealing with the Crimson Company, so we avoid them. We Tirak have enough problems."

Odro held up a clawed finger before I could reply.

"Despite that, we should get started."

This was all moving faster than I could follow. A dozen aches, some imaginary, others not, jabbed at me; mostly along my back. That made understanding this much more difficult.

"Wait. Just wait." I waved my hands to hold off anything more from Odro. "Get started? How do you know so much about that crystal?" I shook my head. "Better still, where did you get it?"

He shrugged.

"It's been among my people for generations. Stories tell that we got it from an old ruin along the Great Chasm. Where? I can't say. The stories weren't about that."

I frowned. There were lots of small ruins along, and in the Great Chasm. Some large, like Long Deep, others nothing more than a ruined watchtower. I scowled at Odro.

"Why?"

Odro gave me a quizzical look, as if I asked if water was wet.

"Why what?"

"Why teach me anything about that crystal? I saw how you reacted when I explained...," the words caught in my throat. They tasted bitter, but I got them out. "What happened to me."

Odro looked down at the crystal in his hands. For a long few seconds, he just sat quietly. I was about to stumble my way through an apology for being pushy when he spoke up.

"I've dealt with the Crimson Company before. It was at a small place near Osidore, south of the Belari river. It isn't standing now, but once it was a lovely river town. Mostly kobolds lived there." He looked at me with a sad smile. "I spent many summers there visiting friends between my trips aboard the *Wavecrest*."

I had a sense of where this was going, but I didn't interrupt. It looked like Odro needed to say this, so I just nodded for him to go on.

Odro replied in kind before he continued.

"I never really found out why they did it. Money? Land? Who knows? The result was the same. Someone hired the Crimson Company to drive my friends away from their land. Some went, but not all of them. Words were exchanged. Heated words. In a tense moment, someone threw a rock and hit the Crimson Company's leader. It didn't hurt him, but tempers flared; weapons came out."

I pictured Vargas, in all his pompous glory, getting smacked by an irate kobold with a rock. It wasn't hard for me to imagine the man's temper exploding.

"Odro..."

He shook his head.

"I arrived there just after the massacre. The mercenaries weren't very particular who they attacked by then, and to them, I was just another kobold."

Odro sighed. "To me, anyone that hires or works with the Crimson Company is probably as vile as they are. So, if they are looking for the pieces of an Automatic Crystal, you need to find them first. Which means you need to know how it truly works."

"Everything my crew and I have read suggests it's a lens. It can focus light," I gestured to the one in his hand, "magic, even enhance magic."

A sly smile crept over Odro's reptilian face.

"That is what most know, yes."

Odro held up the crystal between us. Lantern light sparkled off the facets.

"It is a lens. But it's more than that. It's also a *mirror*. The crystal can reflect, and magnify, what is inside the person holding it; light or darkness. It reacts to the person, and in a way, the person reacts to the crystal."

He released the crystal, but it didn't move. The stone remained where it was, suspended in the air.

A faint, gossamer glitter of snow-white light surrounded the stone. Odro moved his hand in slow circles through the air. The crystal obediently followed.

I just stared, open-mouthed, at the entire display.

Odro held out his hand, and the piece of the Automatic Crystal of the Eclipse landed in his palm.

"This is where we'll start."

22

Amates 29, 1277. Outside the town of Talabrae's Deep at the edge of the Great Chasm

"Town ahead! Talabrae's Deep!"

Tyre's bellow from the front of the windwagon jarred me awake. I found the world's largest cat nose sniffing at my cheek. His whiskers almost made me sneeze. It took me another minute to drag myself from sleep and form words. Coffee would help. Somewhere close by, people were moving around the windwagon.

"*Yoi T'kalo*, Nicodemus."

This had been my morning ritual for the past eight days of travel, ever since I left the Tirak clutch-clan and their ruins. Being greeted by the Planus smoke cheetah wasn't a part of Ki's order to rest and recover. The big cat had his own opinions.

Nicodemus yawned at me with a squeak. After that, he purred, shoving his whiskers at me.

I shoved his head aside.

"Not now." I pulled myself into a sitting position on the futon mattress, then stretched. The footsteps nearby faded out, and more comfortable sounds took their place. Windwagon rigging creaked in the breeze outside while someone tied down and set an anchor. The usual work when a windwagon came to a stop.

"Where's everyone?" I asked. "Outside?"

Nicodemus ignored my question. Instead, he sauntered onto the mattress while he scrubbed his flank against my arm. After a slow turn, he took my place on the futon.

I shot him a perturbed glare before I got to my feet.

My clothes hadn't entirely survived what I went through after the Crimson Company camp. They could be mended, so I kept them, but had them stuffed into the room's tiny footlocker. I was down to my only spare trousers and shirt. Expeditions were always rough on clothing.

I had slipped those on before Ki knocked on the door frame.

"You're looking better. Color looks good. Death warmed over doesn't become you."

"Doesn't become anybody," I replied with a touch of sass under my tone. Confined to quarters wasn't fun, no matter if I was aboard a windwagon or a sailing ship. At least with a windwagon, I had my own room.

"Did I hear that right? We're at Talabrae's Deep?" I asked.

Ki nodded, then leaned against the door frame with a shoulder.

"We are. Evi plans to go out and have a look around. Tyre already is. He was going to make nice with the local merchants. You and I? We stay here with Mikasi. Just in case."

"Sha'ree drown it all!" I growled.

Ki chuckled.

"I told Tyre you wouldn't like it." Ki's tiefling tail swayed like a calm pendulum. "But I agree with him. This time, it's better safe than running in chin first. The Crimson Company has a big lead on us, and they would've come through here by now." He shrugged. "For all we know, they left some enforcers behind to do some leg-breaking."

I picked up my shoulder bag and fished my journal out of it. My temper was already short from being confined to quarters. The news of having to stay on the *Sheldrake* while others scouted around to make sure it was safe didn't help. Reading sometimes helped me blow off steam, and I really needed to do that.

"I blend in," I complained.

"Not with those eyes, you won't."

I winced, then glowered at Ki. But he had a good point.

When I first got back to the *Sheldrake*, Ki mentioned he could tell that I had been treated by a master healer. I had a few scars from the kobold skirmish, but Odro healed the rest. The reptile spines growing along my arms? Those were gone; not even a scale was left behind. But then, there were my eyes.

My eyes used to be a dark brown. Now, after that magic storm Baron Marius conjured up, they were a dark gold. They weren't quite kobold eyes; Odro had adjusted that much. But they weren't back to normal. Odro warned me this might be permanent, and I should be careful. He wanted me to take my time to get used to them, since they weren't human eyes anymore.

That had been hard to take.

One thing I had noticed was that the light was brighter. Sharper. Mikasi had fashioned up a set of goggles for me with smoky quartz eye coverings. I needed them in the middle of the day. Without them? I'd get a sharp headache.

Then there were the dizzy spells. They weren't strong and didn't happen too often, but it was what encouraged Ki to slap an order of bed rest on me.

"I'll wear my goggles. No one will notice."

Ki stared at me with a flat expression.

I jammed my journal back into my shoulder bag.

"Fine! I'll wait aboard," I snapped.

My anger really wasn't aimed at Ki, and he knew it. I wasn't a good patient at the best of times. Sitting around and waiting wasn't easy for me, either. After I snapped at Ki, I stormed out of the cabin, then paced the *Sheldrake's* common room.

Ki waited a moment by the door frame while I fumed. Once I had burned out some of my frustration, he cleared his throat.

"So, all that 'the crystal reflects what's inside you' this Odro told you about... you believe that?"

I glanced at Ki, then stalked over to my favorite window aboard the *Sheldrake*. Outside, the dark, blue-gray stone buildings of Talabrae's Deep took up most of the view. The mining town was nestled in the rolling hill country of the Bonagrave Hills that hugged the Great Chasm.

Those hills spread out in all directions around the town, except to the east. In that direction, they ran up against the edge of the Great Chasm itself. The rough edge of the impossibly deep canyon cut through the hills like a giant knife. Fog clouds rolled beside the cutting like the waves of a ghost sea.

I watched the fog for a few seconds while my mind wandered. Did I believe what Odro said?

"The whole 'reflection' thing?" I sighed. "I don't know. Ki, I don't deal in magic. It's there around me, like when you cast healing spells, but my world isn't like that. It's facts, numbers. Old relics or documents about people long dead. You know, history."

Ki joined me at the window with two cups of coffee and offered me one. I took a sip to let the wonderful sensation wash over me. The tension bled away. Ki took a slow sip out of his own cup.

"Kobolds and that 'Sacred Philosophy of the Way' they have is complicated. It's a religion, but again... not. Sometimes it's more of a philosophy they try to follow. Maybe there isn't a difference." He glanced outside at the town. "You said that after a few tries, the crystal floated for you, too."

I barked out a short laugh and shook my head.

"Floated? A little." I shrugged. "I think it was probably falling over sideways, laughing at me."

Ki grinned as he looked out the window. I noticed his tail swayed thoughtfully while he pursed his lips.

"That reaction. What you described," he shook his head slowly. "That isn't anything I recognize as magic. At least not the kind I've studied. What did it feel like?"

I frowned at him.

"Feel like?"

He glanced at me with a smirk.

"Yes, feel like." Ki held a hand out the open window. "Magic has a 'feel', Tela. Like warm sunlight against your skin, or the sound of wind rustling the grass. Magic connects things around us, like tendons connecting muscle to bone."

I stared outside. Feel? How did it feel? To be honest, I wasn't sure.

Ki had mentioned that before about casting spells. How all magic had a sensation that depended on what was being cast. I never studied magic, so I didn't pay it a lot of attention.

"I... don't know?" I stared off into space while I dredged up the memory again. Another sip of coffee brought it into focus. "Light?"

"You mean you felt light? Like you were floating?"

I shook my head.

"No. Not like that. Everything seemed clear. It was like the light in the room was a little brighter. The shadows had pulled back and even the dust seemed to fade into the background." I paused and squinted at the air in front of me, recalling the odd sensations. "I remember suddenly being so clear-headed, Ki. Like I had just got up from a really good night's sleep."

When Ki didn't reply, I glanced over to find him staring at me with a deep, concerned frown. The intensity made me fidget.

"What?"

"Mind magic," he said with a dark tone coloring his words. "Rare. Dangerous. At least it's rare anywhere on Planus, like in Ishnanor or even in the Kingdom of Jata. I'm not sure about anywhere else."

Ki could be a little paranoid, especially when it came to ruins and what ancient moss, mildew, or disease was lying in wait to kill everyone. This was different. There was a tone in his voice I hadn't heard him use before.

"Just how 'dangerous' are we talking about here? Magically make you drunk enough to wake up next to a happy, snoring bugbear? Or is this 'fireball inside your head' kind of dangerous?"

Ki sighed.

"Closer to the latter, but more sinister. From what little I've found to read on it, if a spell goes wrong, the magical backlash can roll back into the caster's mind. I don't mean the typical headaches you hear about. I mean, break the caster's grip on what's real. Shatter it like glass. The worst stories say this magical backlash might even act like a sickness and infect other casters nearby."

I nearly dropped my coffee.

23

**Amates 29, 1277. Outside the town of Talabrae's
Deep at the edge of the Great Chasm**

"Infected?" I sputtered. "Like a plague?"

Ki shrugged. Maybe it was all his physician's training, but he seemed far too calm about that.

"Infected? Yes. Like a plague? I have no idea. There isn't much written about mind magic." He sighed before he took a sip of his coffee. "Magic isn't clean, Tela. It's a gamble. That's why I try to be so precise when I cast healing spells. It helps me cut down on the risk; to get the magic working in a smooth, predictable fashion. That's also why I'm so tired afterwards."

I didn't know what to say. Ki hadn't ever talked like that about magic before. He looked thoughtful, so I kept quiet and waited. Eventually, he continued.

"I heard a sorceress say that magic was once perfect; like a flawless gemstone. Today? It's more like a pile a broken glass. Shattered, razor-sharp fragments churning around over each other in a barrel."

He shrugged. "Maybe that's what magic storms, or a backlash hitting a spellcaster, really is? Just all that 'broken glass' clattering around and spilling out of the barrel."

A deep, ominous silence filled the air while my thoughts ran in circles.

Magic backfiring and infecting people? I didn't like any of those implications. It also made me wonder about Baron Marius and his lunatic ideas over how to best use an Automatic Crystal. Had he been 'infected' by a bad cast of mind magic? Did he already know about this?

I shuddered at the memory of stabbing him, which made him bleed dust, not blood. There was something deeply wrong there that I just didn't understand.

It was a good two sentences past time to change the subject, so I grabbed at the first topic I could find. Anything to make me quit obsessing over what happened at the campsite.

"Talabrae's Deep. We could enter the Chasm from here. *If* the Talabreans let us past the Churlgrave Gates and into the Direnight Passage."

Ki raised his eyebrows before he gestured out the window with his mug at the jagged, ugly rise of rocky hills on the Chasm-side of town.

"Big 'if'. Last I heard, they're still under constant threat from predators and other things crawling up out of those tunnels."

He shook his head. "The Talabreans keep a close guard on those tunnels, though. Maybe if we ask their Slate Watch politely, they'll let us through?" Ki shrugged. "Of course, they'll shut and lock the gates behind us."

I took a deep breath before I finished off my own coffee. Ki was right. The locals take guarding those passages seriously. They don't let just anyone through.

The Talabrean people are descended from dark elves and dwarves that lived below ground in the Deepland caverns. It took Awldor shattering from the Great Collapse to drive them to the surface. The mutated horde that chased after them made them learn to work together. But it hasn't been easy. Things from the Deepland are still trying to get to get above ground. When they do? People die in a bad way.

Enter the Slate Watch. They are the Talabrean's answer to that ugly problem. The Slate Watch are basically professional monster hunters. They study the mutated things that try to kill them, using what they learn to hone their skills at how to deal with the seasonal invasions.

I don't like that word 'monster' because most use it wrong. More than half the time, the 'monster' is just some animal trying to get by in the world. The person calling it a monster is the invader, not the wild animal.

But, from what I understood, the Talabreans use the word correctly. What keeps trying to crawl out of the Deepland? That's closer to a rabid creature the size of a wagon that can spit acid and tear metal with its claws. Sometimes the Talabreans get a break and it's just a swarm of ancient, mindless undead migrating up from below; if undead actually migrate.

I watched while a thin, streamlined cloudglider took flight out of the Leapport district in the distance. It lurched up after being tossed into the air by the wagon sized slingshot. With a snap, the crew spread the cloudglider's sails, and the ship caught the wind in the Great Chasm.

Cloudgliders are large, catamaran-like flying boats with silk sail-wings to keep it in the air. They're a regular sight along the few Great Chasm rim settlements. The miles-deep Great Chasm is the only place on Planus I'd ever heard of them being used.

I remember them from the last time we came through Talabrae's Deep. They're still impressive.

"You know, that's another idea." I pointed at the flying boat while it unfurled its sail-wings. "A cloudglider. We could make up for the lost time. Maybe even get ahead of the Crimson Company."

Ki rubbed the bridge of his nose.

"I remember those. It could work provided there's enough room to maneuver," he waved a hand idly toward the window, "or even land."

"We landed last time," I replied. "It was a little rough, but we landed."

"A little rough?" Ki raised his eyebrows. "I don't think we remember that the same way."

I shook my head. Just then, a crunch of metal on stone in the distance caught my attention.

To the right of Leapport, where the cloudgliders launch, a spider-shaped wagon lumbered into view between the buildings. A stonejack. Another result of Talabrean creativity. It rumbled on its eight, metal-braced legs while the crew aboard worked the lines, winches and more that made the thing work. Slowly, the vehicle clambered over some rocks before it scaled down the canyon's cliff face, out of sight.

"We could catch a ride on a stonejack," I suggested. It was another attempt to keep distracted from my previous thoughts, which would not quite go away.

Ki's sea-blue complexion turned a light gray-green. It practically reached the horns on his head.

"What?" I asked.

"The walking wagons they use for cliff mining? Dangling off the edge of a miles-deep canyon, held up by a single line?" After a deep breath, he sighed. "Negotiating with the Slate Watch sounds simpler."

I snorted, grateful for his typical paranoia about the world trying to murder us. It was comforting in a really strange sort of way.

He squinted at me.

"Tela, other than ignoring the whole 'die by splatter', I think there's something here at Talabrae's Deep that could help us before we head into the Chasm."

I had to think about that for a moment. Equipment? Supplies? We might need those. But I got the impression Ki wasn't talking about that. It wasn't like I knew Talabrae's Deep like the back of my hand. I had only been here once before, years ago. Suddenly, I understood what Ki meant.

"Hunter's Hall!" I said with a grin. "Their library, the Obsidian Armory! That's here in their Hunter's Hall!"

Ki grinned back. "The same. Remember the last time? They had a few records on Long Deep. Like that partial map which led us to the bottom of the Chasm. It's been a while, so they might have collected more by now. After all, the Slate Watch keeps detailed records on *anything* that slithers through the Great Chasm."

Baron Marius jumped back into my mind. The quiet part of me wondered if the Talabreans had anything about him? Like that 'dust for blood' condition? It was worth a look. I pushed away from the window.

"I'll get my coat."

"Tela," Ki said sharply. "Tyre said to wait, and he's right! This isn't the time to walk into an ambush to set it off."

I wasn't sure if it was what Ki said, how he said it, or just bad timing. But something inside me snapped. I turned on my heels and scowled at Ki.

"That's it!" I snapped. "Ever since I've been back, people have been treating me like I'm going to shatter into little pieces if I get bumped wrong. All because of what happened."

The urge to pace made me fidget. "I'm not a glass statue and I will *not* go sit safe on a shelf! I've been through worse and bled from worse!"

Heat rose to my cheeks while I clenched my fists. I had kept my temper on a short leash recently, but right then? It broke that leash and roared to life.

"I *told* you what happened with Baron Marius! Also about Vargas having me dumped out on the prairie like garbage. At least I was half expecting that from Vargas!"

Ki started to interrupt, but stopped himself. Instead, he stood still and looked pensive. Me? I had a head full of hot frustration, so I just kept going.

"I get what you and Odro told me. I do. But I *need* to know what that bastard did to me! Especially since this," I waved a hand at my eyes, "is *permanent* right? Isn't that what you and Odro said? Also, I have to know just *what* Baron Marius is! He bled *dust* Ki! Dust! People don't *do* that!"

To his credit, Ki stayed where he was and listened. He didn't interrupt me, try to explain it all away, or anything. At most, he fiddled with his coffee cup and pursed his lips while I ranted like a madwoman.

I forced myself to stop yelling at the world through Ki, then took three slow, deep breaths. After that, my temper receded enough that I could talk with my calm, inside voice.

"Ki, given all that's happened, there is no way we won't run into Vargas, the Crimson Company, *and* Baron Marius again. We know about Vargas and his little 'condition'. The Crimson Company isn't anything new. But the baron? Remember, what we don't know could kill us. Right now, it feels like we don't know a lot."

We stared at each other for a long time after I stopped talking. A last few words bubbled up from the back of my mind. This time, my voice was small, quiet. But in the near silence of the *Sheldrake*, they sounded far too loud in my ears.

"The baron. That man. He hurt me in a way I don't entirely understand, Ki. I refuse to be that helpless again. Especially since we both know we're going to *have* to deal with him at some point."

Kiyosi didn't reply. Instead, he walked over to a small table bolted to the wall frame to set his cup inside a small bin. That done, he turned to face me; his tail swayed idly behind him.

"Then we'd better grab Mikasi and get your coat," he said with a small smile. "Daylight's burning and we've a lot of searching to do."

24

Amates 29, 1277. Searching the Obsidian Armory library and learning a few new things...

It turned out Ki was right. The Talabreans *had* been busy with their studies. Honestly, I wasn't that surprised. They're under constant threat by slimy things oozing up from the darkness, looking to kill them every month. The Talabreans' work kept themselves safe.

Once we entered the library, Ki, Mikasi, and myself split up between the tall shelves of books and side rooms. We figured that would let us cover more ground that way. Which in this library? There was a *lot* of ground.

The Obsidian Armory has always fascinated me ever since I first set eyes on the place. It reminded me of the Windtracer Records Hall in Ishnanor. Only, in this library, instead of being a collection of works on the Ancient Order, the Great Collapse, and so on, it's focused on magic, creatures, and the Deepland itself. Also, the design of the place was interesting on its own.

It's a two story library built out of the local blue-gray briskstone and supported by a frame of dark wood. Though calling those timbers 'wood' is generous. Talabreans use actual wood from trees, but most of their lumber is red-brown planks cut from the building-high Bitter Fog Dire-Tubaria mushrooms they grow.

Leather or vellum covered books of all shapes, colors and sizes, weighed down the shelves on each floor. Where there weren't books, there were small jars that held preserved remains of creatures the Talabreans and their Slate Watch Order had fought over the generations. Those remains were either parts of, or entirely whole, mutated monstrosities floating in cobalt blue liquid. Despite the ghoulish decor, there was a comfortable scent of old paper in the air.

An alchemy lab was on the first floor. This seemed to be busy with members of the Slate Watch working out a formula for one elixir or another. A light greenish-gray fog trailed out of the open door to hang like a thin, rotten cloud in the air. It smelled of lilacs with a hint of cooked chicken and burned leather. That wasn't exactly a delightful odor.

There had been enough twisted magical transformation in my life to last me a while. So I avoided both cloud and lab on my way through the Armory.

I searched the shelves until I had a small collection of books. Five in all that covered everything from flying threats in the Great Chasm to a heavy discussion of wild magic based necromancy. The last one I had to sign for in order to even touch the thing.

The book was kept under lock and key in a vault the Talabreans called the 'Undercroft' which was underneath the Obsidian Armory itself. Two guards from the Slate Watch, and a locked black metal door, kept people from accidentally wandering inside. Only the most dangerous, or ancient, books were stored down there.

They were particularly careful about this book of wild magic necromancy. Apparently, last year, a necromancer used it to cause some mischief. The Slate Watch wasn't about to let that happen again.

That was why one of the Order's hunters, called a 'sentinel', was assigned to escort me through the library. It was one Sentinel Ruathan Bravolo. He looked every bit the part of a Slate Watch sentinel, from brigandine armor, alchemist belt pouches, and well-used weapons to the wine-red hunter's coat with the sword and eye emblem of the Slate Watch.

No matter where I wandered between the shelves, the Talabrean dark elf was a few steps away. He was always right where he could keep an eye on me, or really me, and that necromantic book. It took a little time to get used to having an escort; especially one dressed for a fight.

I can't say I enjoyed the experience.

At one point, I stopped in my tracks and turned on the sentinel. The Talabrean man, who was at least a head taller than me and looked like he could out-muscle a mule, tensed like a bowstring.

"I get it," I said. "About the book, being careful, and all of it. But if you're going to stalk behind me, it would help if you carried a few of these, then helped me find a worktable." I thrust two of the larger books at him.

To his credit, he didn't complain. Instead, the man simply inclined his head with a polite, but amused, smile. He tucked the books under one arm and gestured ahead of us.

"This way, Windtracer," he said. "I know just the place."

We settled on a long, Tubaria-wood table on the second floor that came complete with a large jar as a decoration. The two nindel, or meter by Ancient Order measurement, tall glass jar held one of the many preserved creatures here. This one was a small, three-eyed chicken that displayed a disturbing amount of fleshy, reddish-purple tentacles flared out around its head. It floated blissfully in a sapphire-blue slush.

Despite the decor, it had plenty of space, so I settled in to read and ignore the chicken-thing. My escort set the two books I asked him to carry on the table next to me. The book on necromancy was one of them.

"I'll return that to the Undercroft once you're done, Windtracer. Just let me know if you need anything. I'll be nearby."

With that, he stepped to the right of the table to stand watch. Literally. Sentinel Ruathan stood with his feet shoulder-width apart, hands clasped behind him. The Talabrean stood as still as a statue. Except for his eyes. They scanned the room for anything that moved.

I arched an eyebrow at the tall, armored sentinel, then nodded a little, unsure of what to say. Suggesting that he didn't have to stand at attention didn't feel like it would go anywhere.

"Thank you, Sen Ruathan," I replied with a thin smile. "I'll let you know."

I blew out a sigh and grabbed the first book from the top of the stack. It was the *Guide to the Great Chasm*, one of the Armory's older books they kept on hand. This book, last I remember, was less of a 'guide' and more a collection of journals from prospectors. It was also thicker than I remembered.

The *Guide* was a heavy book with a worn, blue-green cover of reptile hide. The scaled leather reminded me of Odro's people. I winced. In the back of my mind, I hoped this wasn't one of his relatives. After a quick look at the index, I flipped open the chapter about Long Deep and got to work.

Last time I was here, there were only a few pages of notes and a crude sketch of the land around the ruin. Now? Long Deep was almost a third of the book.

A portion of the new pages just retold the story of my previous expedition a year ago. How the Talabreans found us battered, bloodied, but alive with a bundle of Ancient Order documents.

Ten of us went down. Only myself and two others came back. Reading the Talabrean's account dredged up some unpleasant memories. I shook my head to get my focus back on what I was looking for.

Long Deep isn't the name of the ruin. That's the ancient lava bed around the buildings. No one's really sure what the Ancient Order called the place. The documents we recovered on the last trip down were just a list of accounts. Ten simple pages from an Ancient Order trade manifest, that were more about bushels of Immon apples than the name of a building.

But there was a 'Bathrogg Station' mentioned at the top of one page. It could have been the name of the ruin, but it also could have been the trade good's next stop. No one knows. The Talabreans, and specifically the Slate Watch, are convinced that the proper name *is* 'Bathrogg Station'. For me, it's always been easier to call it 'Long Deep'.

The Long Deep chapter had a lot of notes in the margin. Most were just about recent creatures that had recently moved in, or parts of the ruin that were unstable. Judging by the notes, the Slate Watch had sent two crews of sentinels to the area in the past year. But they never stepped inside. Instead, they were focused on expanding the map of the outside to see how large the ruin was.

I stopped toying with my pencil to take notes in my journal. A lot of notes.

A few minutes later, I had a duplicate of their recent map and more. The Slate Watch had figured the rough size and shape of the entire ruin. It was a lot bigger than any of us at the Windtracer Company suspected.

According to the Slate Watch, Long Deep, or Bathrogg Station, was mostly underground. If those scouts were right, the place extended down several floors below the ancient lava bed into an enormous stalactite that hung over an underground lake or sea. The most any Windtracer expedition, including mine, ever uncovered was a few fortified buildings nestled among the black, sharp rocks of the Chasm floor.

This opened up all sorts of possibilities. We would still need to arrive as close as we could to the ruin. But we didn't have to walk in through the front door if some Deepland creature was camped out there. Instead, there could be a way inside from underground.

I wasn't thrilled by the idea of hiking through the Deeplands; no one in their right mind is. But if it was easier than fighting our way inside, I was all for it. Besides, it also meant another way back out if the front door was blocked.

Satisfied, I set that aside, then grabbed the book on necromancy. The *Xinder Codex*. I noticed Sentinel Ruathan tense up again the instant I touched the book.

"Sen Ruathan, please relax. I'm not going to try to cast anything, sew body parts together, or cause any trouble. I've about as much magical talent as a table leg. This is just me trying to," I hesitated while I picked out my words, "make sense of some things I came across not long back."

The sentinel relaxed a bit. I saw his eyes slide over to meet mine before he nodded.

"Of course, Windtracer. In some ways, as I understand it, the work we do in the Slate Watch isn't that far off from the Windtracer Company. Sometimes we face things that we can't make sense of right away. I'll be here if you need anything."

That was an understatement if I'd ever heard one. When all I did was frown back at him with a perplexed look, Ruathan returned to standing guard. I shook my head, then went back to my studies.

The *Xinder Codex* looked much older than the other books on the table. I'd heard that they brought the first edition out of the dark elven empire around the time of the Great Collapse. It was one of the few books brought out with the Deepland survivors.

It was a leather-bound book with a few peculiar quirks. The smooth, blue-gray binding was littered with dark stains that looked like blood, soot, or a mix of both. Rough, dark red twine stitches cross-crossed the cover, as if someone repaired it in a hurry. It felt soft in my hands, like a fine fur, and was a little warm to the touch.

I fought down a twitch and wondered if I should have asked Ki to read this instead of me. That sent my mind to wandering for a moment.

Ki. I yelled at him back aboard the *Sheldrake*, but it wasn't his fault. He was just concerned, like he always gets. Tyre and Evi weren't acting any different. They were just being careful. I needed to apologize to all of them and get my head together.

"Focus, damn it," I mumbled in a low voice. "Do the research, then apologize. He's not going anywhere. He's right downstairs."

I let out a heavy sigh, then opened the *Xinder Codex*. The first few chapters were written in a code that the Talabreans hadn't translated.

To me, it resembled some of the Ancient Order dialects I knew, but the letters looked distorted. On one page, when I tried to focus on the writing, the letters seemed to move and shift by themselves.

My first guess was a mage-lock. Ki told me about them. That was a bit of mage-craft casters used when they wanted to keep something they wrote private. Despite that, I dove into reading what I could, and copied a few bits into my journal along the way.

That mage-lock didn't make it easy. It also didn't help that the damn book started whispering to me.

25

Amates 29, 1277. Still in the Obsidian Armory, only this time learning more than I bargained for.

"What's that?"

I jerked in surprise, almost knocking the books off the table. Mikasi stood off to my right and had leaned over to see what I was doing. I know this wasn't true, but it felt like he had appeared out of thin air.

There wasn't a water clock nearby, but I felt stiff from sitting in mostly one position. I had been deep into reading the *Xinder Codex*, oblivious to the world. After a slow, deep breath, I put down my pencil, then gave Mikasi a sideways glance.

Mikasi ignored me while he made his way to the other side of the table, then dropped into a chair. There were two books with him. I couldn't quite see the covers, other than they had something to do with stonejacks and cloudgliders.

"A very bad book," I replied while I rubbed my eyes.

When I looked up, Mikasi had reached over to tilt up one side of the *Codex* so he could see the cover. The instant he read it, Mikasi jerked his hand away as if the book had bitten him. Slowly, he wiped his fingers across the front of his blue shirt and grimaced. For a second, he stared at his fingers to make sure they were all there. After that, he scowled at me.

"Why do you have a book on necromancy?" Mikasi asked with a tone that hovered between disgust and alarm.

"Baron Marius."

Mikasi's scowl softened.

"Oh." He traced the edge of the cloudglider book with a finger. "Well. That makes sense. Do you think he's a necromancer? Maybe some sort of undead... person?"

I looked down at the open *Codex* in front of me.

Did I?

The spidery handwriting on the tan, weathered page twitched like it might crawl off and across the table like a rattled ink-spider. I pursed my lips, then looked over at Mikasi while trying to ignore the chicken in the jar that stared at me. Before I replied, I quickly reached over and turned the jar clockwise to the embalmed thing had something else to pay attention to.

"Yes, I do. I just don't know which he is. Either he's undead, a necromancer, or just something else. After dealing with him, what's wrong with him has to be necromantic."

"What are his symptoms?"

Sen Ruathan's low, calm tone cut through the conversation like a hot knife.

Mikasi and I blinked at each other in surprise. Ruathan had been so quiet up until that moment, I'd forgotten he was nearby. It was almost as if he had turned invisible, at least until he spoke up. I suffered a small involuntary shudder, then glanced between Sen Ruathan and Mikasi.

"Mikasi? This is Sentinel Ruathan Bravolo of the Slate Watch. Sen Ruathan? This is Mikasi Zenia of Banye."

Ruathan nodded in greeting.

"Pure ore and good craft."

"Good winds," Mikasi replied, though he stumbled a bit over his words.

I didn't blame him. The Slate Watch with their ice cool, dark humored manner often made most people uneasy, including myself.

The Talabrean dark elf was still standing in a parade rest off to one side, hands behind his back. Only now, he watched us with a sideways glance and a raised eyebrow. There was a hint of a frown around his ghost-white eyebrows.

"So. What are this baron's symptoms?" Sen Ruathan asked again.

That's when inspiration jumped up and slapped me in the back of the head. I had been so focused on 'books' and 'study', I overlooked the obvious.

Why didn't I ask the Slate Watch in the first place?

The Slate Watch studied this sort of thing all the time. They've had years, generations, of experience dealing with undead, rogue necromancers, and magically twisted creations threatening people. If anyone had an idea about what I saw and experienced, they would.

So why haven't I asked?

Because I was more tired and rattled than I wanted to admit out loud. I was so convinced I could solve this puzzle about the baron by myself, it made me miss the obvious. I still wanted, or really needed, to solve this. But it wasn't smart to tackle it alone. That's what a crew, friends, and allies are for.

I frowned while I rummaged through my memories. It should be easy to just explain what happened. But *everything?* Maybe not that much. I wasn't sure how the Slate Watch would react to the idea of an Automatic Crystal of the Eclipse and what it could do.

Then again, what if they already had heard rumors about it? After all, they had a three-eyed tentacle chicken in a jar on a table. It was possible.

So where could I start? The beginning?

I clenched my fists while I wrestled with those thoughts in my head. Finally, I settled on the one moment where I felt things went all wrong with the baron.

It was when I saw that burning light in his eyes that made me so uncomfortable. The one that appeared when he offered to be my 'partner' and why. Everything in the tent had gone downhill from there.

So that's where I launched into my story. I left nothing out, even the uncomfortable parts where I passed out screaming once the wild magic blast slammed into me. By the time I was done, Sen Ruathan's expression had become as dark as a thundercloud. He had also turned to face us, arms folded over his chest.

Apparently, I had his undivided attention.

I heard Mikasi's chair creak while he fidgeted on the other side of the table. That wasn't a surprise. He had heard the story more than once already, and every retelling made him uncomfortable all over again.

"Sorry, Mikasi," I said over my shoulder.

"It... it's all right," he replied uneasily.

Sen Ruathan was stone silent, face pensive, for an uncomfortable, long few seconds. By the time he said something, I had started to fidget in my chair like Mikasi.

"You're fortunate to be alive." He said with a firm voice. "Are your golden eyes the result of the wild magic?"

I let out a long sigh. This wasn't the time to go into the whole 'magic poisoned and nearly died' thing.

"Yes, it was."

Ruathan replied to that with another of his small nods.

"You would find some ideas in that book of necromancy. At least three solid passages, if I recall. But I'm not sure they'll help you. Everything you've said suggests this baron *is* a product of the Dire Arts of necromancy. At this point? If he's what I suspect, he's beyond the bounds of that book."

"What do you mean?" Mikasi asked, wide-eyed, drawn in by the conversation.

Sen Ruathan shrugged.

"One of the Dark Curses; most likely the oldest. The Futhewia Curse. It lets a victim stay forever young, at a price. Their spirit, heart, or 'true self' is extracted and placed into something else. Most of the time it's a small gem or locket. The dark magic of the curse creates a painting of the victim. This painting suffers the wounds and pains in life."

Ruathan shook his head.

"Each time the victim takes a wound, the dark magic re-paints the portrait with the wound. This lets the painting suffer it, not the victim, except..."

Mikasi swallowed.

"Except what?" he whispered.

"The magic repaints the portrait to spare the victim the actual wound, but the victim still experiences the pain." The sentinel squinted. "Imagine being stabbed in the heart over and over for decades. Then, imaging having to live with all those little memories of lethal pain chipping away at your thoughts, stealing a small piece of your mind one tiny bite at a time."

He shrugged.

"A victim is driven to protect that portrait at all cost. At times, they have to feed the curse. This could be a specific task they have to perform, such as murder or causing torment in some way."

"Like forcing a transformation spell on someone," I suggested in a low tone.

"The very same," Sen Ruathan replied. "But in return, they stay flawlessly young for centuries. They're rare, and often mistaken for vampires. Make no mistake, they aren't. They are far worse. Especially because they look like any other normal person until you get too close to knowing them."

Mikasi and I exchanged a haunted glance.

"What is he?" I asked quietly.

"A lich." Ruathan sighed. "They're driven, obsessed, and deadly. Especially if they're an Ancient Soul. Once a lich becomes obsessed with something, they'll stalk it across the face of Awldor to get it. Kill anyone, destroy anything in their way for it. In this case, I'm sorry to say, it sounds like he's obsessed with you, Windtracer. Which means he'll come for you again."

Mikasi scooted his chair farther down the table, away from me. I shot him a sour look.

"He's not after me," I said, remembering the conversation with the baron. "I'm just a means to an end. Baron Marius is fascinated by what I've discovered, what I've written about it."

I shook my head.

"He wants to restore the Ancient Order." I shot a dark glance at Sen Ruathan. "He said 'bring peace to Awldor' and create a 'New Age'. He's obsessed with *that*."

Sen Ruathan raised an eyebrow at me.

"What about the people who don't agree with his vision?"

I pursed my lips.

"He'll bury them. Given what he did to me? He might could do it."

I grabbed my journal to show Sen Ruathan the sketch I made of Long Deep and jab the page with a finger.

"If the relic he's after is actually in Long Deep, and the baron walks away with it? Then I know he can bury anyone that gets in the way of his 'vision'. I went through that firsthand."

No one spoke for a few uncomfortable seconds.

"You have a very big problem," Sen Ruathan said quietly. "You also need more help than just a few books. Come with me, there's no time to waste."

26

Amates 31, 1277. Mid-morning. Depths of the Great Chasm, on the way to the Long Deep ruins. Not exactly a walk in the park.

I thanked all the gods of the high tides that the meeting didn't last long. If one sentinel of the Slate Watch was unnerving, an entire council of them staring at me? That was worse. But it was better than being stared at by a three eyed chicken floating in a jar, so there was that.

They wanted to help after hearing my story. It meant more people looking for the Crimson Company, and better equipment than the *Sheldrake* to navigate the Great Chasm. It turned out we needed that to catch up.

"They beat us here!" Evi growled.

She slammed a fist against the chest-high, dark tan sandstone rock wall in front of her.

"How are they already here? It's like they've been for days. We were only a half day behind them."

The constant breeze of the Great Chasm stirred up a gray-brown dust mixed with damp fog, blowing it across our hiding spot. We were nestled four stories up in a crevasse tucked away in one of the Chasm's rock walls. Ki, off to my right and leaning against the same rocks as Evi, shrugged.

"Exactly. How long have they been here?" Kiyosi asked. "That scaffold in the middle of their camp is bigger than a wagon, even a windwagon. What is that? A siege engine? Are they planning on attacking the ruin?"

I shook my head, then wiped some of the dust from my eyes. Fortunately, I didn't need my sunshade goggles down in the Chasm. Its heavy fog kept the light bearable for me. I pulled out a spyglass I had purchased in Talabrae's Deep before we had left, and studied the Crimson Company's campsite.

The mercenaries had set up in a hollow weathered out of the unforgiving, ancient black lava rocks and ruddy sandstone of the Chasm's floor. Spindly and twisted yellow-white plants grew in clumps, along with spotted cadaverous gray ferns around the hollow's edge. Ominous black seed pods writhed in the gray and purple tree leaves. The Chasm's churning fog gave the impression that the trees were stalking the camp, looking to eat anyone nearby as a meal.

Aside from the gloomy decor, the hollow was a good campsite. It was a green oasis in the middle of the Chasm's perpetual gray, black and tan desolate terrain. Plants growing along the shoreline of a small pond in the oasis actually looked green and healthy.

The scaffolds Ki referred to squatted in the middle of the campsite. I frowned while I studied them. They were two stories tall at most, with four solid corners. A nest of ropes and rigging stretched between the poles and a set of large buckets big enough to hold a person. Those buckets were constantly on the move, raising and lowering into a dank pit carved out of the dirt.

"A mining rig?" I suggested, not that I was an expert on those. "Maybe they're digging their way in?"

Mikasi, perched on a makeshift rock stool in our shared hiding place, pulled out his own spyglass to look for himself. After a second, he giggled.

"It's delightful, is what it is! That's a mining scaffold all right, but someone has made some interesting alterations to it. There's so few gears! Did you see? On the right, that's a type of hydraulis pump I've never seen before."

The inventor looked happy enough to jump up and down. I was glad he didn't. The sound of his boots against loose rock might have gotten the Crimson Company's attention. Mikasi lowered his spyglass before he tugged at my sleeve.

"They're using most of the designs Cesibus invented, but they've made some alterations. I saw a water screw to help channel water from that pond to work the waterwheel and the bucket pulleys. There's even way-stones incorporated into the waterwheel. It's almost like gears, but I can't see from here why they would bother."

Evi let out a deep grunt before she pawed the ground with a hoof in thought. She usually did that when something really caught her attention.

"Way-stones? Like what's used in a compass?"

Mikasi nodded and brushed the rock dust from his hands.

"The same. But these looked really large." He raised a hand, palm out. "About like that. The size of a person's hand."

I exchanged a glance with Ki.

"A counterbalance system?"

Ki shook his head with a frown.

"Not sure. But really, how did they get here so damn fast and why here? It's like they knew where to go all along."

I didn't know for sure, but I had a guess, and is wasn't pleasant. Most of that came from what Odro explained to me about Automatic

Crystals back in the Tirak Ruins. The rest was from those old alchemist journals I had copied. I looked out at the Crimson Company's campsite. After a hard sigh, I pulled out a piece of travelcake from a vest pocket, unwrapped it, took a bite, and started sorting through my thoughts.

"Back in the Tirak Ruins, Odro told me that the Automatic Crystal is more than just something that makes magic stronger. It's also a mirror that can reflect the nature of the person using it."

I finished my piece of travelcake, then knocked the crumbs off my hands.

"I think I understand what he meant. Those crystals can reflect someone's desires, not just their inner nature. Maybe."

"What?" Evi asked. "Like wanting to get another Automatic Crystal?"

I shrugged.

"Something like that. Which is why I think the baron is using his Automatic Crystal shard like a compass, letting it to guide him to other crystal shards." I gestured toward the camp. "If that's what he's doing, that would be how they got here so fast. They knew exactly where to go. Any maps from the Obsidian Armory and copies of the same journals I have would just help confirm it for them."

"So we've lost?" Ki asked. "They're digging down to it right now?"

It was a good question, and I didn't like it one bit.

Thinking about everything we went through to get here, only to be too late? That left a bitter taste in my mouth. I shook my head while I unclenched my jaw.

"I'm not sure. Something is off about this."

"Wait," Mikasi said suddenly, then stared intently at the campsite below. "Mirror. You said a mirror."

I swapped a confused look with Evi and Ki.

"Yes, why?"

Two long, uncomfortable seconds passed before Mikasi looked at us or did anything but stare at the campsite.

"If he's following it like that, then this can't be right." The Banye inventor frowned at us. "Really, if it's a mirror showing him what he wants, then this can't be right. Unless he's accounting for it being a mirror."

What he said almost made sense. I squinted at him, then nodded, not sure where he was going with this. Beside me, Evi and Ki looked just as confused as I was.

"Say that again?" Ki asked for all of us.

Mikasi sighed, dug out a pocket mirror and a piece of paper from inside his vest. There was a half-finished diagram on the page. Some sort of idea Mikasi had probably been working through. He held the mirror up against a line of letters, which reflected backwards.

"The crystal reflects what's inside the baron? What he's wanting? Like a mirror?" Mikasi held the mirror and paper out toward us.

No one said a word for a solid five seconds. The only noise was from the digging contraption and workers in the campsite. As if on cue, I saw from the corner of my eye Baron Marius leave the largest tent. He held up his crystal shard in front of him before making a series of intricate motions in the air above it with a free hand.

A glittering yellow glow appeared around his hand, and inside the crystal he carried. That glow in the baron's shard looked just like what happened when lantern light hit Odro's crystal.

Most of the baron's spell shone through the crystal and illuminated the dig site. The rest of the magic? That bled off in all directions around the baron.

What caught my attention was the faint, glittering, crystal-shaped ghost that appeared behind the man for a second. The baron smiled, looking satisfied and apparently oblivious to what I saw, then walked toward the dig site.

I glanced between the baron, the dig site, and Mikasi's little example with a pocket mirror and a piece of paper.

"*Aile Shavat,* hell and high tides!" I growled under my breath. "They're digging in the wrong place."

This time, Ki and Evi stared at me like I'd lost my mind. I silently thanked Odro for taking the time to teach me about Automatic Crystals before I waved a hand at Mikasi's mirror.

"Odro taught me a lot about an Automatic Crystal in a short time. A good bit of how the crystal reacts comes off the user's intent, but he also told me it depends on how you hold the thing."

I dug through my shoulder bag and pulled out my journal. "See? A fully intact Automatic Crystal supposedly has these pegs. That would mean they really are knobs to turn the facets. Like focusing a spyglass."

Ki's grin spread from ear to ear. He reached forward and gripped my shoulders.

"He's got the crystal turned the wrong way!" Ki said. "They are digging in the wrong place!"

Evi chuckled. It was a deep, pleased sound I always heard her make before she headed out to start a fight she expected to win.

"Then where do we need to go?" she asked.

I studied the Crimson Company's campsite, their dig, and where I saw a magical glimmer appear in the air from the baron's spell through my spyglass.

"If I'm right, it's almost the opposite direction from where they're digging." I turned toward the nearby jagged gray-tan cliff face of the Great Chasm. There, almost half-buried by ancient landslides, was exactly what I hoped to find.

"Due east of the camp, at the base of the Chasm rock face." I handed my spyglass around to others who didn't have one. "Between the two natural rock pillars and past that old landslide, I see something in the shadows there. Like part of a carved archway or door with some lettering. The Crimson Company wouldn't be able to see it from where they are."

"Wait," Ki replied. "If Baron Marius doesn't know about the mirror effect on his spell, how did he hit you with a spell cast through that shard? Luck?"

I shook my head.

"No. I think he's working off pieces of information like we all are. I bet all he knows is how to focus a spell through the shard."

My thoughts were running faster than I could talk, but I managed.

"All right. Here's the plan." I pursed my lips. "Evi, go find Tyre and the stonejack we came down here in. Tyre's had enough time to hide it. After that, track down the Slate Watch sentinels and let those scouts know what we found. Make sure that stonejack is ready to move. We're going to need a fast way out of here."

"Will do," she replied with a nod.

"Ki, head over to that door. See what you can make of those carved letters. You're better at languages than I am. Mikasi, help him."

Ki nodded. "What about you?"

I jerked a thumb at the campsite.

"Heading down there."

Everyone started talking to me at once. With Ki, it was ranting. I shook my head while I held up my hands.

"According to the Slate Watch, Baron Marius is a lich who might have been around since the Great Collapse. The man is deranged and obsessed in a murdery sort of way. He's also not stupid. He'll eventually figure out what we know about the crystal shard and the mirror effect."

I gestured at the Crimson Company camp. "Worse yet? Vargas. Ki and myself know just what Vargas is capable of. He's a former *Windtracer*. If anyone can figure out they're digging in the wrong place, it will be him. If I slip in and sabotage their digging scaffold, that should buy us some time before they realize they are on the wrong path."

Ki scowled and put his hands on his hips.

"Or, it could get them wondering why they were sabotaged, which could lead them right to that idea they are in the wrong spot."

"I'll make it look like an accident," I countered.

"The plan makes sense to me," Evi agreed.

Ki threw up his hands.

"I have such a bad feeling about this."

Mikasi squared his shoulders. "I'm going with you," he piped up at me.

I shot him a glare.

"No, you're not. They wanted you in the first place, and I'm sure it's for what you know about that Ancient Order inventor, Cesibus." I shook a finger at him. "Like, for example, what you just told us."

Mikasi folded his arms over his chest.

"Still going with you," he declared. "Tela, you helped me get away from the Crimson Company, even though it nearly got you killed. Let me help you."

"Mikasi," I complained, but he held up a hand.

"Wait, I'm not done. I everyone thinks I'm addled, or have my head in the clouds. That's fine. But really, do you have the first idea how to wreck those machines in such a way that it looks 'natural' how they broke down? If you do it wrong, then what Kiyosi said would come true. They would get suspicious. Between the two of us, we can make it look like a real accident."

"Once in a while, he makes good sense," Evi rumbled.

I shot her a perturbed glance, then sighed.

"All right, fine. Mikasi comes with me."

Ki shoved two vials into my hands.

"Here, at least take these with you."

They were two finger-length vials that held only three or four shot glasses of colored liquid. One was a cherry red color. The other? A deep yellow that churned on its own inside the container. Ki pointed at them.

"I brewed these up last night. The red one is a concentrated healing syrup. Just a drop or two will close up most average wounds. That second? Be careful with that. It's Helian Fire."

Mikasi took a small step back. I ignored him while Ki continued.

"You know how it works. Toss it and run. Once it breaks open and that liquid hits the air, it'll burn on anything, even water, for a long while until someone dumps sand or vinegar on it."

I knew these potions pretty well. Ki only made them when he was really worried about might happen. I nodded, then tucked them away in a belt pouch.

Ki gripped my hand before we split up.

"So, what's your plan for when you get down there?" he asked.

I brushed one of the dark, tight braids away from my face.

"I don't know, I'm making this up as go along."

27

Amates 31, 1277. Later that same morning. A brief hike between the rocks and into the lion's den...

The wind howled like an angry ghost by the time we reached the bottom of the canyon. We moved quietly, or as quiet as the occasional loose rock allowed. Fortunately, the silvery-white fog covered our hike and muffled most of the sound. The closer we got to the canyon floor, the thicker the fog became. I had never seen fog this thick. It was almost like smoke. At one point, I wondered if it was following us, but I tossed that idea aside as a case of nerves.

Mikasi, Nicodemus, and I eased past twisted, black bark trees like shadows. A wind I could barely feel rustled the canopy of purple and gray leaves overhead while the fog drifted around us. Before, up on the cliff, the trees looked thin, if not a little sickly. They were a much larger up close, especially their seed pods that looked the color of burnt charcoal.

Those pods varied in size and smelled like smoky, burnt sage. Some were a no bigger than the palm of my hand. Others? They were as large as a full-grown person and every one of them twitched if we got near them. That didn't do a thing to ease my nerves. Nicodemus didn't like them, either. Any time a pod writhed, his fur would bristle. Mikasi just stared at the things thoughtfully.

What little I remembered, or really anyone knew, about the Great Chasm was that nothing was as it seemed, and *everything* wanted to kill you. So, in my mind, the Crimson Company fit right in.

"Mimic trees," Mikasi whispered. "Be careful. Don't touch them, or let them touch you."

That last part got my attention. I froze since I was about to do exactly that to move a limb out of my way.

"Why?" I whispered slowly.

Mikasi waved his hands at one of the nightmare trees.

"From what I read, that's how they 'eat'. These trees shuffle along, stalking what they want until they get close. Then they change shape and color to look like a tree that belongs nearby. Something that looks safe, I guess. After that, they either wait for what they're hunting to touch them or they reach out with a root. Either way, they poison their victim, then swallow them in a seed pod when they're helpless."

I raised my eyebrows before I gave the tree next to me a sideways glance.

"Don't even think about it," I snarled under my breath.

It could have been my imagination, but I thought I saw the tree recoil a little. I wasn't fond of the Great Chasm and this didn't help my opinion any. But it gave me an idea. I knelt down, being mindful to keep clear of the mimic tree's tar-black roots. I pointed to the large waterwheel and water screw ahead of us.

"Here's what I'm thinking. We loosen the ropes, maybe a bolt or three, then come back here. We can use these monsters to cover our escape."

"The ropes, yes," Mikasi replied. "But I think we should leave the bolts alone. Ropes can come untied, or depending on the rope, they wear out faster than any bolt or wooden peg." he shrugged. "I would believe it was an accident it if it was only the ropes."

I nodded. "Ropes it is. Hopefully, that's enough to distract this lot." A thought made me glared at the tree next to me. "It would be nice if this pack of nightmares around us could walk over there and help."

Mikasi frowned in thought while he scratched behind one of Nicodemus's ears. The smoke cheetah purred back at him.

"There's an idea," Mikasi said.

I blinked at him.

"What?"

He smiled.

"The mimic trees helping. I think they can." He waved a hand at the Crimson Company's campsite. "See, the poison the tree uses is an oil. There's a little on the bark, but it's mostly on the roots and leaves. Especially the leaves. What if we collected some of the fallen leaves to smear oil on levers and other places a person would touch to fix anything?"

"Hold on, you said these trees poison their victims," I whispered quickly, interrupting him.

Mikasi nodded. "Yes, they do, but its only puts someone to sleep for, oh, about an hour."

I shook my head. The more I learned about these trees, the less I liked.

"Right, I don't like the Crimson Company, or their tactics, but are you sure this will *just* knock someone out? I'm not an assassin looking for my next kill here."

Mikasi held up his hands at me.

"I *promise* I'm sure. See, I once got lucky and bought a few leaves off a ruin poacher who survived coming out here." His cheeks turned a deep crimson. "A day later, I accidentally dropped a leaf in my tea when I wasn't paying attention. When I realized what had happened, I tried another leaf to be sure."

I rubbed my eyes. If it had been anyone else who had told me that story, I'm not sure I would've believed them.

"You've convinced me. It's a good idea." I pulled a pair of tan, battered leather gloves out of a belt pouch. "Let's get some leaves and wreck a waterwheel."

My partner in sabotage grinned. "I'll gum up the gears in the water screw!"

The dark leaves, or at least the ones I picked up, were about the length of my hand and the color of burnt rust with purple streaks. They were soft, a little bloated, with the faint odor of spoiled eggs. It felt like holding a few pieces of rotten fruit or nearly dried out sea sponge. I tried not to think about that too much.

Using the thick, gray-white fog as cover, I kept low and raced across the open space between the mimic trees and the camp's waterwheel. There were faint footsteps nearby, but nowhere near me. They didn't sound to be in any hurry. Just the soft crunch of boots against gravel. It had to be a sentry, keeping a watch in all this mess. I felt sort of sorry for whoever that was. Keeping an eye out for anything from wild animals, bandits, or wild magic abominations trying to slip into camp was an important job. It was just one filled with long stretches of dull.

I crouched down between two stacks of crates and a rain barrel that sat at the base of the tall waterwheel. Most waterwheels I'd seen were as big as a two-story house. This one was a good bit smaller, maybe half the size.

That didn't surprise me. There wasn't much in the way of actual trees, or even Dire-Tubaria mushrooms down here in Great Chasm; so lumber was scarce. I could tell by the rough craftsmanship, the

Crimson Company had to make do with what was around. Like the way-stones that Mikasi spotted earlier.

It was an 'undershot' waterwheel. The water screw pulled water out of the pond, but was only tall enough to pour the water out against, and below, the wheel's paddles. This wasn't a great design, but I understood this was the best they could do with what they had on hand. The way-stones were a clever addition. They were stuck in the middle of the wheel.

Way-stones can attach to metal but they can also attract or repel each other depending on which side you use. Some genius had the bright idea to use that last part to their advantage. The way-stones in the waterwheel arranged, with the opposing sides facing each other. That way, they acted like gears and let the waterwheel turn easier with the weak water flow.

It was all still a really fragile design, but I wasn't one to judge, given how many times I've had to throw something together in an emergency. Mikasi was right. Moving those would shut things down, but would get everyone's attention right away.

A crunch of footsteps on gravel again grabbed my attention. Unlike before, this was a closer. A lot closer, on the other side of my hiding place, to my right. Somehow, the fog had grown even thicker, so I couldn't see anything more than odd shapes and shadows. But that was enough.

The shadow of a tall man loomed large in the gray mist. He looked as big as a door and just as wide. A whisper of his sword leaving its scabbard shot a chill along my spine. I tensed, clutching the pulpy leaves in a tight fist.

"Damn fog ghosts," the man snarled in a deep voice before he sheathed his sword.

At the mention of a ghost, I stared hard at the soup-like fog around me. It was fog. Thick, but just fog. Then I saw it.

Ten paces away from me, a milky-white figure materialized out of nothing. It, or he, was silvery-white with gaunt features, wearing clothing I'd only seen in old portraits. Here, it was the uniform of a high-ranking soldier from the Ancient Order.

I kept still as stone, crouched behind my shelter of crates. After a few seconds, my legs ached, but I ignored the pain as best as I could. Better a pain in my legs than deal with an irate sentry and that thing in the fog.

The ghost materialized in and out of view. It drifted close to a barrel and continued past it. A light crust of frost appeared over the top of the barrel. Slowly, the ghost wandered in the open space between the sentry and me. It, or he, glanced at the Crimson Company mercenary, but didn't move closer. Instead, the ghost watched the man thoughtfully. Another ten seconds passed before the sentry walked away into the fog. The specter trailed a few paces behind, with a pensive expression.

Ghosts. Fog full of *ghosts*. Why did it have to be ghosts?

I waited until the fog swallowed them both, before I shuddered hard enough to almost knock me over. After a deep breath, I forced myself to focus on the water wheel, then got to work.

Moving fast, I darted out from cover and over to the base of the wheel. After a quick glance at the maze of ropes that held it all together, I traced down three that looked the most important. I tugged at those until they came loose. Not all the way untied, but enough so they would give out on their own in a few minutes. After that, I pulled loose a rope around the nearest way-stone, just to make the pending disaster that much worse.

I'll admit, I rushed the work, so it wasn't at all my best. But I wanted out of that camp and the haunted fog more than anything. I checked the loose knots once more, then smeared mimic tree oil over the knots, rope, and the surrounding wood.

"Hey!"

I almost jumped out of my skin. The last thing my nerves needed at that moment was a voice hissing behind me. Caught between running or fight, my instincts went with the latter. I spun around, ducking low, and swung a hard uppercut with my right fist.

Lucky for both of us, Mikasi was as nimble as his pet cheetah. He jumped out of the way, hands up in front of him. Nicodemus tensed, back arched, ears alert for a threat. I was glad the cat didn't have me on that list.

"Hey! Stop! It's me!" Mikasi hissed. "Did you get it done?"

"Yes," I whispered back, exasperated. "All done. Now..."

A crunch of rock to our right interrupted me. I tossed the crumpled mimic leaves aside, then waved Mikasi down behind the crates next to me while I pulled off my gloves. To his credit, he didn't ask. He simply grabbed Nicodemus before the two of them joined me behind my tiny shelter. I held up a finger in front of my lips to warn Mikasi to keep quiet.

The sentry had returned, but someone else had come with him. Honestly, it was the last person I wanted around.

"You. Jameson, isn't it?" Vincent Vargas snapped.

"Jameson, aye. Is there trouble, Captain?"

I peeked around the crates. Through the fog, I watched Vargas, dressed for combat, rest his right hand on the pommel of a dagger at his belt. He nervously tapped it with his fingers.

"She's nearby, I just *know* it."

Jameson shook his head with a sigh.

"Captain, if I may? You dumped her in the middle of nowhere to die. If the heat, or that spell the baron cast, didn't get her, the coyotes did. Tela Kioni is dead by now."

Vargas shook his head with a stern frown.

"No. It would take more than that to kill her. She'll have found a way out of that. That's why I wanted to leave people back in Talabrae's Deep to keep watch. Tela Kioni is nearby... somewhere. Just like I know, we're digging in the wrong place."

Mikasi started mouthing words at me in alarm. I waved a hand frantically at him to be still. Nearby, Vargas continued.

"I do wish the baron would listen to reason." Vargas rubbed a hand over his face and let out a ragged sigh. "Have you seen anything?"

Jameson shook his head.

"Just the same fog ghosts as always."

The two men continued their conversation while they walked off into the mists. I didn't make out the rest of what they said and didn't care to. What I heard was more than enough.

"Go!" I hissed in Mikasi's ear. "We're got to warn the others, we're already out of time!"

28

Amates 31, 1277. Taking a wrong turn for the right reasons.

There's distracted. Then there's what happened at the campsite be-hind us.

Mikasi, his cheetah, and I reached Kiyosi at the weathered gray-white marble doorway, when a muted crash echoed through the canyon. Angry shouts far behind us were icing on the cake. I knelt down at the collection of canvas bags next to Ki, fished out my worn canvas shoulder bag, and slipped it on.

Kiyosi had pulled his attention away from the inscription in the marble over the commotion.

"What was *that?*"

Mikasi skid to a stop, gasping for breath. Nicodemus fared better. The smoke cheetah padded up to glance around at the doorway and its partial rock slide. In hindsight, calling it 'partially covered' was generous. Those rocks were from a landslide, but now that I was right next to them, I saw there was a sizable gap on the right side. Plenty of room for a person to squeeze through.

"Oh, probably the waterwheel coming off its base and crashing down," Mikasi said in a low voice. "I think they noticed."

Another crash followed the first, accompanied by the sound of wood shattering like twigs. More shouts, a lot of them, filled the air. Then, the silvery-gray fog thinned out enough that we saw the mercenaries' waterwheel. Free of its moorings, the large wheel trundled heavily through the middle of the camp and flattened several tents and one cooking fire. The thing came to a stop at the camp's center, where it teetered sideways to crush one last tent.

Ki frowned at the two of us.

I shrugged.

"What? They're distracted. Wouldn't you be?" I took a quick glance at the marble doorway. "What's the translation?"

Ki rubbed the bridge of his nose.

"Age and weather have eaten at some letters, but I'm guessing this is a side door for workers to get into the tunnels. It mentions an underground storage vault named 'West Branch', which fits if we're right about Long Deep being used as a trade center."

"Perfect! Then we're probably on the right path." I squeezed past the rocks to the other side. "Mikasi and I both heard Vargas complain about this entire situation. He's already sure they are digging in the wrong spot, but the baron won't hear it. So we're running on borrowed time. Vargas will find this door quick enough. Come on!"

"Damn the tides!" Ki swore.

"At least they're distracted." Mikasi shrugged, grabbed a pack, before he followed me past the rock. Nicodemus leaped in right after him.

"We have a very different definition of 'distracted'." Kiyosi groaned. "At least the inscription on the frame didn't suggest any traps."

"Did it mention anything other than 'vault' and 'West Branch'?" I asked.

Ki grabbed the last bag, a stained brown canvas backpack, then slipped inside after us.

"No. There had been more, but it's long since ruined."

I grinned while I fished the Sun Orb out of my shoulder bag for light.

"Then we find out for ourselves."

Ki shook his head while we picked our way down the dark, tiled hallway.

Some of my cheery disposition was bravado. A mask to deal with any fear of the Crimson Company, their undead patron, and the current situation we were dealing with. But there was more to it than just a 'brave outlook'.

Ancient ruins are history, and everyone experiences that history differently. Ruin Poachers see an ancient building with its locked doors, even stained glass, and only see money. Something to break down and sell in one smuggler's den or another. I've lost track of how many times a Windtracer expedition was sent to steal a relic from a thief, looking to make some fast coin.

For me? A ruin, really any ancient building, is as much the prize as any relic inside the place.

Every piece of tile, mason's mark, or dash of paint is a story told by the people who lived there. A voice wanting to be remembered. It was someone's present, or future, frozen in place. Preserved hope passed down so that people like me could call it 'history' and let those people live again. Maybe even rekindle that hope in someone else.

The hallway was wide enough for two people to walk next to each other without a problem. It was also tall, with a vaulted ceiling. This wasn't a surprise. The Ancient Order used that style of architecture a lot. It was the design of the ceiling arch I didn't expect. I held the Sun Orb up as high as I could reach.

"Reinforced," I said and glanced at the others. "Ceiling uses reinforced arches."

Ki glanced overhead while we walked. Mikasi looked up and shrugged.

"Support the weight of the rock and cliffs overhead?" he suggested. "I mean, this is basically a mine shaft," the inventor tapped a nearby wall, "even if it's lined with some nice, colorful little marble tiles."

I lowered the Sun Orb, then continued forward.

"That's true, I guess," I replied with a wary glance at the architecture. "Still, something seems different." I shrugged. "It could also be because of where we are. Nothing down here in the Chasm is 'normal'."

We continued at a brisk pace in silence. Smooth stone tiles the size of my thumb lined the walls. Blues, greens, and creamy pearl colors glittered underneath centuries of dust and grime. A stale, bitter scent of rock dust and mildew hovered around us while we hurried along. Occasionally, I saw the remains of ancient markings painted on the tile. A slap of a word here and there. Directions? Someone's attempt at a mural? I wasn't sure.

At the doorway on the far end, we stepped into a wide, round room. Empty wooden shelves and what might have been a cart suggested 'storehouse'. The only crates were the ones smashed on the floor long ago.

Overhead, the ancient remains of thick spider webs ran from one edge of the arched ceiling to the other. It was a dust-filled gossamer sunshade for ghosts. A curious stone circle with the remains of a wooden timber suspended over it as thick as my body dominated the middle of the floor. Chains descended from the arched ceiling between the cobwebs to hold the wood aloft. Rags of old rope still clung to that wooden beam for dear life.

Several doors gave us ways out of the room, but none had anything marked on them that made any sense. I pulled out the map I had copied from the Obsidian Armory in Talabrae's Deep and did some quick comparisons. That didn't help much.

"It's well preserved," Mikasi said in amazement. "But what's that supposed to lift things to? Does the ceiling open?"

"No idea. Maybe crates to carts?" Ki asked. "These doors all look large enough for simple carts. We know the Ancient Order loved using those small, one person types."

A distant set of voices echoed through the darkness from the entrance. One of those was Vincent Vargas.

"Hell and high tides!" Ki snarled. "Crimson Company. We've got to move!"

"But where?" Mikasi asked. "Which door? They all look the same!"

Ki and Mikasi both looked at my map before they ran to separate doors to try the handles. Some were still locked or swollen shut. Others clung to their hinges in a desperate attempt to remain useful. Me?

I looked up at the webbing. It was a lot of webbing. Fortunately, nothing moved up there, but I noticed something odd. The webbing glimmered with a faint golden hue as if it reflected something off the floor. Bits of the same color traced along doors and around the abandoned shelves on the far side of the room.

"I wonder."

Slowly, I partially covered the Sub Orb. The room came alive with that faint, golden light.

Lines traced along the floor, spilling out from under my feet in all directions. It raced along the seams in the stone tiled floor to reach across the room. That light touched the doors, raced around shelves, and best of all, ran round a set of still intact wooden levers off to my right against one wall. We had missed those at first in the dark.

Ki and Mikasi gasped at the sight. I couldn't help but grin once more.

The room was lit up with lines of golden starlight that traced the shape of the stone tiles. I wasn't sure how well Mikasi or Ki could see, but for me, it made the room as bright as the first rays of morning.

"What is *that?*" Mikasi asked, fascinated, fear of the Crimson Company forgotten.

"Paint," Ki replied while he knelt down by one of the glowing lines. He tapped one dusty line with a dagger. "It's... glowing. Just like the Sun Orb."

"Magic?" Mikasi asked.

Ki shook his head.

"No, not like we know it." He looked across the room at me. "Tela, it's centered on you. I think this paint is reacting to the light of the Sub Orb. How are your eyes?"

"Perfect," I said with a huge, stupid grin on my face. "The room is clear as day now. I think... this makes sense. My eyes are better suited to this kind of dark."

I was caught up in the moment and couldn't help myself. Words tumbled out of me like flowing water.

"The tiles... they're a mural! It runs along the walls in a pattern and makes letters with arrows by them. Those over there read 'platform thirty four', more say 'storeroom'. The arrows point to the doors and to the floor. Ki, by the kind tides. I get it now..."

Despite the looming danger of the Crimson Company, I closed my eyes and imagined the room as it was; as the room *might* have been. Slowly, history unrolled. People and things washed into view like a painter brushing details to a half-finished canvas.

It was magnificent.

I watched people walk through those doors. Workers in coveralls, worn boots, and more chatting about their day. All sorts, a cosmopolitan mix, went about their day. Some moved boxes and crates between shelves. Others stacked dry goods by doors or took boxes out one of the five doors leading away from the room. At times, a cart would trundle past, pulled by a horse-sized Feathix iguana.

Suddenly, everything made so much sense. I opened my eyes and uncovered the Sun Orb to let the mysterious magic paint between the stone tiles soak up more light.

"We didn't come in through some back entrance for workers," I said in a hushed tone. "The Great Chasm wasn't even really there yet. This was all underground! The Great Chasm crushed some other part of all this right at that door we came in through."

Then I remembered the map the Slate Watch drew of the area that included the underground lake.

"These people were trading with someone living underground. The Slate Watch drew a lake in the Deepland caverns under all this. Ki! Mikasi! The Ancient Order was trading with someone in the Deeplands! Not some outpost. It was a kingdom below ground in the Deeplands!"

Voices of the Crimson Company had grown louder, along with a crack of split rock.

"They've broken out that partial land slide from the entrance," Ki said.

Mikasi looked around nervously.

"That's fascinating, Tela, but really, which door does that mean we need to take? They're coming!"

I looked around the room, before my eyes fixed on the stone circle in the middle. It glimmered the brightest in the golden twilight.

"None of them," I said, then raced for the levers.

There was something written above those levers, but I didn't know the words. There wasn't time to translate it, either. I glanced over at Ki. He frowned, glanced at the levers, then nodded once.

I ran my hands over the stone letters. Something deep inside whispered to me as if from far away, like remembering part of a memory. My hands settled onto the far right lever. Ancient wood felt hard, almost stone-like under my hands, but my fingers found worn spots in the wood. I shoved down. The lever groaned a little at first, then obeyed. Something in the wall rattled against the stone. My guess was a counterweight.

In the middle of the room, the stone circle split into 'leaves' and spiraled open. Overhead, the chains on the ceiling lowered the ancient wooden beam. Somewhere out of sight, I knew there had to be a wheelhouse for the chain itself. This place was a lot larger than I thought.

Meanwhile, in the pit that had opened in the floor, a round platform of stone with a metal frame rose out of the darkness. I pointed to it.

"Quick! Get on!"

"What?" Mikasi exclaimed and stepped back from the pit and platform.

Ki raced over to him and grabbed the inventor by the shoulder to give him a little shake.

"Trust her! Just go!"

Mikasi raced to the platform with Nicodemus right beside him. Ki was fast behind him.

"Hopefully, they'll take the easy route and head out one of the doors up here," Ki mused.

"They won't have a choice," I said, then shoved my lever sideways.

The ancient wood resisted at first, then gave with a sharp crack as it broke free. Immediately, the counterweight in the wall rumbled back into place with a scrape of metal against stone. Footsteps down the hallway from the entrance broke into a run.

"Tela! Run!"

Ki didn't have to tell me twice.

The instant that counterweight fell, both platform and stone circle moved. The platform holding Ki, Mikasi, and Nicodemus lowered quickly, while the stone circle started to close over them.

I ran. It was only a few paces away, but it could have been Ancient Order kilometers. A lot of them. I was only partway there when two crossbow bolts sang past, with one almost catching my shirt. I ducked out of instinct and nearly stumbled.

On my left by the door, two Crimson Company crossbowmen were already reloading. From the hallway, three swordsmen spilled into the room, followed by Vincent Vargas and Baron Marius. The swordsmen ran right for me. But I had no plans to wait for them.

"It's her! That Windtracer! Stop her!"

"Tela! Come on!" Ki shouted at me.

I tossed the broken piece of lever at the swordsmen before I turned to race for the pit. There was a yelp and more than a little swearing, followed by a clatter of wood on stone. No idea who I hit. I just hoped it slowed them down a little.

The stone circle was almost closed when I reached it. There was barely enough room for me. I clutched my bag and jumped into the hole.

While I fell, I glimpsed the other side of the room. Neither the Crimson Company nor Baron Marius looked happy. Except maybe Vargas. I thought I saw him smirk a little as I dropped out of sight.

I hit the platform below me hard, before I dropped to one knee. Above us, the stone leaves circled shut with a solid sound of heavy stones slammed together. Just like that, everything went almost silent. No Crimson Company, cobwebs, ghosts, or the ruins above. It was just us, a Sun Orb, a rattling metal-framed stone platform, and a long way down to darkness.

At least, that's what we thought.

29

Amates 31, 1277. Finding new lows to our highs.

The marble gray platform trembled like it might shake off its support chains. Fortunately, the rusted chains held on while they lowered us down in a light cloud of ancient dust. But the clank and rattle were bad enough to wake the dead, if any were nearby. I hoped not.

I landed harder on the platform than I wanted to after my dive through the door above. It hadn't been a long drop, but it was enough to rattle my joints. Worst of all was the leg cramp when I stood up. Ki caught me before I fell, then helped me over to a rusted metal railing. I clutched at the ancient metal while my calf squeezed in painful knots.

There was this stale scent to the air like old mildew. Not enough to steal my breath, just ruin my nose for a bit. That seemed odd, since I expected more grit and dust. But it wasn't odd enough to worry about. I chalked the smell up to an underground stream while I tried to ignore the stench.

The stone platform we rode on was a set of smooth, interconnected marble tiles, like the ones on the floor above. Together they formed a large stone circle about fifteen nindel, or Ancient Order meters, across. I was more convinced than ever that the Ancient Order used this as a ferry system. A way to move people and cargo between the surface and the Deepland realms.

But where underground? I had no idea, since we didn't have much light. There was my Sun Orb, of course. It pushed the darkness back five or six nindel past the edge of the platform, enough to know this was an enormous cavern. But luckily, it wasn't the only light around.

The cavern ceiling was alive with drifting waves of soft, glowing smears of purple, blue, and white lights. Those came from odd shaped lumps on the ceiling that I couldn't quite make out.

It was a colorful display, but not that much brighter than dock lanterns in a light evening fog. The dancing lights reminded me of lightning that jumped between storm clouds.

"Those look like mushrooms," Ki said while he watched the lights. "Glowing mushrooms."

He frowned for a few seconds while he rubbed the thumb and fingers on his right hand together.

"I can feel that there's some magic involved, but not much." He squinted at the ceiling. "Maybe a touch of wild magic?"

"It's mostly not," Mikasi chimed in.

He joined us on our side of the platform while we stared at the ceiling.

"Those are Spindletongue mushrooms," he said. "I read that Deepland folks cultivated them before the Great Collapse for a kind of street lamp. They used a lot in their cities. That glow?" Mikasi shrugged. "They do that in the dark when air moves over them. Supposedly they give off a little Deeplands energy, but not enough to turn you into a purple goo or anything. If you tie enough of the small ones together, they might make a good lantern. A gloomy one, but enough to see where you're going."

I nodded, lost in a cauldron of dark thoughts about Long Deep, the Deeplands, and us heading into the jaws of that danger. The Deeplands itself was a great way to get killed in a thousand different ways. Abominations oozing through tunnel walls, colorful wild magic fog glowing off rocks and plants that might twist a person inside out. I shuddered, as did the platform under our feet while we descended.

Ki tapped me on the shoulder, which dragged me out of my thoughts.

"We could use some more light. I'd rather we see what's coming than get surprised by it." He gestured to the Sun Orb. "Mind if I use some of that?"

I held out the Sub Orb in his direction.

"Go ahead."

Ki scooped his hand through the air next to the Sun Orb and dragged away a little of the light. It flowed around his fingers like water scooped out of a bucket. Using what didn't drain away back to the orb, Ki pulled the light into long, glowing strands. In no time, he had a bundle of glowing 'yarn' drooped over his hand. That he pulled taught, then literally finger-knitted his spell.

It was the primary way he cast any spell. He worked fast, but it still it took him a little under a minute to finish. Once he did, there was a flash of light, then the spell spread its wings and leaped into the air. Ki's creation flew in a slow circle over our heads, casting light all around us.

"A bird?" Mikasi asked, watching the spell with keen interest.

"Parrot," Ki corrected him, then shrugged. "I like parrots."

I shook my head with a thin smile. The darkness down here wasn't that bad for me. Whatever Odro had done when he healed my eyes let me see better in the dark than before. But that didn't mean I could see clearly in pitch darkness. We all needed to see where we were going, and now there was suddenly a lot to see.

The view was incredible, and I almost forgot our lives were in danger. No one spoke right away. All we did was stare at the ruins in front of us and everything around them.

"It's a giant underground lake!" Mikasi exclaimed while he peered over the railing. "There are little islands down there. I think some have buildings on them surrounded by some giant Spindletongue clumps. It looks like a small fishing port."

"Never mind that. Look out and up," Ki said in a hushed tone.

He pointed at the stalactites on the cavern ceiling. The smallest was the size of a building, but the largest could have held an entire town. From the looks of it, I think it once did.

They were like polished stone fingers that stretched for the dark waters below. Light from the Spindletongues and the flicker of our own light danced off smooth stones of blues, greens, and browns. Windows with ornate frames lined the stalactites in orderly lines. Water spouts carved into the stone directed water to where it would help the stalactite grow but not damage the living spaces. Suspension bridges were everywhere.

"It's an entire settlement carved out of those small mountain sized stalactites with suspended bridges connecting them together." He squinted. "I think there are more platforms like this one, but I don't see any chains to raise and lower them. But still, it's an entire town. Maybe a small city."

I pulled the journal from my shoulder bag. The view was breathtaking, but I realized it was also the missing puzzle piece I didn't know I needed. After I flipped open to the map of the Long Deep ruins and the surroundings, everything felt like it slid into place.

"Hello, Long Deep," I said while I tapped the map in my journal.

Ki met my glance.

"Tela, are you sure?"

His eyes cut over to the stalactite city with its sweeping support arches and dark windows like thousands of dead eye sockets. I noticed the tip of his tiefling tail sway with curiosity. It may have been the place where I almost died, and he did die, but that didn't curb his interest one bit. I was sure a rant about ancient mold out to kill us would come later.

I scowled and shook my weather-beaten journal at him like a floppy bludgeon. Ki raised his eyebrows and held up his hands in defense in response. The tip of his tail curled in silent laughter.

"Fine. It's Long Deep," he said. "But last time, how did we miss those rooms, balconies, upside down arches?" He gestured at the nearest stalactite building that loomed out of the darkness. "All of that?"

"Running for our lives," I replied dryly.

The ancient metal railing complained when I leaned on it.

"All trying to rescue Vargas from his greed and stupidity while running for our lives."

Ki nodded while he pursed his lips.

"There was that."

"Flying buttresses," Mikasi exclaimed, lost in staring at the ruins. "Those are upside down flying buttresses. That's somehow distributing the weight of the hollowed out stalactites. Brilliant!"

Mikasi lightly tapped the railing with a hand before Ki or myself could reply.

"So, you both have been here before. We know we have to get to the Automatic Crystal before the others do. If you didn't see it before when you were here, it has to be down in these chambers, yes?" The inventor pointed in excitement to the largest stalactite building that was larger than the rest. "I'd say that one."

I flipped through my journal, then looked out to where Mikasi pointed. In everything I had dug up on the Crystal, from journals to what Odro taught me, I had nothing more than 'Long Deep' for a location. Certainly not an upside down building.

Still, there was something about that idea that rattled around in my head. My gut screamed he was onto something. I raised my eyebrows at Ki, who just shrugged back.

"I suppose it could be. It's the tallest," I hesitated, remembering that it's a stalactite on an enormous cave ceiling, "well, longest of the buildings. That could be the town center."

Mikasi squinted at the two of us.

"Don't you see it?" After a second, he shook his head with a small frown, then waved a hand at the upside down building. "Take a good look at those buildings. The architecture, the design and how it flows. I'm no expert, but that isn't entirely Ancient Order design. Think about those buildings standing right side if they were above ground."

We tried, or at least I did. I felt like I almost followed what he meant.

When we didn't reply, Mikasi added, "the Ancient Order weren't the only ones who designed this. People used to living underground were involved. They had to be."

The moment Mikasi said that, I understood. I noticed Ki did, too, by his astonished expression.

"The Ancient Order built what was above ground to meet a Deep-land city-state that wanted to trade with them." I tapped my journal against the railing. "If you're right, that makes the 'tallest' stalactite the 'city spire'." I glanced down at the underground lake, then back at the largest stalactite. "Or a lighthouse."

"Where better to put something like an Automatic Crystal if you want a clear field of vision to aim a spell," Ki added.

I nodded along with the conversation while my thoughts ran like a racehorse.

"That would be why we never found it last time. We explored the Ancient Order side. Those papers we recovered talked a lot about trade goods being moved through the area. We've all thought that was to other settlements above ground."

"Yes!" Mikasi exclaimed with delight. "Exactly! So how do we get there? Or in there?"

Ki shook his head and held up his hands.

"Wait, this is a lot of guesswork. Why wasn't this in anything the Talabreans wrote about? Their ancestors are from here."

I raised an eyebrow at him.

"Do you know the name of every town sitting on the Planus continent? I'm doing good to remember when the fruit carts set up each week in Ishnanor."

"All right, fair enough. So how do we get over there without getting killed by whatever's living there? Because you know there has to be an entire herd of Deepland abominations sliming their way through those hallways."

Ki was right. I sighed and tapped the railing with my journal again while I stared at the upside down buildings.

"The bridges and platforms," I replied. "We'll use those. That way, we can see where we're going and know if something is following us. If we head inside, we could get lost. I don't want to go through that like last time."

Mikasi frowned as he studied the network of bridges that connected the stalactite buildings.

"Those seem stable enough. Those bridges might even let us get ahead of the baron and the Crimson Company, too. They'll have to find their way down through the ruins above."

I closed my journal before I slipped it back inside my shoulder bag.

"That's a long shot, but I'll take it. The baron will eventually figure out that using his piece of an Automatic Crystal as a diving rod has that 'mirror' effect. By now, he probably has. That could lead him on a pretty direct path to the Automatic Crystal. So we'd better hurry, but keep our eyes out for whatever's living down here that doesn't like visitors."

The platform rattled itself to a bone-jarring stop on one of the sweeping marble bridges. The stone was a bone-white marble carved in an artistic pattern. To me, the whole thing looked like a sculpture of flowing water. A frozen river with a walkway in the middle with ornate guide rails shaped like foam and waves.

A thin layer of dust proved it was ancient. But, there wasn't any weathering. No cracks from age. Just some worn down stone in the middle from use. The bridge almost looked new. I shook my head. It was another testament to just how much knowledge had been lost since the Great Collapse.

It wasn't one connected to the 'central tower' or lighthouse, but it was close. We just needed to cross this bridge. After that, navigate around a medium-sized stalactite building half the size of a city district, then go onto the bridge to the underground lighthouse itself.

Simple. What could go wrong?

Which were, I knew, famous last words.

As I stepped off the platform onto the marble bridge, Ki put a hand on my arm.

"Will you be all right?"

I blew out a long breath. It didn't take a lick of the anxiety from my shoulders. I stared for a long time into the face of my oldest and best friend since childhood. The last time we were here, he died. I was luck that I found a way to revive him last time. No one needed to die now. I swore I would shatter that Automatic Crystal into powder first.

"I have to be. We have to be. Otherwise, a lich will get his hands on a relic that could kill a lot of people."

30

**Amates 31, 1277. Still underground in the ruins.
Felt like mid-afternoon to my stomach.**

Using the bridges was a good plan. It was a great plan. Unfortunately, everyone else had the same plan.

"Did they see us?" Mikasi panted while he ran. Nicodemus trotted easily along beside him.

An arrow shattered against the bridge next to him. Mikasi yelped while the splinters shattered around us. I skid to a stop long enough to flip a middle finger at the archer on the bridge overhead. It didn't really help our situation any, but it made me feel a little better. I raced to catch up with the others.

"Oh, they saw us," I replied once I caught back up.

"Hell and high tides, don't they have enough to do?" Ki snapped.

Ki's question was a good one but mostly answered itself. A good three stories above us on another bridge, the Crimson Company had spilled out from a door into one of the stalactite buildings.

We kept outside, following the Ancient Order signs posted on each bridge for directions. Unlike us, the Crimson Company chose to cut a path through the ruins. Which meant they woke anything with ears and an appetite for eating the living. Case in point was the pair of pony-sized dripfang prowlers that were hot on their heels right at that moment.

Dripfangs are a nasty piece of work. Imagine an ill-tempered crocodile that can cling to walls and ceilings using hooked claws. A reptile covered in luminescent algae spread over its rocky hide that let it blend in with its gloomy surroundings. It was an ambush predator that either dropped on prey from above, or 'fished' them off the ground with a prehensile tail and crush them. I blame an Ancient Order mage on a drunken bender for creating something like that.

"Door!" Ki shouted and pointed ahead of us.

Our bridge was curved like most others in Long Deep. It hugged the outside of a five story stalactite and had occasional stairs that led inside the suspended building. The bridge was narrow, a walkway at best. The stairs told me it was probably Long Deep's version of a 'side street'.

Past the bend, we saw this side street ended at a set of steel bound, wooden double doors set into the 'lighthouse' stalactite. Letters were carved into the door frame on either side. I couldn't make out what the writing said. The glowing mushrooms overhead gave off enough light to see the letters, not read them.

"Go!" I urged while I dodged more shattered arrow fragments.

We really didn't need any encouragement. The Crimson Company wasn't out of arrows yet, and eventually, their aim would get better. I bit back some of my favorite profanity and mumbled a quick prayer that those doors were unlocked. We really needed off that bridge. It was getting messy.

Then the spurt of arrows stopped. We kept running, but I dared a quick glance over my shoulder at the bridge overhead.

It had become a bloody battlefield.

A third dripfang had joined the fight. The creature had scaled a nearby building, then slipped along under the bridge before it jumped into the middle of the mercenaries. Screams were everywhere.

"*Siren's tits*," I snarled while I skidded to a stop.

"What are you doing?" Ki exclaimed.

"Something stupid. Worry about that door."

"No," Ki snapped. "Tela, I get it. I remember when we were trapped by dripfangs the last time we were here, too. They're what? Three stories up on another bridge? What will you do, throw a dagger? Throw your whip?"

"Stuff it. You know that won't reach. Just prep a light spell for Blind Man's Bluff," I snarled while I dug through my bag.

"What?"

"Do it, Ki!"

Ki's glare made it really clear he didn't like this one bit. But he did as I asked, anyway. While he pulled light into magical yarn and wove a spell, I found what I hoped I still had with me. A length of cord as long as both my arms. I hauled the cord out, wrapped it around my palm four times, then quickly braided the rest.

In a minute, I snatched up a marble chunk and put my improvised shepherd's sling to work. I let fly with my broken marble stones and connected on the second try. The stone slapped the haunches of one dripfang with a loud pop. Started, the creature spun around with an angry hiss. That's when Ki cut loose with his spell.

Magic leaped between Ki and the dripfang to strike the creature square on the snout. It belted out a furious hiss that was almost a roar, while glowing yellow light blocked its view. I'm sure to something like a dripfang that lived mostly underground, that magical light hurt like all hell.

I didn't wait, but snatched up more marble stones and let them fly. There wasn't a wide gab between that bridge and ours, but the railing and the sweeping curves made any attempt to aim tough. But I managed another two hits on a second dripfang with the same result.

"Tela, they've got this. Let's go," Ki exclaimed while he ran for where Mikasi struggled with the double doors.

I managed two steps before the window to my left exploded, frame and all. A hailstorm of stone, wood, and glass filled the air like a deadly cloud. I tackled Ki just before that mess swarmed us. We avoided the worst of it, but there was still plenty of debris that rained down around us.

The worst either of us had was a few bruises, small cuts, and a heavy coating of chalky gray-white dust from age. I rolled over, then scrambled to my feet. Ki was a second behind me. The first thought I had was that this was another dripfang from the same murderous hunting pack. It was much worse than that.

"Oh, hells," I muttered under my breath, "a fang weaver."

Thirty nindel away at best, no more than a short sprint, was a nightmare combination of pony-sized scorpion and a scowling, shaggy-haired human. A giant nasty ball of anger walking around on too many legs. I swapped my Sun Orb to my left hand then fumbled for my whip. Right then, I desperately needed reach.

"Ki, warn Mikasi about the fang weaver. Help him with the door, I'll keep this thing busy."

"Not alone, you're not," he snapped. "I'm sure Mikasi knows already. A fang weaver is hard to miss."

I didn't argue, even though I wanted to. There just wasn't time.

The fang weaver sprang forward, tail up and black claws out. It raked the air with those claws while we dove to either side. I got to my feet, stepped back, and cracked my whip. The popper slapped an ugly red welt on the thing's shoulder.

On the other side of the weaver, Ki snatched faint strands of light from the air. Quickly, he wrapped them around his hand, then slammed a trio of glowing yellow-white arrows into the creature's side. Unfortunately, they barely made it through the creature's thick hide.

Despite that, it took a step back. The fang weaver was a little bruised, slightly singed, and a lot ticked off.

"This is going to be a long fight," I sighed.

Ki glanced to his right where he left Mikasi, then gave me a quick nod before he jerked his head toward Mikasi and the doors. I got the message, or hoped I did. Mikasi had the doors open. Time to make a run for it.

The fang weaver lashed out before we could run. It swiped claws at the two of us, then stabbed at me with its tail. I jumped right, avoiding the tail, then cracked my whip against its midsection. As for Ki, he ducked under its claws, then launched another trio of magical light arrows into the thing. The bolts slammed into the fang weaver's wide, armored back while my whip crack made it almost double over. It hissed in rage and kept coming.

It was a bloody dance over the next few seconds while we traded blows with the beast. It was fast, but we managed to keep a heartbeat ahead of those claws and tail. At one point, the claws missed me but tore my shirt. Ki got battered twice when the weaver clubbed him with its tail. Then there was the ugly moment when it spit two of its paralytic mouth fang-spikes at me. I was just lucky my shoulder bag got in the way at the last second.

By then, I could feel the fatigue setting in with desperation lurking just behind it.

I arched backwards and avoided claws to the throat. In not quite a flail, I stumbled back, the jumped left to avoid the tail. Before I could get my whip into motion, the fang weaver lunged in and backhanded me across the mouth. The world exploded in stars while I flew backward and hit the bridge hard and had the wind almost knocked out of me.

Nearby, I heard Ki yell something before there was the sizzle of magic. It sounded like fire, something Ki only used when he was really upset. I heard the fang weaver let out a shrill shriek of pain. I shook my head while my vision cleared and I stumbled to my feet.

"This is stupid," I muttered. "We're getting nowhere. This thing's got more armor than a Quillback rhinoceros. It's like trying to slap down a wall."

I touched the back of a hand against my mouth and winced. That wasn't going to feel good tomorrow.

Suddenly, Ki sailed through the air before he hit the bridge hard right next to me. He grabbed his chest where the fang weaver had clubbed him again with its tail, then wheezed while he tried to get his air back. The beast skittered right for us, but before it closed in for the kill, I snapped my whip near its face. That made it back off a few steps. It hissed, smoke curling up from the fresh magical burns along its right shoulder.

"Ki, you alive?"

"Yes," he coughed. "I just feel like the dog's breakfast."

I cracked the whip again when the weaver tried another step. Then once more before it got settled, only that time I aimed for the burn wound.

That it felt.

It grabbed the burn and skittered back a few paces. Just as it got settled, a bright yellow-white light erupted on the fang weaver's face.

The creature shrieked in surprise, then stepped back while it tried to wipe the spell away.

"Run," Ki shouted in a hoarse voice. "That won't last long."

It was music to my ears. I curled my whip around my chest and ran. Ki was right beside me. Seconds later, we heard the fang weaver chasing after us.

We reached Mikasi, Nicodemus, and the open doors in no time.

"Get inside," I panted at Mikasi as we ran up.

"*Wait!* There's something you need to know," Mikasi waved a hand at the doors that had swung open into the room.

I glanced back the way we came. The fang weaver had shaken off most of Ki's spell and was headed right for us. The manic, staccato sound of his eight feet against the marble tiles punctured the air. It was like being chased by a stampede of hammers. A sound that ran right up my nerves.

"Quick, what?" I asked.

"The doors," he replied. "I have a feeling something bad happened here to the locals."

"How bad?"

"Bad," he said with a dark tone and quick glance at the doors.

I followed his gaze and didn't like what I saw. They were elderwood doors belted in two places by iron or some other sort of dark metal. Deep cuts crisscrossed the center of the wood in a haphazard pattern from axes, blades, and even a few claws. Some were big enough that they had to be fang weaver claws.

A design burned into the door had been cut apart a long time ago into a shabby mess. The doors hung from a dingy, gray-brown door frame that still clung to a few pieces of ancient paint.

Two things leaped out at me. First, I didn't see a lock. Second, there were letters haphazardly burned into the door frame. Blurry letters that *moved*.

They looked all too much like the blurred like the letters in the *Xinder Codex* back in Talabrae's Deep. More important was that every letter along the door frame had started to glow like a metal bar heating fast in a forge.

I grabbed Mikasi by the shoulder.

"Mikasi, how did you get the doors open?"

"Balanced the counterweights," he stammered, then pointed at a loose tile at the floor on the right side of the frame. "It reset the mechanism. The latch, or lock I guess, is some sort of water clock."

I stared at doors, damage, and door frame in shock. Realization set in and I didn't like what it whispered to me.

"It's running away?" Ki gasped while he caught his breath. After a second, he glanced around while his tail twitched in curiosity. "What in the high tides scares that thing?"

"Quick, get inside," I said.

I raced inside the room, then pulled on one of the doors. The others ran after me. Ki grabbed the other door. Mikasi helped me with mine.

"What's happening?" Ki asked while he yanked on the heavy door.

"A water clock kept these doors shut. How many rooms do you know need a timed lock in a city? Especially an Ancient Order city?" I jerked my chin at the door frame outside the room. "Look at the door frame. Mikasi was right. Something bad happened here. Whoever closed these doors didn't want them opened back up."

I pointed at the door lock that was on the inside of the doors.

"Especially, not from the outside. Shut the doors!"

Around the door frame, outside the room, the mage-lock letters glowed with the yellow-orange fury of the sun. The bright light felt like getting needles stabbed in the side of my head.

Ki yelled out something, but I missed it as the magical inscription erupted in a tidal wave of light, heat, and sound that consumed the entire bridge. At the same moment, my entire world turned into a thick haze as I fell back into darkness.

31

Amates 31, 1277. Past the double doors, where we found some answers, and a little bit of a surprise.

"Tela! Can you hear me?"

Ki's voice sounded muffled. Like he was yelling out of a deep well or from the bottom of a canyon.

"Blink if you know what I'm saying."

That made no sense to me at all. I would've scowled at him, then shooed him away, but I couldn't figure out where he was. It was dark and thoughts felt a little thick. I shook my head, which felt like I was sunk in mud up to my ears, but I managed. After that I blinked, which really meant I opened my eyes, then blinked.

Ki was kneeling next to me and hovered over me like a mother hen or a physician. Probably a little of both.

"Tela?" he asked again.

I tried to ask what had his tail up in a knot, but the words came out wet and jumbled. Like having a mouthful of soup and trying to talk. Instead, I rubbed the side of my jaw, then managed to sit up off the floor with some help from Ki. After that, the world, such as was, came into poorly lit and gloomy focus. I tried to say something again. This time I managed real words instead of slobbering burbles.

"What?" I scowled at him. "Yes, I hear you," I grumbled.

The thoughts sloshing around in my head were like runny scrambled eggs. I rubbed by face before I said anything else.

"Mikasi and Nicodemus? Are they all right?"

Ki smiled while he leaned in to check my eyes.

"They're fine. That spell trap hit the fang weaver, not us. Burned it up like paper in a bonfire. The light from the spell was more than your eyes can handle. You still have your goggles?"

"Yes." I took in a deep breath, then let it out slowly. Even I could tell that I needed to tuck in my cranky, because it was starting to show. "It just seemed more important to shut the doors at the time."

"Always the protector," Ki said wryly. "Next time, put them on, please? You can't help anyone else if you're in no shape to do that."

I gave him a sideways glance at that and pursed my lips. He wasn't wrong, but I had a small headache pinching me.

"All right."

Standing up was more effort than success, but with Ki's help, I managed. He kept a hand on my shoulder until I was steady. Talking was still a bit more effort than it was worth, so instead I just nodded my thanks. After that, I rubbed the side of my head and looked around.

The only light we had was the Sun Orb and Ki's parrot-shaped light spell. Together, that still wasn't a lot of light to see by, but it was enough. Mikasi had my Sun Orb with him while he wandered the far side of the room. Ki's glowing parrot circled lazily overhead.

In the flickering light, the room was draped in shadows and dust. The room was almost round, shaped like an octagon with a vaulted tan ceiling. It reminded me of a theater. Exhausted Sun Orbs covered in dust, dangled from chains overhead. They were suspended over a spiral staircase that headed down to another floor.

Dark shapes lived near the walls on the far side, close to where Mikasi wandered. They looked like tables with what appeared to be thin drawers underneath them. Brown, grease-like stains smeared parts of the top and sides. That could have just been a trick of the light, but they looked real, and ominous enough, to me. Tall cabinets stood on either side of the tables.

"This isn't like any observatory or lighthouse I've seen," Ki asked in a low tone. "What is this place?"

"The tables and these cabinets make me think of an alchemist's workroom," Mikasi said from across the room.

He stepped carefully around a pile of rags, stained brown, covered in centuries of dust, and frayed with age. Once he reached a cabinet, he tugged open a door to peer at the glassware inside.

"It might also be a surgeon's workshop," he added with a somber tone and worried glance back at us.

I blinked while my eyes quickly adjusted to the dim light. Details about the tables grew sharper. They looked about the right length for a surgeon to use in an emergency. But that idea didn't sit right for me. It was something about the way the stain spilled over the wood, but I couldn't put my finger on it.

"Both, I think. After all this time, it's hard to tell. But I'm not sure that all those stains are blood. Blood splatters in a very particular way." I glanced between the tables, cabinets, and the spiral staircase. "Those tables were also added later."

Ki glanced over at what caught my attention.

"Late period, but not long before the Great Collapse. Especially with those dovetail joints. They certainly don't match the decor." He frowned at me. "What are you thinking?"

I glanced up at the vaulted ceiling, then around at the walls. Each wall of the octagonal room had a floor to ceiling panel covered in elaborate carvings. Some sort of scene. I crossed over to the nearest one that was at the left of the doors in. Ki wasn't far behind me.

"What I think is that those tables were hauled in here for an emergency. A big one. I don't think they'll help us figure out where to go from here."

On the wall was a landscape. Bridges, people, carts, all frozen in time while they went about their day in the underground city we were in. Even better were the words inscribed below the panel in late Ancient Order dialect that read 'Bathrogg Station'. At least that cleared up once and for all where we were.

The carving was impressive down to the finest detail, from bridge railing to clothing. I wanted to put my hand against that wall so badly. Just to feel the shape and texture of the polished wood. Get a sense of history and maybe feel a connection to the woodcarver all those centuries ago. It was a masterpiece.

But the idea that we weren't that far ahead of the Crimson Company or their lich benefactor loomed in the back of my mind. We needed to figure this out and move on. Besides, the wood might be fragile. I needed to be very careful, since you can't study crumbled wall panels.

Also, I was willing to bet hard coin they could be laced with traps or some other mechanism. There was a good reason why this profession hadn't killed me yet, even if some days it comes close.

"Which I think is down," I added. "Because if this is an upside-down lighthouse, down makes the most sense. But not that staircase."

Ki shook his head. "Of course. Too easy."

A sharp metallic snap behind us got our attention. We whirled around to find Mikasi next to the spiral staircase with a broken wooden rod in his hand. I had no idea where he found it. The stick looked like something had bitten off the end with a passion. Savaged wood was bent and splintered off at the end. Nicodemus crouched nearby, hackles bristled all the way to the tip of his tail. Mikasi was as white as a sheet.

"Trap," he said and pointed at the stairs. "Snap blades." The inventor wiggled the broken stick in the air for emphasis.

I glanced at Ki. "Way too easy. But I think these panels might be the way out."

He looked back once more at Mikasi, raised his eyebrows, then studied the wall panel closest to us.

"Could be. It wouldn't be the first time the Ancient Order hid a message in a mural." He leaned in and squinted at the wall. I could almost hear his mind working. "Wall murals often get crusted over with mold after centuries, not that Ancient Order artists cared about this. But this is an engraving, not a mural. Why the wood?"

"Better detail?" I pointed at the wall panel. "I'm pretty sure that's the bridge we crossed to get here. Which means those are the doors into this room right there in the panel, dead center."

"I don't think it's just for better detail," Mikasi said from near the central staircase. "Those are a lot of surgeon tables that were added. If it was for an emergency, maybe the panels were brought in, too?" He shrugged. "Like they wanted to save them from whatever was happening?"

I swapped a glance with Ki.

"They were running for their lives," Ki said as he looked back that the panels. "They wanted to save these panels from what? A disaster?"

I shook my head.

"Invaders, or something like it. Bathrogg Station was under attack. The people of Talabrae's Deep were running from down here in the

Deeplands after the Great Collapse, or at the end of it. There's no way to get these panels out." I pursed my lips. "Maybe with magic?"

Something about that didn't sit right with me. The panels weren't resting against the wall as if just left there. They were upright and attached to the walls in a neat trim order. Understanding reached up and slapped me in the back of the head.

"Ki, they didn't bring them here to save them," I said slowly. "Even if these had some religious significance, something bad happened here and people were in a hurry. When do people take the time to organize and attach portraits to wall in an emergency? These panels are here for a reason."

"Concealed doors?" Ki suggested.

I scratched the back of my neck.

"Maybe? But the panels are the key here. Look at the panels. I mean really *look*. These panels are a giant map. This is why there was just a water clock on the doors in here. That water clock was a thief trap. A dodge. We didn't find a lock because this entire room is the lock."

"Oh, by the tides," was all he managed to say. "We're standing *inside* the lock," Ki repeated slowly, wide-eyed.

"It's a way to tell who's a friend and who isn't!" Mikasi exclaimed. "Cesibus wrote about these. He even designed a few. I've studied them, but I never thought I would see a real one." He hurried over to the closest wall panel. "We just need to follow the map and look for any 'hidden latches' along the route. This is a map of this city, so I would think that would be windows and doors. Anyone from here would know what to look for. Outsiders wouldn't."

He put his hands on his hips and scowled at the panel.

"So we need to think like someone from Bathrogg Station and pick the right doors, I suppose. Maybe, think like Cesibus? That might work, too."

I glanced over at Mikasi and watched him while he searched the wall panels with a frantic, eager intensity. In seconds, he uncovered five door-shaped 'switches' in the engravings.

"Ki, this is why they were after Mikasi. *This* right here." I said in a low voice. "They knew this was here." I shook my head. "No, that's not right. The Crimson Company had no idea."

"Baron Marius," Ki replied in a flat, low tone.

"The same," I replied. "That lich either heard of this place or read about it. But he knew just what to expect."

"What if he knows because he's been here before? Or was here back then?" Ki asked quietly.

I gave him a sideways look.

"Not something I want to think about."

Ki didn't press me on the topic, and I was glad of it. Debate about the baron could happen later when he wasn't a constant threat. Maybe also after I had set him on fire at least once. We let the conversation drop and instead helped Mikasi search the panels.

The inventor's idea paid off. No sooner had we started than there was a muffled click from Mikasi's direction. I glanced over to see that he had pressed a small door, no larger than two fingers, near the bottom of the wall panel in front of him.

"I think I found the right door out."

A low tumble of ancient gears groaned to life.

"You were right," Ki said, posture tense while a vibration rippled through the floor.

I just nodded in reply and fought to keep my balance. It would have been nice to hang onto a table, but the furniture in the room wasn't any better off.

But my suspicion had been right. I just didn't know how right I was and if Cesibus had designed this, I questioned the man's sanity.

Just then, the entire room rotated to the right like the giant tumbler of a combination lock.

32

Amates 31, 1277. Past the panels and below. We didn't find trouble; it came looking for us.

The room spun three more times to the sound of rattling gears before a way out opened up. It wasn't the spiral staircase. That stayed a spring-loaded, hungry meat grinder. Instead, the way out was a dark, dusty door hidden behind one of the medical cabinets. There was another spiral staircase behind it, only without the spring blades ready to snap out at us from all directions.

All told, it was a good sign they were on the right path. Ruins were often thick with locks and inventive ways to get killed. Those were always far less complicated than a room-sized combination lock. Still, it made my head throb.

But the floor below was well worth the headache.

I left the stairwell, took two steps into the new room, then froze. This room was round, similar to the one above, but lacked the engraved wall panels. Instead, there were wide, broken bay windows, some the size of a small carriage, that had a breathtaking view outside. Not that there was much to see. It was just giant, glowing blue mushrooms on the cavern ceiling and the massive underground lake with its dark water splashing in the distance, far below.

Everything else in the room? It looked like a carpenter's shop thew up. The chaos was so much. I had a hard time taking it all in. So I focused on the view, and a set of tall, aged cabinets made of a dark wood that stood between the broken windows.

It wasn't hard to imagine what the room looked like centuries ago. The place was fascinating. I flexed my hands, as I had an itch to sketch the room. Common sense tackled that urge and shoved it into a closet. We didn't have time for that.

"Whatever happened upstairs, happened here too," I said in a reverent whisper. "A last stand, maybe?"

Ki left the stairs behind me, sent his parrot-shaped light spell to fly near the high ceiling, then walked over to a nearby broken table. The room was bathed in a soft, yellow-white glow. The added light didn't make the place any more cozy.

That nearby table, like most of them, had once been a long affair, like the ones in the room above, but smashed into large pieces. He knelt down and touched the jagged edge of the ancient, shattered wood. A dried, dark stain of some suspicious liquid was painted across the savage splinters. It was dribbled along the wooden planks that made up the floor.

"Most likely. Rough fight, too. This almost looks like it was hit by cannon shot."

He squinted at a nearby window. A chill wind streamed through the room, filled with the dampness of cavern and underground lake.

"Could have been a made with a fireball, too." He shrugged. "Not a better thought."

I walked a little farther into the room, but studied the scene outside. Anxiety over the Crimson Company haunting our back trail nagged at me. But I ignored it and focused on the destruction. Ki's glowing parrot was a good source of light, but it was constantly in motion. This left the pulsing cobalt light from the mushrooms outside and overhead. My magic-altered eyes could see better in the dark, but even for me, there were a lot of long shadows. Most of those slowly danced from the moving lights.

"A ship? That lake is pretty far down. We're not suspended that far down off the cavern ceiling."

Ki shrugged. "Tela, given everything we know about the Ancient Order, would you count out flying ships?"

I started to say something about the logistics of a ship trying to fly, but didn't. Ki had a good point. Everything found so far, from relics to records, pointed out that the Ancient Order was way ahead of us in, well, everything. Which is what made it even more scary, and interesting that the Ancient Order had been wiped out by the Great Collapse.

But none of those thoughts were the least helpful, and more than a little depressing. I put my hands on my hips and blew out a sigh.

"No, not really," I admitted ruefully, then squinted at the room.

Mikasi blew past us in a hurry and into the disaster of a room. Nicodemus was close on his heels. The halfling looked at the room with unvarnished fascination.

"So, it's the right place, yes?" Mikasi asked. After a quick glance around, he frowned. "Maybe they hid it?"

"I'm sure of it," I replied. "But just not sure where."

I stared at the room and made myself take in the details. Ki and Mikasi busied themselves searching in other parts of the room. For Ki, it was the tables and what might have been footlockers underneath them. Mikasi was interested in the cabinets.

Most of the walls really were large windows. They were all shattered, though some still held some of their wide panes. Large, jagged pieces that looked like teeth with a spiderweb of cracks through the glass. Between the walls were the wooden cabinets I saw when we entered or stone walls of the same mottled brown-gray stone of the original stalactite of the building.

The more I saw, the more Ki's idea about the room being attacked made sense. Though I struggled with the flying ship part.

Nothing I saw suggested the attack came from the room above. Maybe from outside. Besides, if it had been an attack from the other room, that 'lock' to get down here would have already been opened. So that wasn't at all right, but neither was this room.

The intact cabinets that lingered at the edges of the room seemed familiar, but also highly out of place. It was like seeing a wet bugbear walking into your room wearing nothing but a towel and a twinkle in his eye. Not that I had any experience with that I wanted to talk about. But the cabinets did remind me of the relic restoration tables back in the Windtracer Records Hall. It was the old dusting brushes and scraping picks on a nearby cabinet that stirred the memory.

A light crash of wood snapped my attention back to the moment. I saw Mikasi over by another cabinet, holding one of its doors that had broken, rotten hinges. The halfling was two shades of dim crimson.

"Are we sure it's here?" he asked, then sheepishly set the broken door down at his feet.

I blinked as my eyes flicked between the broken cabinet door and Mikasi. Quietly, I bit down on a dozen replies about respect for history and not searching fragile, ancient cabinets like a bag of old socks. Slowly, I let out a small sigh.

"It's here," I told him with more confidence that I felt. A thought I couldn't pin down flashed through my head and bolstered that reply. I nodded, more to myself than anything. "I just *know* it is."

Ki, who was over by another of the broken tables, squinted at me. It looked like a memory had come back to him.

"Because of the baron and his 'dowsing rod' trick with his crystal?"

"The same," I said before I navigated some of the broken furniture, then pointed up and a little to the right. My mental map of where we had traveled sprang into life in my mind.

"We came down on that stone platform about over there. After that, we took the first marble bridge into the city. Using that platform as a guidepost, that would put the Crimson Company's camp a little to my right. Maybe four degrees?" I shifted my hand in that direction.

"So his dowsing rod stunt pointed this way and I think right here," I continued. "Also, if the Ancient Order was using Automatic Crystals for anything like sending messages, this would be the likely place for that." I waved a hand around me. "Somewhere."

Ki stood while he brushed soot and wood dust off his hands.

"This place looks like a battlefield. Where would you even hide something like that? We barely know how big it is."

I let out a heavy sigh.

"All right, think, Tela," I growled at myself. "They had one here. Why? Wait, no. That doesn't matter. There was an attack, and they didn't want it found. So they stashed it somewhere but might want to come back for it later." After another frustrated sigh, I rubbed the sides of my head to fend off a headache. "Siren's tits! Where would you hide a large crystal in here?"

I scowled at the room, which didn't seem all that impressed. So, instead, I pursed my lips.

"Where would *I* put it?"

Broken tables were mostly congregated in the middle of the room. Even burnt wooden shards of the ruined furniture were there. None of them were close to a window or a cabinet. That was odd. Even an attack from the stairwell would have scattered parts of the tables right up to the windows.

Ki was right. There were signs everywhere this place had been a battlefield, and the defenders didn't win. It was like looking at a painting where the artist left out one important, but tiny detail you couldn't quite place. Which just nagged at you until your skin twitched. Or maybe that was only me.

Then it hit me.

Missing pieces.

I turned to stare at the ancient brush and picks on that nearby cabinet while my thoughts raced. This wasn't possible, was it? It couldn't be right.

"You haven't heard a word I just said, have you?" Ki asked with no small amount of tartness to his tone.

I twitched and blinked. Given the thin smirk on Ki's face, I figured I looked like a stunned owl with golden eyes.

"What?" I asked, probably a bit too sharp.

Ki shook his head a little, tiefling tail swaying thoughtfully.

"I said that this 'battlefield' looks too perfect. Too organized." Ki waved a hand at the tables. "Hells, it's like a stage play."

That brought a grin to my face. Ki saw it, too. Either we were both wrong, or both right. I went with 'right'.

"Exactly! Look for papers! Journals! Something!" I exclaimed while I ran over to the cabinet that held the picks and brushes.

There was a loud bang off to my left. Mikasi had slammed his head on a cabinet door when I shouted. Ki glanced over in concern, but Mikasi waved him away. The halfling backed a step away from the offending cabinet and grimaced, rubbing the spot where his head had met the edge of a door.

"Like blueprints?" he asked in a small voice.

"Even a scrap of cloth with words on it," I said while I carefully, but quickly, sifted through the cabinet's dusty contents. "This entire room is a disguise. A blind. If I was in a hurry and needed to hide something, this is what I would do. Also, I'd leave a hint for me to find it again if I made it back here."

Ki tossed aside the lid of a shattered long box.

"Exactly," he agreed. "If this was a battlefield, where are the bodies? Given the mess upstairs, someone was here. Maybe the corpses *were* blown out the windows over time, but all of them?"

Inside the cabinet, I found loose blank paper, more brushes, and a stack of ancient cloth. Interesting, but not what I was looking for. I gently nudged those aside and winced when some papers crumbled from being disturbed.

"The windows, too," I added. "The frames are bent outward a little and the glass is broken. If something attacked this place from the outside, glass would be everywhere. Still would be everywhere. But there isn't any. Where is it?"

Ki nodded, but Mikasi looked around in surprise. The inventor went back to his searching in earnest. I tried not to flinch at the sound of a solid clunk or the crack of porcelain hitting something a little too hard from Mikasi's direction. Instead, I focused on my hunt for any scrap of hint about a hiding place for the Automatic Crystal.

We found it five minutes later.

A pair of journals, wrapped in sealed oil cloth, were nestled behind an ancient wooden drawer. Inside the ancient papers were drawings of an Automatic Crystal with a long list of numbers and what looked like calculations in the margin. Measurements? Improvements? I wasn't sure, but we could figure it out later.

They also had a detailed layout of the room. Elaborate drawings of what everything looked like before the stage play of destruction was set up. We dragged broken tables aside, using those drawings as a guide. What we were looking for, and what I hoped to find, was not quite in the middle of the room.

Below one of the tables was a set of pale, bone-white lines carved into brown stained floorboards. Almost a half-finished diagram, it was carved in a series of concentric circles on the floor with the occasional dots around them. For a second, I wondered if it was a worn out summoning circle. But when I tapped the edge of one delicately carved line, a curved section in the floorboard shifted. This jostled its neighbors. They could be moved.

It was complicated, but the scratches were faint enough that the whole thing was easily overlooked. Unless you knew what you were looking for, or at least had a good guess. We were in the latter camp. We gathered around the markings.

"I don't understand," Mikasi said slowly. After a second of staring at the scratches, he squatted down for a closer look. "Another lock?"

"Another one," Ki replied. "A scrambled puzzle, I think. But if it's for a door, I can't see where the edges are." He rubbed his eyes before he glanced at the ceiling. "We are running out of time. I can just feel it."

I nodded.

"Agreed. Ki? Look for the seams. If you can find them, we can try to pry the door open," I said, then glanced over at the inventor. "Mikasi, look for the mechanism. There has to be something that opens this. I'm betting it's not here, but nearby. I'll work on the diagram pieces."

To be fair, I had no idea how to do that, but this has never stopped me before. I sat down on the floor next to the diagram and got to work.

I frantically searched both the Ancient Order journals and my own, while I racked my mind for any loose ideas.

Everyone who studied the Ancient Order had their own ideas on how their culture worked. They left behind enough in ruins, documents, and relics that people agreed to disagree. Their understanding of magic, really devices and magic, went beyond what we knew. Often, most researchers would stare at a relic, shrug, then poke at it until it did something.

A good way to lose a scholar if you ask me. Not that I'm any less guilty of poking at the unknown. I'm just lucky I've not been turned into a chicken wearing socks by now.

But this? The markings on the floor were so *familiar* it hurt. I had seen those before. Where? It was recent. I flipped quickly through the journals in front of me. Fast enough that I worried I tore one. Then I stopped on a set of sketches of an Automatic Crystal. Both mine, and those by whomever, wrote the Ancient Order notes.

What I drew was a guess at best. But what was in the Ancient Order papers didn't look like a guess at all. The numbers, which looked like chicken scrawl before, suddenly made a kind of sense to my addled head. They were measurements, with a lot of corrections. Then I noticed a phase scribbled in the margin of one of the old journals. It was written in Atani, the common dialect of the late Ancient Order, like the rest of the book next to a line pointed at the Crystal's surface.

"Unknown metal," I translated.

The meaning hit me like cold water to the face.

"They weren't using it," I said in a low voice. "*That's* why nothing makes sense about the Automatic Crystal. The Ancient Order wasn't using it, they were *studying* it. They didn't know how it worked, either. So they needed to store this quickly, but carefully."

No sooner had I said that to myself than a memory snapped into place. The cargo loading room we found once we first entered the ruin on the canyon floor. It had similar circular lines like this on the floor. I touched my Sun Orb to them. They came alive with a ghostly, pale white glow for a moment, just like the magical paint in the cargo room.

"Ki! Mikasi! Look near the cabinets or by the stairs for..." words failed me, so I gestured at the stairs and waved a hand in that direction like it would help explain anything. A few words finally tumbled to mind. "A lever. Pulley system. Something. Like what was up in that cargo dock room we found."

"Where we first took the platform down into here?" Ki asked with a frown while Mikasi ran past him. "That's here?"

"Yes! That!" I nodded. "Find those, pull them. I'll adjust these pieces here. This room has something like it. I think it's how we open this."

Ki frowned as he took a deep breath, but I cut off his reply with a scowl to let him know I was serious. We didn't have time to debate this. He raised his hands as if to ward off the argument before he retreated to help Mikasi.

While they looked for hidden levers, I placed my Sun Orb against the carvings on the floor. This time, I held it there for a few seconds. The paint instantly glowed with a soothing, soft, ghost-white light. Once the glow was strong and steady, I pulled back the Orb. I couldn't help but grin as I got busy trying to work out the correct order for the carved puzzle pieces.

It turned out they were, of course, an outline of an Automatic Crystal. I wasn't sure if the maker was in a hurry or wasn't feeling imaginative that day. But once I slid the last piece into place, the circular outline of the Crystal, complete with hints of bumps and knobs, glowed once with a sharp, bright white light.

A muffled thump followed by a rattle of gears filled the room. Slowly, a seam parted between the glowing outline on the floor in front of me. The small panel, large enough for a person to stand in, swung down to a dusty crawlspace below the floor. I jumped back, eyes locked on the opening.

It was there. Covered in centuries of dust, but it was there. The Automatic Crystal was a round ball, just like in the drawings, but a good bit bigger than I imagined. Three times the size of a person's head, at least. Underneath the dust, the surface looked made of dark lacquered wood, or even metal, plates. White crystal glimmered between them like seams. Tarnished metal studs, just like from the sketches, sat in the middle of each plate.

I almost cried while a platform magically, and silently, raised the large crystal and metal ball out of the floor in front of me.

Instead of crying, I nearly screamed when I looked up from the relic.

"Thank you, Tela. I always knew you would be the one to find it. Really, I'm just surprised you lived to do just that."

The voice was smooth. Sickly sweet, like a poisonous syrup. But in the few times I had heard him talk, Baron Marius Apollinare was like that. I figured it was a lich thing.

He stood on the far side of the room near the stairwell from above, brandishing his piece of an Automatic Crystal. It already glowed with a promise of magical mayhem. Four thugs from the Crimson Company were with him, and, of course, Vincent Vargas.

They all, except for the baron, looked battered and a little bloody. Leather and brigandine armor sported enough claw marks and tears,

I was surprised any of it held together. Even Vargas looked like a dog had scooped him up by the scruff of the neck to shake him like an old towel.

One of them, a wiry man with a weathered, scarred face, also had his hands on Kiyosi and held a knife to my friend's throat. Mikasi was nowhere to be seen. I just hoped the little inventor had found some place safe to hide with his cat. With any luck, they would be safe until this got sorted out. If it got sorted out.

"Now. I'll be taking that, my dear, since you've unearthed it for me," the baron said while he started across the room. "We can discuss a new arrangement after that once I've *helped* you think about your future."

"Tela!" Ki tried to step forward, but the thug with the knife didn't let him move.

Not that I needed much encouragement, anyway. The moment the baron took a step forward, I jumped for the crystal. I remembered what Odro told me about light, intent and all with this thing. If the baron was going to use a spell on me again, and it sounded like he might, I wanted to be as ready as I could. Also, I could use this to bargain for Ki's life. The latter was far more important to me right then than the former.

Only that was when everything happened at once.

People were shouting, yelling, or running at me. Ki managed to put some space between himself and that knife. With a quick twist, he slammed an uppercut into his kidnaper's throat. The man wheezed, then sliced out at Ki.

Vargas, over by the stairs, hadn't moved. The man looked furious, but I wasn't sure if it was at me or the baron. Hard to tell, since one of the Crimson Company had just fired an arrow to try to slow me down.

"No!" Baron Marius shrieked. "I told you. Don't fire at the Crystal! Not here!"

It was good advice for dealing with any relic, since they were often fragile. But the Automatic Crystal seemed in better shape than that, since the arrow bounced off in pieces. Arrow fragments clattered to the floor somewhere nearby. I didn't pay it all that much attention. There were more important things going on in front of me.

The Automatic Crystal had come alive with light and magic the instant I, or maybe it was the arrow, touched it. A bright snow-white glow with a touch of sea blue deep inside lit up the white crystal seams between the plates. It was pretty, but that wasn't what made everyone stop in their tracks.

That happened because the Automatic Crystal in my hands started to unfold on its own.

33

Amates 31, 1277. Just when I thought I had everything figured out...

It was a kobold.

Actually, it wasn't a live flesh and scale kobold but only a statue of one. This had the same size and shape as a real kobold, only with interlocking dark metal plates for a 'skin' like an alligator's hide. Palms and other 'soft' parts were still the same clouded quartz crystal. Each individual fist-sized piece of the Automatic Crystal had slid, turned, or rotated along the knobs that dotted its surface. They had clicked together like a puzzle to fashion arms, sinewy paw-stepper hind legs, a reptile-shaped head and tail.

All in all, the process took only two seconds from start to finish.

Everything in the room came to a dead stop, even the fight between Ki and the mercenaries by the stairs. All eyes were on the statue with a combination of fascination, shock, and a little fear over what had just happened. No one spoke or moved, save for one exception, which didn't surprise me one bit.

"Finally!" Baron Marius almost cheered, a grin smeared across his face. "After all these centuries, I've found one still intact!" A dark shadow passed over his face a moment so fast, I almost missed it. "Also, no Cesibus or Alchemy Council to get in my way."

Cesibus? That was something to think about when my life wasn't in danger.

"Don't get too happy. It's not yours," I said in an even, flat tone. "It's going to a museum."

I saw that all too bright light in the baron's eyes as he shot a glance in my direction. There was a lot of greed there, but something else that was even more dangerous. It was the same damaged, predatory shine I saw when he tried to twist me inside out with a spell back at Banye. A chill slithered down my spine as he raised his glowing crystal shard in front of him like a totem. Its light cast his wine red waistcoat and fine clothing into stark relief against the gray grunge of the room.

He took a slow step towards me.

So, I threw a dagger at him.

In my defense, I wasn't feeling all that diplomatic toward someone who tried to murder me once before.

The blade slammed deep into the baron's chest, right between the lapels of his waistcoat. He staggered back a step with a grunt, reaching for the weapon, while bloody hell erupted around us.

Two Crimson Company mercenaries rushed to his side. One stopped by the baron, while the other one, a tall, square-jawed wall of muscle, ran right at me. I yanked the whip off my belt, then cracked it in the air between us. Air popped like a thunderclap. The big man in the leather jerkin bolted sideways like a startled jackrabbit while he covered his face with an arm.

"Don't even try it," I snarled at him.

I cracked the whip twice more, just to buy myself some more space. The Crimson thug wanted nothing to do with that whip, so he gave ground. But from what I could see, the second he had the chance, he was going to rush me again. I pulled the last dagger from my belt and held it low in my left hand. Just in case he got too close for comfort.

Past my current thug-shaped problem, the baron yanked the dagger out of his chest, then shoved the man next to him roughly aside. The mercenary recoiled in wide-eyed horror at the sight of the smoking dark hole in the baron's chest. Powdery gravedust poured from the wound like a waterfall of gray sand that smeared itself across the baron's silk white shirt.

Baron Marius shoved the terrified thug aside into a stack of broken chairs.

"Get away!" he snapped irritably, then hurled my dagger across the room. The baron fixed a hungry, irritated glare on me. "This? Again? Tela, this habit of ruining my clothes is getting expensive. You're becoming more trouble than you're worth."

That predatory stare of his would have scared milk to cheese, but I stood my ground. At least, until a blast of yellow-white light from the crystal shard in his hand punched me in the stomach. Next thing I knew, I was on the floor, laying on my side. I opened my eyes.

Panic slapped me into action as a shadow fell over me. The Crimson thug I had threatened reached for my shirt. I rolled to the right. My whip handle made a satisfying crack against the side of his jaw when the hard leather knot bashed him like a flail. He backed off fast, and I scrambled to my feet.

The baron grabbed the wounded man, then tossed him aside to the floor like a big sack of garbage. I retreated a few steps, wanting no part of that. Baron Marius was a lot stronger than I imagined. Which made a wicked sort of sense since he was undead.

"Both of you, stay back!" he snarled at the two thugs. "She's *mine!*"

I flinched, then stepped back again. It was the tone in his voice that did it, with that all too raw, hungry look in his eyes. All the memories of horror and pain when he ripped into me with a spell flooded my vision in lurid detail. All of it from sight to smell, and everything down to the screaming. Mostly my screaming.

Somewhere near the stairs, I heard Ki shout for Mikasi. The halfling gave a sharp reply I couldn't make out. They both sounded either in pain or panic, not sure which. Past and present blurred into a murky mess, covered by ghosts from the past. Friends were laughing, crying, then screaming and dying, while the Long Deep ruins around me swallowed them whole.

Friends I had brought here years ago to die, just like this time.

A shadow of motion made panic shake me back to reality. It was the baron. He was almost on top of me.

"Hold still this time," he said, his words slithered like cold slime. The man's crystal shard turned a familiar sickly yellow. "It won't hurt much."

I lashed out with my whip. The handle made a sharp, solid smack across his jaw. He stumbled back, wide-eyed, grabbing his jaw from what I assume was instinct. I advanced on my tormentor with whip and dagger, like a woman possessed. Where I didn't stab, I beat mercilessly with the wood and leather handle. Most people are at least a head taller than me. But that meant I learned a long time ago to make every hit count so it would both hurt and sting.

Seconds later, the lich quickly stumbled away from my frantic torrent of pain, hands raised in some sort of weak defense. His shirt was a shredded mess, but so was he. What wasn't cut had been broken or bruised. Gravedust streamed out of a dozen cuts.

Exhausted, I gulped down air while sweat poured down my face and through my braids. I wiped at it with a hand. Dust smeared across my cheek.

Lich or no, even he had to have a limit on how much punishment he could take. I just needed to knock him out long enough to give us a fighting chance in here. I lunged after him.

"*Ah'sa'kee!*" I screamed in kobold.

A pale yellow-white blast of light exploded from his crystal shard. I dove for cover behind the ruins of a nearby table but never made it. Hot magic hit me in the chest like a hammer. One moment I was on my feet, the next I skid across the floor. My back crashed into one of the ancient cabinets at the edge of the round room. I was just lucky it was that and not one of the open windows.

Wood splinters shot everywhere when the fragile, ancient cabinet doors gave way behind me. A shower of antique pottery rained down. I curled into a ball and covered my head against the porcelain avalanche.

Once the last bowl fell, I stumbled to my feet. I felt like a cracked pane of glass, bound together by cheap, frayed twine. Everything from back to boobs, joints to lower ribs, felt like a spectacular bruise. Ki was going to chew me out again. I coughed to knock the dust out of my chest, which earned me a sharp stabbing pain in my right side. All the other aches joined in a second later.

An agonizing scream snapped my attention back to the room. I spun around, pain forgotten for the moment. It was the baron, but sadly, he wasn't the one screaming. A small problem I really wanted to fix.

The scream was from one of Vargas' thugs. An elven man, a head or so taller than me, wearing battered crimson brigandine armor. Baron Marius had forced the man to his knees and had a hand latched on the thug's throat. Red, bright magic flowed out of the baron, through his crystal shard, and over the mercenary like hot syrup. Everywhere the power touched, the mercenary writhed in agony, screaming as if it boiled him alive.

Without a second thought, I ran right at them. Did I know what the baron was doing? No, and I didn't care. But it was about to stop.

Four paces out, I cut loose with my whip. The popper struck the baron like a lightning hammer. He grabbed his wounded hand. The crystal shard clattered to the floor while the Crimson mercenary collapsed like a forgotten sack of potatoes.

Baron Marius shot a poisonous glare at me that would scare milk into cheese. But his bloody spell faded into a bad memory, and that's all that mattered at that moment.

"You. Again!" He snapped the words out like his favorite profanity.

"Me. Again," I replied with all the venom I could muster. Sure, I was exhausted, but anger made up for the difference. "It doesn't matter who or what you are, I will end you before you hurt anyone else or even touch that relic!"

The baron snarled at me, then lunged for the crystal shard. He was fast, but to my surprise, his former victim was faster. The mercenary grabbed the baron before lich took a step. Off balance, Marius hit the floor face-first. I vaulted them both, then kicked the crystal shard to the far side of the room. It clattered to a stop somewhere near Ki and Mikasi.

I spun around to find myself squared off once more against Baron Marius. He had kicked free of the elven mercenary, giving the wounded man a bloody nose on top of the magic-burns. The elf lay there curled in a ball, wracked by agony.

It was like facing a mad, undead bull. I had lost my dagger somewhere near the now-shattered cabinet. All I had left was my whip, a battered body, and a lot of pent-up rage. If I stood up straight, I was only five nindel two. The baron was a head taller like most everyone else, broad-shouldered, with undead strength for days. I took a deep breath before I readied my whip and planted my feet. This was going to hurt.

"End me?" Marius snarled, shoulders bunched like a predator ready to strike. "Get in line, Tela. You aren't the first..."

Then, in a blur of red and gray, the baron was gone. Something slammed into him with the force of a runaway wagon. A tinkle of silver clattered to the floor at my feet. I glanced down, stunned, trying to keep up with the moment.

It was a lone silver spider pendant. The one Vargas wore everywhere.

He had let the curse take him. The same curse that had infected him the last time we were here.

Vargas had thrown the baron to the floor not far away, using all four of his new, fur-covered, spidery arms. Fangs were eager to rip the lich to shreds. But that lich wasn't about to go down easily. There was a muffled crack when Marius snapped one of Vargas' arms. The mercenary leader let out a soul-shriveling shriek of pain.

That sound snapped me out of my haze. I scrambled over to the Crimson Company mercenary that lay at the foot of the Automatic Crystal. The elven man was covered in ugly purple blotches of magic burns. Blood streamed down from his nose. He looked like he had been shoved through three kinds of hell and left some of himself behind.

My old friend, pain, returned and politely explained that I wasn't that much better off. I dropped to my knees. A sharp pinch, almost a stab, jabbed me in my lower ribs. I gasped, but refused to double over.

"You have bandages? Burn creams? Healing salves?" I asked between sharp gasps.

Smoke curled up off the man's ruined armor, clothes, and body. He blinked at me, eyebrows pinched over a confused frown, while he tried to focus on my face. After a second, he shook his head.

"Bandages," he rasped at me, voice raw. "Left belt pouch. Rest is in my pack. By the stairs."

I practically lunged for the man's belt pouch. He grabbed my wrist. "Why?"

The intensity of his gaze with that one word made me hesitate. I stared at his intense look with my own.

"Because you're hurt," I snapped while I pulled my hands free. "I don't like any of you or Vargas, but what the baron did? What he was doing?" I shook my head while I jerked out the bandages. "It wasn't right. Not a bit of it."

What really wasn't right was all the things I didn't say. That I couldn't stand for these ruins to swallow anyone else whole. Not even Vargas or his cut-throat crew. Too many had already died here. It needed to stop.

I quickly ripped away the man's sleeves, then loosely covered the burns with as much cloth as I had. There were more burns than cloth, but I did what I could. After that? I rummaged through my battered satchel in a panic.

"Something!" I snarled at both the world and myself. "Lady Deep, if you've *ever* listened to me, I need *something*, dammit! Anything!"

A hand gently touched my shoulder, and I nearly screamed.

I honestly thought it was Ki or Mikasi. It wasn't either of them. The soft rattle of wind chimes blew through the air. In that music, there was a gentle voice that spoke in perfect kobold.

"I heard you call," the soft voice sang. "You're hurt."

I glanced over at the hand, then up at its owner, and found myself staring into a pair of golden, crystal, kobold-shaped eyes.

It was the Automatic Crystal statue.

I had been wrong. Everyone was wrong, yet also a little bit right.

The Automatic Crystal of the Eclipse was a golem. Tears stung my eyes.

"I can help with the burns," it sang softly in my mind while its eyes glowed at every syllable. Flashes of light that I somehow understood as words. "I know how."

For no reason at all, Mikasi's words from that day in his workshop back in Banye leaped out and ambushed me.

"A language of light," I repeated in a hoarse voice. "He was right. By the Lady Deep and her Nine Misbegotten Children, he was right..."

The Automatic Crystal of the Eclipse was *talking* and I could *understand* it.

It was help, just not the kind I expected.

34

Amates 31, 1277. No one said this would be easy. If they had, I would've called them a liar.

The crystal golem knelt down next to me, then stirred the musty air between us with its right hand. Golden sparkles of light chased its gemstone fingers until they became flowing threads of light. Without warning, that gentle circle of light washed out over the both of us like a glowing stream, before it settled onto the mercenary's burns. The elven man visibly relaxed with a heavy sigh of profound relief when the power from the spell melted into the burns like a soft cream.

Was I caught up in the moment? Oh, of course I was. Three kinds of death lurked nearby like pickpockets looking for a mark, and here I was all doe-eyed over an ancient, talking crystal golem that could touch magic. History had just come to life right in front of me, and I was all here for it. Besides, for a few seconds, I actually felt *safe* for the first time in days or weeks.

But the small war around me had kept going.

A loud crash behind me of ancient wood and fragile pottery shattered the delicate moment into nothing more than dust.

I scrambled to my feet, then spun toward the chaos, whip in hand. Pain from my lower ribs and a dozen bruises punched through me like an arrow and stole my breath. It made me stumble, but somehow I willed myself to stay upright. Better to be on my feet facing whatever was coming, not lying face-first on the floor. It was easier to stab new problems standing up. Sadly, I had no idea where my daggers were at the moment.

But thank the tides, it wasn't a new problem. Just the same damn one, only worse.

The battle had wandered all over the place while I had been huddled up against the Automatic Crystal. In this latest round, the baron had slammed Vargas into one of the cabinets at the edge of the room with some sort of spell. Remnants of red-gold power dribbled off both Vargas and the cabinet for the floor. Two paces to the right, and Vargas would have been tossed over the side to his death.

I bit back the urge to run over and harass the baron, just to give the others some sort of chance to recover and regroup. It wasn't the dumbest idea I'd ever had, but it was right there at the top. If I ran over there, there was every chance I'd get myself killed, or worse. I didn't want to think about the 'or worse' part. Besides, it was about as useful as trying to set water on fire.

"We can't keep this up," I muttered under my breath. "Just can't. We're hurt. Exhausted. Vargas has his curse to keep him going for now, but for how long? Marius is undead. He's getting faster at shrugging off whatever we do to him. We're barely slowing him down."

A tear crawled down my face. I wiped it away with a snarl.

"This isn't like last time," I snapped at the thoughts in my head. "There *has* to be another way. What in the hell and high tides am I missing?"

I shot a sideways glance at the Automatic Crystal.

"Can you do *anything* about this?" I stabbed a finger at the baron. "Like pin him down or something?"

The golem shook its head while it continued to work on the mercenary's burns.

"The Maker was very clear," its eyes flashed while it sang at me. "I was made to help, not hurt. One of those people is cursed by Deeplands wild magic, and the other is undead. I'm useless to the undead. They can't touch me."

That last comment was like a cold slap of water across the face.

I ransacked my memories of days, even weeks before. Bits and pieces of information I had heard or learned clicked into place like keys in a series of locks. Things suddenly made way too much sense. It had been in front of me this entire time. I wasn't sure if I was about to scream, cry, or attack Baron Marius with the nearest pointy object. The lich had earned a good stabbing for what he tried.

"*That's* why he tried to alter me," I snarled at the ruins, room, and the small war around me. "It's why he wanted Mikasi. Cesibus set all this up to keep Baron Marius away from the Automatic Crystal. Hell and high tides, if I didn't just lead him through all of that to what that bastard wanted. Especially after he tried to break me..."

Another crash sent a hailstorm of wood across the room when Vargas was hurled into yet another cabinet. Shattered glass and pottery shot out in all directions like a bladed hailstorm. An ornate thin stone tablet that was more stained glass than stone slipped off a ruined top shelf and hit the petrified floor. It shattered on impact into thousands of pieces and set my mind in motion.

The world moved like syrup. A flash shot across my mind's eye about the tablet. There, a first century Ancient Order glassmaker took painstaking care to assemble a stained glass portrait. It was once a record of an important event in history, now? Lost.

Something inside me snapped. I stepped forward with murder in my heart, when a golden band of magic lashed out in an attempt to pin the baron's arms down. The lich dashed to his right, then snapped the spell like strands of tinsel. He snatched up a broken cabinet door and hurled it back at the caster. It slammed into Ki like a hammer. Both hit the floor like discarded trash. Neither one moved.

"No!" I screamed.

Memories flooded the room. I couldn't breathe or move. It was all so much, just too much, like being drowned in history. Memories of my last expedition choked off my air. Voices of old friends screamed out for me as they died all over again in the ruins. Slowly, those ghosts appeared around me.

I knew them all.

Every single one.

I had lost them all here in this very ruin.

"Lady deep, not now," I begged with a ragged voice. "Please, no."

Suddenly, my vision cleared, or at least enough to see the state of the disaster surrounding me. One Crimson Company archer had a broken leg trying to reach Ki, but his companion had pulled him to cover. They were both behind one of the countless piles of ruined furniture. The rest of the Crimson Company that had come down was missing or already dead. Ki lay still on the floor with a bloody shirt, but I saw his chest move as he breathed. Vargas was a magically twisted mess, who looked like he had fought a small war and almost lost.

He was a punch drunk wreck even despite his cursed transformation. Clothing, even armor, hung in shreds. Spiny, slate-gray fur matted with blood stuck out at odd angles from under what he wore. The four spider-like, crooked, fur-covered arms were at hideous odds with what was left of his human body. A scorpion tail the right size for his shape twitched while he rubbed face and protruding fangs across the back of a human arm.

As for the baron? The fight had carved him up like a cooked ham, but his undead nature had already mostly patched him up. He turned his attention toward me and flexed his hands like claws that dripped with deep red magic.

"Now. Where were we, my dear?"

"You getting dead," I shot back.

"Already done. Care to join me?"

His words dripped over me like a cold, thick slime. I fought down a shudder that ran through me. All I had left was one last appeal to sanity, which was mostly me stalling to think of something to stop this.

"It doesn't do what you think, Marius," I snapped. "The Crystal belongs in a museum. It could teach and help. This is not a weapon. Cesibus *had* to have told you at least that much."

Baron Marius stopped walking and glared at me. The magic still boiled around his hands, but from the look on his face, I hit a nerve. A big nerve and maybe even the chink in his armor.

"Shut up, woman," he snarled.

Something blazed in those undead eyes. Fear? Alarm? Whatever it was, that was new.

"You weren't even alive," he growled, eyes blazing. "You don't know what you're talking about."

I allowed myself just a little smirk.

"Don't I? Mikasi studied Cesibus and his works for *years*. You needed him to get past what Cesibus set up to keep you out. The rest of us, maybe even the Crimson Company, have been down here before. We were fodder to clear the path for you."

"The others, perhaps," he said in a cold voice. "But you? Oh, I have such plans for you, Tela." Those last words had such a seductive undertone I felt like I was covered in slime again. My mind was going to need a hot bath and a stuff drink if I survived this.

Across the room, the last Crimson Company archer met my gaze, then scrambled for a better place to fire from. Vargas shook his head while he pulled shafts of wood from a ruined, furry arm.

I shifted position, which put me closer to the Automatic Crystal. It was all part of my plan. A great big, stupid plan, but still a plan. The baron narrowed his eyes at me, immediately suspicious.

"Oh, I know you do," I replied in a dark, even tone. "I get it. You've been stalking me. Studying me like a bug. At some point, you figured out I could spin pieces of history around in my head until they fit together like a puzzle. So you wanted to magically alter me in a way that I could talk to the Crystal through that talent I have. Use me like some link to it. But you also knew you had to break me, so I'd cooperate."

"I needed you more... agreeable. Pliable," Marius replied in a dangerous, low tone. "At least until you were broken enough that you would submit to anything I wanted. Specifically, make the Automatic Crystal to use its power to reshape other's minds in the same way."

The last piece of the puzzle clicked into place. That was how he planned to get around a city's anti-magic shield generated by a Schutz Crystal or a Blackstel Shield. Just walk the Crystal and myself right through those defenses before tuning us loose. I shuddered and glanced away a moment to gather my thoughts.

All around me, the ghosts were still there, like an audience. Marius acted like he didn't see them. Some of the ghosts glared at the baron, others looked at me expectantly. They all acted like I was supposed to do something amazing.

No pressure, right? The dead are so damn judgmental.

"I was made to help, not hurt," sang the Automatic Crystal. The golem got to its metal and stone feet to stand just behind me and to my right. "I will *not* help you cause harm!"

There was so much emotion packed into those last words, I thought they would pop open. This wasn't just a golem. I wasn't sure what this dark device really was, but it was anything but 'just an old relic'. But that wasn't important at the moment. I'd think about it tomorrow, provided I was alive and in my right mind.

"What did it say?" snapped the baron with a suspicious glare.

"Crystal here says it won't help you. That it wasn't made that way," I translated.

"It doesn't matter what you think," the baron snapped at the golem, then started toward us. "You don't think. You're just a device to be owned and used!" He flexed his hands, which made the magic bleed faster from his fingers. "As for you, Tela, if you would hold still, this won't take long."

On the other side of the room, out of the baron's sight, the lone Crimson Company archer made a quiet, frantic wave for me to dive aside. I replied with a small, quick shake of my head.

A knot rolled around in my bruised guts. I needed the baron closer. A lot closer. So I held my ground and sighed.

Each step the lich took toward us was pure agony to watch, and I swallowed the urge to scream. Finally, the baron was close enough to touch. He towered over me with that same self-satisfied, smug look on his face. I cleared my throat when he started to reach for me with that magic-coated hand of his.

"Baron?" I asked with what I hoped sounded like a soft, submissive, maybe even meek voice.

He paused, face pinched in suspicion again.

"Yes?"

"Gotcha," I said with a smirk.

The baron stepped back in alarm when I yanked my goggles down over my eyes and jerked my right hand behind me. I pinched the air between the Automatic Crystal and myself. Across the room, the lone Crimson Company archer let fly an arrow that stabbed the lich in the back left shoulder. Marius yelled in rage as he ripped the arrow free.

Pain flared through my chest and sides, but I moved my hand in a circle through the air like I'd watched Ki do a hundred times. After all, casting magic, how hard could it be?

Every thought in my mind focused on what I wanted to happen. The 'intent' that Odro taught me only a little about back in the ruins.

Did I really know what I was doing? No. But that never stopped me before.

A brilliant yellow light exploded to life behind me.

"This is a bad idea!" The Crystal sang in alarm before it took a step back.

"I'm all out of good ones!" I snapped back in reply.

Quick as I could, I yanked my hand back out in front of me. Bright yellow threads, like spun sunlight, wound around my fingers. Interspersed between them were stands of blue-white power so pure they were almost silver. Inside, a part of me groaned. I'd already done something wrong. But there wasn't any time to think about it.

Baron Marius dashed forward in alarm. His hand was almost at my throat. I wrapped those magic threads around my fist and swung for the baron's nose.

He was terrifyingly fast.

I was faster.

My fist, wrapped in healing magic and more, slammed into the Baron's undead mouth and nose. A small sun of power exploded between us and burned the lich as if he had been dumped in acid. My goggles protected my vision from the flash of light, but I shut my eyes anyway. There was no help against the heat, that left me a bit toasty.

I opened my eyes in time to see a storm boil to life between myself and the baron.

An uncontrolled storm of wild magic.

In my defense, I never said this was a good idea.

35

Amates 31, 1277. A storm can get you moving better than a cup of coffee. This just wasn't anything like a storm...

The wild magic storm slapped the ancient floor with blue lightning like it deserved it. Everywhere a bolt touched, petrified floor planks shattered, cracked or blasted into pieces. Blackened chunks flew everywhere. What didn't get scorched, was assaulted by wild magic, which led to far worse results.

After all, no one expects lightning to leave lava behind in petrified wood.

I pulled myself off the floor while I eyed the dark green storm clouds overhead. They boiled like some vile potion that wanted to eat the sandstone ceiling. Without warning, the room shuddered like it wanted to fall apart. It stopped almost as soon as it started, and I let out a small sigh.

If we fell into that lake below us, it was so far down there wouldn't even be paste left.

"This," I groused. "*This* is what I get for messing with magic."

I tried to ignore the obvious impending doom while I ran over to Ki. He groaned in pain as I dropped to my knees next to him. Before I could touch him, he opened his eyes wide with a gasp. I practically dove onto him with a tight hug.

"*Aile Shavat!* You're alive!"

Kiyosi squirmed a bit with a whimper as his right arm under me shuddered.

"Tela? Healer tip. Don't hug the patient right where they're wounded."

I let go fast, then sat back to lift my goggles and wipe at one of my eyes.

"Shut up! You're not dead. That's what matters."

Ki barked out a short laugh that turned into a dry cough while he struggled to sit up. Then he noticed the storm clouds along the ceiling. His blue skin turned a deathly pale.

"Gods, is that a *wild storm?* Inside a *building?* What happened?"

I pulled my goggles back down, then glanced over my shoulder at the storm. Blasts of blue lightning jumped like giddy demons between the green clouds. Everywhere the storm touched the ceiling or thin window frame supports, stonework seemed to crack and twist with a sharp pop.

For a moment, I saw glowing yellow lines race out along the ceiling. The whole pattern looked like a spiderweb, then it was gone.

I pointed at where the lines had appeared with my right hand. The same one wrapped in silver and gold magical threads, like a twisted set of glowing brass knuckles.

"Did you see that?" I asked, as I glanced back at Ki.

He didn't notice. Instead, he stared at my hand in pure horror.

"I, uh, had to improvise?" I tried to explain with a pained expression.

Ki pushed up into a painful crouch, face drawn, eyes wide.

"Hell and high tides, that... that is *magic*, Tela. A really twisted spell around your hand. What did you *do*? Do you know how..."

I scowled at my best friend in the world, then shoved a finger from that same magic wrapped hand in front of his face.

"Not. Now. Less talkie, more escaping! Run for the stairs! You can lecture me later," I snapped, then stood up and looked for the others.

Across the room, the last two Crimson Company archers had started to make a slow retreat from the storm. Mikasi and Nicodemus found their way to the Automatic Crystal and the wounded elven mercenary. The rest of the few Crimson Company down here was half-conscious near the stairs.

Blue lightning shot out from storm clouds and shattered cabinets with a touch. More of that strange spiderweb glow raced over the ceiling. This time, cracks were left behind.

"Mikasi!" I shouted over the wild magic blasts.

The inventor spun around while I motioned frantically with both hands toward the stairs out of this death trap.

"Get everyone out! Now!"

I frowned at the battered room, including its gray, mottled stone stairs that were the only safe way out. Nothing made sense anymore. Especially the wild storm.

"All I did was punch the baron," I complained under my breath. "It isn't like I punched the room."

Then I saw it.

I almost squatted down on the floor and screamed in frustration.

Each time the lightning struck the floors, walls, or ceiling, a spiderweb of power raced out above the storm. In the center of that spiderweb was a thin thread of light drawn from the ceiling to where I had found the Automatic Crystal. That thread sputtered and sparked where it met the door that had concealed the dark device.

It looked like a frayed tripwire made of light. The wild storm poured out from where that thread touched the ceiling.

"Lady Deep and her Nine Misbegotten Children!" I yelled at the world while I rubbed my eyes underneath my goggles. "Why didn't I see this?"

Ki was on his feet but hadn't run for the stairs like I told him to.

"What?" he asked, out of breath.

"Why are you still here? Run, you stubborn mule!" I snapped at him, then waved a hand at the frayed glowing thread. "There's a tripwire!" I let out a ragged sigh. "I think I set it off when I cast this made up spell."

A thousand questions played across Kiyosi's face. He looked at where I pointed, puzzled. But instead of ask, he limped fast for the stairs out. Not far away, Mikasi had already shepherded the rest to the exit.

I glanced at the thread of light, then at Kiyosi. He couldn't see it.

"Mikasi! Do you see that?" I yelled over the storm and pointed at the thin, glowing thread.

The inventor looked at where I pointed, shook his head and shrugged. Then he followed the others up the stairs.

"They can't see it," I said, stunned. "By the Lady Deep, it's my stupid eyes again. That has to be why I'm the only one who sees it." A frustrated sigh ran out of me. "At least there aren't poison darts, too."

Suddenly, the room shuddered hard enough that parts of the ceiling fell down with a hard thud. I flinched from the impact.

Overhead and all around, the storm tore at the room. Ancient, polished stone from the ceiling melted like soft wax or crumbled to dust in patches. It was chaos. But now that I had an idea of what to look for, I saw a pattern to it all.

Normal wild storms were a massive wave of wild magic mixed with a hurricane or other storm. Often they erased towns or even cities that didn't get their Schutz field active in time.

But this wasn't a normal wild storm. Somehow, the Ancient Order had found a way to contain a wild storm. To stuff it into something, then use it as part of a trap.

"That webbing. The wild storm is following the webbing," I murmured as I broke into a run.

Almost everyone had left this room and run upstairs, save for two. One of those I sort of felt responsible for. The other one could go to hell.

"I can work with this!" I shouted to myself. "Follow the webbing! Stay in the gaps!"

After a quick stop to snatch up a certain silver pendant, I raced off across the room toward Vargas. He was right where I last saw him. The man was still transformed from his curse into a furry, spider-like scorpion thing with anger issues. He was beat up, tore up, and bloody on his knees next to a ruined cabinet.

I didn't see the baron anywhere. That bothered me. But this was more important. That lunatic would have to wait his turn.

Now that I knew what to look for to avoid the storms, I raced across the room as fast as my bruised body would allow. The instant the clouds flashed with power, the webbing appeared, and I stood in the gap between the lines.

Wild magic and raw power slammed down around me in thick sheets. I've never been so terrified in my life. But, step by step, I made it through.

Vargas climbed to his feet as I approached, then charged at me with a mad roar.

"Damn it! We don't have time for this!" I yelled at him while I avoided one of Vargas' black claws.

Vargas swiped first at my throat, then my face. I ducked down, twisted behind him, and swallowed a gasp of pain from my side. When he spun around to lash at me once more, I lunged forward and punched that amulet into his chest. His arms snapped down to claw my back through my shirt.

Magic came to life when the amulet touched him. The result was immediate and disgusting.

Vargas sagged like a overheated candle. Spidery arms melted down behind him into a gray goop that soaked into his back. The rest of him probably did the same. I didn't want to look. So, I stared at the floor.

Two seconds flew by then Vargas grabbed my arms with his own normal, boring, human hands. I glanced up from the floor to meet his eyes. He was still beat up, bloody and cut. But now he was confused, and human once more.

"Tela?" he croaked at me. "What?"

I shook my head. "Not now. Keep the amulet on this time. We're getting out of here."

Vargas sputtered in a daze, while I pulled him to his feet. Then I guided him across the room, being mindful of the glowing spiderweb pattern. Our window of escape had narrowed quick. The storm had started to swallow the room whole and break it apart.

Run, then stop, then run again. It was painfully slow.

"We'll never make it," Vargas growled. The confusion had worn off, so his usual sour disposition returned. "Another one of your great big plans?"

"I swear by the Lady Deep and the High Tides, I *will* punch your teeth in," I snarled back while we limped toward the stairs and safety. "In case you overlooked it, this is a rescue, you pompous ass."

"Fine. We get out and life goes back to normal," he growled in my ear.

"Vargas, you and I haven't seen, smelled, or tasted normal in years. Shut up and limp faster. I'm trying to save us both."

We made our three-legged foot limp across the storm-cracked room in record time. But we didn't arrive alone.

Vargas and I had just climbed onto the stone stairs when the baron lunged out of the shadows. The lich banged my head against the stone and latched onto my throat.

I punched at his hands with my magic threads, but it didn't do any good. The baron was a mess of tattered clothes and ruined body. His skin was a mottled mess caught in a constant, painful cycle of healing, then rotting back to putrid undead flesh. His eyes burned like bloody orbs of mystical hate that bored into mine. I could still see my ghosts while they ripped into him from behind. It seemed to make the baron more wild and unstable.

"The Dark Device is *mine!*" Baron Marius hissed in my face like a fiend. "*You* are mine!"

I flailed against him as the air squeezed out of me.

"Let! Her! Go!" Vargas punctuated each word with a kick to the side of the baron's head.

The baron's hands came free of my throat on the last kick. His head rolled to the left.

I slapped his hands away with everything I had, then slammed the mess of magical threads around my knuckles into that lich's throat. Every thought, my full intent and desire, shot through my mind. I wanted to end this evil creature right here and now.

The magical threads snapped apart, then speared into the baron's head through his jaw. I watched a bright flash burst to life in his eyes as the spell vanished from my hand.

I heard whispers in my mind, and somehow I knew what I had hit the baron with.

It was a mind storm. I had caused a mind storm like Ki had warned me about. Why? Intent. Dire warnings aside, I *wanted* to.

With my free hand, I grabbed his ragged collar, then hissed in his undead ear.

"The Crystal is not your toy," I rasped at him, my throat raw. "I am not your toy!"

The baron let out a soul-tearing shriek of pain.

I screamed in rage, braced myself against the stone stairs, then kicked him with both feet in the chest.

Baron Marius Apollinare slipped off the stone stairs and fell backwards into the teeth of the wild storm. Power lashed and twisted him like soft bread. All around us, the storm filled the room at last, then slammed down on the petrified wood like a hammer. The entire room, except the stone stairs, shattered into an avalanche of death aimed at the void below.

Just then, a crack tried to split the stone stairs up the middle. Off balance, I slipped over the edge toward the waterfall of falling debris and nothingness. A hand shot out and grabbed my shoulder at the last moment. I grabbed back and tried not to scream.

Vargas and I have disliked each other for some time. So much so, that we've tried to kill each other more than once. But right then, we clung desperately to each other while the last of the ancient room and the wild storm fell away to the dark void. We stared, wide-eyed, as it took with it a creature of twisted, real evil to the depths of Awldor.

I scrambled back onto the last safe stone step with some help from Vargas. The moment I settled onto it, I shuddered. All the events of the past days, and even weeks, crashed in on me like a tidal wave.

Slowly, I pulled my knees to my bruised chest, then softly cried.

"It's over," I whispered between exhausted sobs.

"Yes, it really is," Vargas said with a soul-wrenched sigh. "You saved us. Even me."

I nodded and sobbed.

Now, we could go home.

All of us could finally go home.

36

**Darolio 2, 1277. Morning coffee aboard the
Sheldrake. Looking at the past to see my way
forward...**

I walked across the common room of the *Sheldrake,* then carefully sat
down on the bench by my favorite window. Tyre's coffee smoothed
down my frayed nerves. Sadly, it didn't do much for my aches and
pains.

The bandages on my back itched, but so did all the scars. Magic
healing worked wonders, but the body always remembered. At least I
had fresh clothes that weren't torn to ribbons.

Outside, I watched the sunrise kiss the blue-gray buildings of Talabrae's Deep, while its people went about their day. It was a soothing
portrait of normal. Not a single one of those people had any idea how
close they came to a brush with disaster. That was fine by me.

I pulled down my goggles against the morning sun, then enjoyed
another taste of coffee.

The crowd along the caravan docks grew while the town woke
up. Merchants and mercenaries packed their caravans or windwagons
while they prepared to leave. Between the crowds, I saw a familiar

figure stroll toward a caravan that flew the Crimson Company banner. Five well armed mercenaries stepped out to meet him.

I knew that man all too well.

He was human and impeccably dressed. Everything from his sleeveless long coat and wine-red shirt to polished boots was clean cut. Even his long blond hair had been styled back into a tight braid.

Vincent Takeda Vargas stopped before he reached the Crimson Company caravan, then turned to look over his shoulder at me. With a small nod, he lifted a hand in my direction.

I returned the wave. Vargas walked away to join his mercenaries, while I took a sip from my cup. The coffee really was fantastic. It tasted like freedom.

My thoughts wandered a bit before I pulled a familiar small crystal from a pocket of my new vest. It was the crystal shard that Baron Marius had used as a spell focus. Mikasi had given it to me once we were back in Talabrae's Deep, saying it bothered him.

"You caused a lot of trouble," I sighed at the stone.

I rolled the quartz-like stone between my thumb and forefinger while I stared at it. Its facets caught the sunlight, twinkling brightly.

"How did Marius get this to work?" I mused. "I wonder..."

Slowly, I tilted my head a little to one side, then frowned. After a long breath, I focused my altered eyes on the heart of the stone, the broken shard of an Automatic Crystal. Either I'd see something, or get a headache in the process.

Deep inside the stone, a yellow-gold glow surrounded a twist of dark smoke like a cocoon. That black smudge jumped and thrashed against the golden light. It was like a demon dancing on the head of a pin.

"Well, I'll be," I murmured. "So, it was right here all this time. Who would've guessed?" A dozen thoughts spun through my head all at once. "I need to figure out what to do about you."

I dropped the crystal back into a vest pocket when Ki strolled up the *Sheldrake's* ramp. He looked better than he had a couple of days ago. Rest, some healing magic, and fresh clothes had done wonders. Ki slowly stretched the stiffness out of an arm, then joined me at the window.

"Now for home?" he asked wistfully.

"Home," I replied.

"Tyre said you wanted to make one stop?"

I watched the activity outside and nodded.

"Just one." I pulled in a deep breath. "I need to get my head straight about a couple of things. It won't take long."

Ki nodded, then glanced outside with a frown.

"So. You cast a spell."

Tension dug its claws in and crawled up my spine. I hadn't been looking forward to this conversation.

"I did." A sigh bled out of me. "Not that I wanted to, but I needed to."

"You could have died."

I sipped my coffee, then nodded. "I know."

"One of those spells was healing magic. I recognized the sun-gold threads you spun," Ki said as he frowned again. "The blue-silver ones... that was mind magic, wasn't it? What Odro taught you?"

"I think so." I studied Ki over the edge of my coffee cup. "He taught me the basics. I spun the threads off that."

Ki nodded thoughtfully. "That makes sense. I didn't get a good look at the monstrosity you weaved..."

"Magic brass knuckles," I corrected him.

He smirked and gave me a mock salute. "... a good look at the magic brass knuckles you weaved, but it matched what I saw."

"You know," I told him thoughtfully, "I think the only way I could've cast that spell was because I stood right next to Crystal."

"Where is the Automatic Crystal, anyway?" Ki asked.

I half-shrugged. "In the far back of the *Sheldrake*. Tyre, being himself, decided Crystal needed his own room. Naturally, Mikasi is back there now peppering Crystal with questions about inventions and Cesibus during the Ancient Order days."

"Of course he is." Ki shook his head, chuckling.

A low rumble shuddered through the *Sheldrake's* wooden floorboards, before Evi trotted up the ramp and closed it behind her. The centaur gave us a quizzical look, then seemed to decide it wasn't her business.

"Tyre says we'll pull out in ten minutes," she said. "We're getting up to lift now."

I smiled at her. "Thanks, Evi."

Ki leaned against the window while his tiefling tail twitched against the floorboards.

"How did it feel to pull threads? To cast a spell?"

I pursed my lips, then looked out the window. Gently, the *Sheldrake* rocked while she lifted off the ground until she was in the air higher than a warhorse was tall. Somewhere nearby, I could hear the hiss of the windwagon's boiler.

"I don't know," I replied softly. "Powerful? Larger?" Memories of that moment played out in my mind all over again and I shook my head. "Mostly, I felt desperate. Is that what it feels like for you?"

Ki raised his eyebrows at that, then nodded. "Just about. Not quite desperate, though. Spinning out those threads, weaving them into a spell. It can get to you if you're not careful. You think you can do *anything* if you can just spin out enough magic threads. Weave just a *few* more. It gets addictive."

I took a deep breath, then tugged at one of my braids. The ends of my black hair were singed and curled a little. A result of being caught too close to a wild storm. It could have been worse. The storm could have made me grow a tail, blue skin, and all like Ki or any other tiefling.

"Baron Marius."

Ki nodded emphatically.

"He was a damn good example of getting too caught up in all that power," he replied softly, while he tapped an idle rhythm on the window ledge. "It's why I warned you about a spell backlash."

"A mind storm," I said. "A storm in someone's mind. Ihodis and I talked about it back in Ishnanor. When you told me about a spell backlash, it sounded about the same to me."

"Magic storm," Ki said as he tested the phrase. "Good way to describe it. Makes sense."

"There is no way in hell or high water that I'm using magic again," I said flatly. Magic was terrifying. I'd had enough of it.

A long silence settled down, both of us lost in thought. The *Sheldrake* shifted position while Tyre's buffalo team tugged the windwagon barge out of the docks and toward the open prairie.

"Tela? My offer still stands," Ki said softly.

I gripped my coffee cup with both hands, mouth set tight in a flat line. Ki watched me for a long moment.

"Only if you feel like it," he added with a long-suffering sigh. "I just thought..."

"We were dying, Ki," I blurted out. "The baron was taking us apart, piece by piece. He was *enjoying* it. Using it for some sort of magic I've never seen before. It looked glowing blood."

I felt that old desperate frustration from the ruins slither up my spine before it bit down on my chest.

"I think maybe I was already dead before we got there," I said in a low, small voice.

Ki's brow furrowed. "You mean what happened in the tent? When the baron poisoned you?"

"Yes, back in the tent." I gripped my coffee cup like I was going to choke it.

"Ah."

"It wasn't just some magical poison," I snapped, then pointed at my eyes. "Nobody has their eyes turn into *this* from poison."

Ki raised both hands in a peaceful gesture.

"Fair enough, they don't."

"Sorry." I glared down at my coffee, which really didn't deserve it. "Marius tried to kill me. I've had plenty of people try to kill me, but this was different. The baron tried to twist me into some undead, doe-eyed thing that would obediently do whatever he wanted."

I shuddered, then stared at my coffee again.

"Nothing was the same after that. I wasn't the same." While I talked, my jaw tensed. "I have kobold eyes that let me see magic threads. The Crystal? I'm the only one who can understand him right now. Can 'see' its words and language. Understand that chime music it sings are words. So, yes, I think I died. Maybe just a little."

The prairie passed by the window and I found a rather boring rock to stare at. For a dull rock, it was pretty soothing.

"Then there was Long Deep. The ruins. All the ghosts," I whispered before a long breath slid out of me.

Silence came back to join us.

"Ki?" I asked in a small voice.

He looked over, then raised an eyebrow at me.

"I think I want to take you up on that offer," I whispered. "To talk about... it."

"The tent?" he asked.

I shook my head and shrugged.

"That, and a few other things."

My best friend in the world nodded like some wise old sage.

"Where do you want to start?"

"At the beginning." I pursed my lips.

Talking about my pain was hard. I'd rather outrun a boulder.

"Back during the last expedition to Long Deep before this one." I looked over at Ki. "You know, the time when you died."

37

Darolio 10, 1277. Never ask a question unless you're ready for the answer...

"You knew, didn't you?"

We had stopped outside the Tirak ruins deep in the plains, just like I asked. The moment I stepped off the *Sheldrake's* ramp, five sentries from the Bluescale kobold tribe, covered in dust and brown cloaks, popped right up out of the ground. Three of them ran over to give me a gleeful group hug. It was nice to be remembered.

A short ride down a hidden wooden lift brought me to Bluescale town below ground, inside the ruins. Sun orbs hung on the walls lit the way along sandstone hallways to where I wanted to go. It wasn't long before I stood in the same room not so long ago, where a friend saved me from a magical poison.

Quietly, I fumed at that friend from across the low, rough-hewn worktable. Odro sat on a blue floor cushion, calmly grinding something in a gray-white stone bowl. I didn't know what it was, other than green.

I dropped the baron's crystal shard on the table. It clattered against the polished ancient wood, then lay still. Light from nearby sun orbs glittered merrily over its facets. A happy lie if I ever saw one.

"Really. You knew, didn't you?" I asked again.

Odro gave the crystal a dark, sideways look before he glanced at me. The amused twinkle in his eye, and a grin that tugged at his kobold snout, told me everything I needed to know.

"Damn it, you knew!" I threw up my hands in exasperation while I snarled at the ceiling.

"No, not really," Odro replied with a dry chuckle. "But I had a good guess based on everything you'd told me, and what magic had been used on you."

"Odro! You could have warned me!"

All I got for that was another dry chuckle.

"Over a vague guess?" He shook his head. "Certainly not! Tela, you weren't in any shape to believe me. I'm a healer, among other things. It was much more important to make sure you didn't die. After that, it was more important to make sure you knew how to say alive, given what you were facing."

He swirled the green powder around in the bowl, then picked up an empty jar. Carefully, he poured the powder from bowl to jar while he gave me a wry look.

"So, why would I warn you about some faint guess that I desperately hoped was *wrong?* You had enough to worry about, Tela. I wasn't about to pile on more."

I rubbed my face before I let out a wordless, frustrated snarl. Then I paced twice beside the worktable, as if that might cool me down. It didn't. I flopped onto a nearby saffron-colored floor cushion next to Odro.

"You still should have said something." I drew a long, deep breath. "But, I understand. All right, for the sake of argument, what was this guess you hoped was wrong?"

Odro paused in his pouring, then set the bowl down beside the jar before he folded his hands in his lap.

"That a group called the Gatekeeper Society might have been involved and was after the Automatic Crystal of the Eclipse."

A quartet of small kobold children ran into the workshop and surrounded me in a disorganized mob of bouncing giggles. They proudly presented me with a bracelet of small, round blue and white stone beads on a cord with a single, tiny ivory figure of a kobold.

"*Win'āut*," I said in my best Belari-scal to thank them. The mob of giggles ran out of the room.

I squinted at Odro while I put the bracelet on. "The who?"

"The Gatekeeper Society," he repeated.

I grimaced.

"Ew. Really? They actually picked that name on their own?"

Odro nodded with a deep laugh before he returned to pouring powder into the jar.

"Yes, they did. Really, I'm not surprised even a Windtracer doesn't know about them. I doubt even the Archivists Guild does, either. Gatekeepers try hard to work from the shadows, and not draw attention to themselves."

He paused, frowned, then returned to his pouring.

"What little I know is that the Gatekeeper Society was formed over a thousand years ago, not long before the Great Collapse. They thought the Ancient Order had lost its way. Gone astray from its 'true values', and they were sure they could 'fix' it. Remake it into how they thought it should work, using magic, of course, to force people if necessary."

"Of course," I said dryly.

Odro arched an eyebrow ridge at me.

"But their plans never worked. The Ancient Order's society never changed. It didn't matter who they twisted with magic, or what part of society they warped. Eventually, the Keepers thought they needed more magic to bend the Order to their will. To make society see things *their* way, no matter who wanted what."

Ki's words from the other day came back to me.

"Just spin out enough magic threads," I said softly, rubbing my eyes. "Weave just a few more. Then a little more after that. It never stops, because it's never enough."

Odro gave me a wizened grin. "Ah, exactly. I knew you'd understand."

I pursed my lips while I tried to wrap my head around it all. This implied a lot, and I didn't like any of it. Busy sounds of life and conversation reached me from the rest of the kobold town. The calm, normal sounds made my thoughts wander, turning around in my mind what Odro had said. I chewed on my lower lip a little while I stared at nothing.

"Baron Marius was one of them, wasn't he? He talked a lot about 'restoring the Order' and 'remaking history'."

The kobold healer poured the last of his green powder into the jar, then brushed his scaled hands clean.

"Oh, yes. From what you've told me, I believe he is," Odro gestured to the goggles around my neck, then to then my eyes. "All of what he tried to do to you? As I understand it, that's typical for Keepers. Bring change, even if by force, even if you need to kill."

I toyed with the beads of my new bracelet while my frown deepened.

"Marius was a lich. So they're all a kind of lich then?" I couldn't quite keep a low growl out of my voice. Pent up anger is a rough bag to carry.

Odro folded his hands in his lap again, then shrugged. "Who can say? But given what little I've read, I think they are. Especially after you dropped *that* on my worktable." He gestured to the stone. "It's the baron's, isn't it?"

I gave that stone my own sideways glance.

"He sent any spell he wove right through it to make it more potent."

Odro quietly stared at the stone for a few seconds. Then he coughed and slowly shook his head.

"Of course he did. Tela, did you look into it? I mean really look deep into it? Use your gift? Your sight?"

I squirmed a little on the floor cushion.

"How did you..." I stammered.

The healer waved a hand at me. "Did you?"

"Sort of," I replied warily. "There's something in it. A dark and cloudy thing that acted like it was trapped."

"Yes," Odro pointed a finger at me. "You saw Baron Marius. The *real* Baron Marius. His true self that suffers all the pain and death for him so he lives forever. A magical portrait frozen in a crystal. It's very possible he was weaving spells and using his own life force to make them more powerful. A type of twisted necromancy. Since his curse doesn't let him die, it's a never-ending supply of power that the curse replenishes, so long as he abuses himself."

The air turned thick with anxiety until I thought I would drown. I remembered the magic storms and its wild magic tearing into the baron before he vanished.

"He's not gone." My voice was a hoarse whisper. "That's why you keep talking like he's still around."

"I'm sorry, Tela," Odro looked at me sadly. "No, he's not. Not even after all that you did and went through. Marius isn't destroyed. He'll be back, and he'll want that stone. Then he'll come for you."

I let out a frustrated snarl while I slapped the worktable hard enough it jumped.

"*Aile Shavat!* Fine. Hammer!"

I jumped to my feet and looked around. There was a set of metal hammers on a small table next to the door. I stormed over, then snatched up the largest one with a bloody snarl.

"I'll smash the damn thing. Crystal goes smash, baron does dead for real. Easy!"

Odro darted up from his cushion, then into my path before I could try my idea.

"Tela, no. Please don't break my workshop," he asked with his hands out. "It takes more than a hammer or even a spell to shatter that kind of crystal. Also, don't think you can just toss it into a magic storm, or whatever volcano you stumble across. It's not that easy."

I rolled my eyes, then threw the hammer onto the worktable.

"Hells and high water," I snapped. "All right, how do you break it?"

Odro dropped his hands, then quickly walked across the room to a small, weathered bookcase tucked away in a corner. I remembered seeing it the last time I was there. The wooden shelves were heavy with old books and scrolls, and had a small vine engraving along its edge. After a bit of rummaging, Odro pulled out a stained blue canvas journal.

"Ah ha, this one!" he exclaimed while he walked back over and handed it to me.

The weathered book had seen better days. But inside, its pages were filled with description and diagrams about a wildly complex device.

A small, table-sized thing with a tiny barrel and small, sharp knives attached to long arms. Odro tapped that page with a claw.

"The Ancient Order had a way to carve and even melt down crystals, usually to mix them in with other things. This device is what you need."

I nodded while I looked over the design. The diagram came to life in my mind, turning and whittling down magic crystals as quick as you please. The remains would sift out into the small barrel.

"I'll find it, then toss the baron's crystal in."

Odro sat back down on his cushion, then scowled at me.

"Just be careful. Carrying a corrupted crystal can slowly corrupt the holder." He shook a finger at me. "Don't ever use it, and make sure no one else does."

Mikasi's complaint that the crystal bothered him suddenly made all too much sense. I grimaced like I ate a lemon.

"So, there's no way to protect yourself from it?"

"I only know of one way. Mind magic." Odro shrugged. "The only magic that the Gatekeepers supposedly never understood. I'm sure some of them learned to protect themselves against it, but to spin the threads and weave it? Not that I ever read."

All the baron's twisted plans ran back through my mind in lurid detail. I slid a thumb slowly over the aged pages of the stained journal.

"That really was why the baron wanted the Automatic Crystal. To get at mind magic and it use on people," I said slowly. "I was right."

Odro let out another dry chuckle. "It's also why he wanted you, and you know it. Even if you're too stubborn to admit it, even now."

I blinked at that. "Sure, I can spin puzzle pieces of history around in my head, then figure out how they go together. That's why he tried to twist me inside out with that spell."

"No," Odro said as he held up a finger at me. "Though I'm sure that encouraged him. The baron recognized someone with natural talent in mind magic when he saw it. Just like I did. Through you, he could have gotten control over the Automatic Crystal. Connected you to it like some single twisted, dark device serving him. Used your natural talent to control the Crystal, and then others."

I snapped the canvas journal closed.

"Don't even go there," I warned him. "The high tides will freeze over before I cast anything more than a fishing line from now on. Anything." I growled.

The healer shook his head. "Tela, it's your choice, not mine. You do need to train, to practice. Yes, I can help you since I'm one of the last few who knows how. The more trained you are, the better off you'll be against the Gatekeepers. But if you don't want to," Odro sighed, "then you don't have to. If you ever change your mind, you know where I am."

Frustrated, I ran a hand over my braids, then glared at the floor. The complex gently swayed on its suspension ropes, like a houseboat in water. Life wasn't easy, and I never expected it to be. But damn, it would be nice if life played fair, just once.

"This is a lot to take in, Odro," I muttered. "Let me think this through."

"Of course," he warmly replied. The old kobold healer reached out, gently clasping my arm with a smile. "Take all the time you need. The Gatekeepers now know about you, but as I'm sure you've noticed, they're terrible at finding things... or people."

I shot a stubborn look at Odro, then blew out a long breath.

When I returned to the *Sheldrake,* my thoughts were churning like a whirlpool. Odro had given me a lot to think about. I paced the common room but got nowhere, so I tossed my shoulder bag to the floor, then sat on the wooden bench by my favorite window to think.

"What do I do?" I mumbled to the prairie outside.

The prairie didn't seem to care much, since it didn't bother to reply. In fact, the prairie was silent on the whole matter. So, I fell back on what I was used to.

I pulled out my weathered journal and pencil from my shoulder bag, opened to a blank page, and wrote.

"Summer, 1277, deep in the rain forest of the Chivit Continent
It wasn't my best day."

About the author

Windtracer: Adventures in Awldor is the work of C. B. Ash, who also writes as Kummer Wolfe and K.M.R. Wolfe.

C. B., or as most know him through the nickname and pen name of Kummer Wolfe, spends his days going in several directions at once.

With degrees as a Physical Scientist, Mathematics, and Computer Science, it seemed only natural that he started out rather young teaching martial arts. Well, it made sense to him. Beyond that, he's also dabbled as a musician, artist, and spent a good deal of time in tech working out web designs, engineering, and software architecture as a consultant. Traveling to view the world through its real lens... people.

No matter where he went, there he was with a notebook and pen in his trusty bag, taking notes. Sometimes even with a tablet, writing out stories and characters. Which is, at the core of it all, what he enjoys most.

But don't worry! He does sleep sometimes, or at least that's what he says. Otherwise, people might start to wonder about him...

If you're looking to find him, maybe even get a sneak peek at what he's writing now? Head on over to Substack! He's got serial fiction

stories, worldbulding, and so much more: https://kummerwolfe.su
bstack.com/